ADVENTURES IN VEGAS

A CROSSWORD PUZZLE COZY MYSTERY

LOUISE FOSTER

Adventures in Vegas; A Crossword Puzzle Cozy Mystery

Copyright 2020 by Louise Foster

ISBN 978-1-955458-05-4

❀ Created with Vellum

This book is dedicated to the healthcare workers and volunteers
who've given so much of themselves
to help others.

TROUBLE IN SIN CITY

I'm Tracy Belden and I'm getting out of town. Fast.

A quick meeting with a client in Las Vegas will pay for a weekend getaway for me and my guy.

It's a perfect plan.

I didn't count on my client being killed or having someone shoot at me.

Now I have to do my job. More importantly, I have to finish my crossword puzzle.

1 Across; 7 Letters;
Clue: An event causing sudden damage or distress
Answer: Calamity

"Go away. You're a potential boyfriend, not a hired gun."

Though nerves added an edge to my tone, Kevin Tanner's sapphire eyes held no acrimony. "At least I finally have potential."

After ten years as besties, he and I have been a couple for a few months. I couldn't be happier. I returned his smile with one of my own as I fought to hide my impatience.

Twenty minutes after the appointed time, my contact, a whistleblower with files to share, was a no-show.

Not good.

Not only was I worried for him, the man's tardiness was eating into my getaway weekend. Okay, so this trip was supposed to be strictly business. I can multi-task. Once I got the stolen files, I'd overnight them to Crawford, my boss; then, the weekend was mine. Well, mine and Kevin's.

A man matching the client's description started toward me. I perked up. Then the tide carried him away like an eddy of sand caught in the current. I sighed in disappointment.

So far, Kevin was the only male interested in me. At twenty-eight, he's seven years my junior, part of the reason I'd resisted his advances for so long. He also resembles a six-foot-two-inch black-haired Greek god with a body honed by construction work.

This would be our first weekend away as a couple, but it couldn't start until I collected the documents and got them to safety. The lucrative exchange would pay December's rent and, if I were frugal, buy a few Christmas presents.

The client would be here. He'd been delayed, that's all. I didn't want to think about the alternative, that he might have been caught in the act.

"You sure you'll be okay?"

"I'm thirty-five, not thirteen. I got this." Tracy Rae Belden on this side of the conversation. Short brown hair. Run-of-the-mill gray eyes. Able to blend into a crowd without trying. "Las Vegas is your hometown. Go cheat the casino."

I buried a pang of regret at his ten years of honesty. He could have paid for the entire trip if he'd chosen to use his talents.

"Did that. Broke even." Born to a family of con-artists, Kevin had been cursed with a conscience. A defect that made him useless to his grifting relatives. "I thought you'd be done by now."

"So did I." Pleased at the impatience underlying his words, I couldn't ignore a growing worry. The client had already wired a big retaining fee to my boss, Crawford. He had no excuse for not showing. "Harrison said no one suspected him. I'm beginning to wonder if the guy got caught."

Kevin froze like a panther who'd sighted prey.

I followed his line of sight. Touching his arm for balance, I stood on my toes. At six-two, he topped me by five inches. "Is it--"

"Not your guy." His narrowed eyes tracked his quarry through the crowd. Curiosity glinted in his gaze. "Someone I once knew."

I craned my neck at a fast-moving female with short brown hair. "You mean that girl in the cute boot-cut jeans?"

He took two steps, then stopped. His hand reached toward me as his eyes remained on the target. "Belden, you're okay if I – ?"

"I'm fine." I gave him a shove. "Go."

The crowd swallowed his muscular form in a heartbeat, leaving me wondering who had struck a nerve. Could it be a family member? The acrimonious break with his relatives had cost the Feilen family big money. From what I knew, they weren't the forgiving type.

With a new worry on my list, I leaned against a pillar disguised as a palm tree, crossed my arms, and studied the crowd. Harrison, the lawyer client, had my description as I had his. His pink tie was the one standout detail. Otherwise, I was trying to find an attorney at a legal convention. Forty-three. Caucasian. Brown hair.

Seriously? The convention at the Aquarius Hotel this week was Legal Aspects of International Business or some such ilk. Dozens of men matching that description had hurried by in the past half-hour. Not one had made a move toward the Blue Nile meeting room, our rendezvous spot.

Crawford, my boss and a former police detective of twenty-five years, hadn't heard from Reginald Harrison this morning. I'd gotten no answer on the guy's cell number.

Fifteen minutes after Kevin left, I resorted to making bets with myself to pass the time. I lost half-a-mil, which summed up my luck with gambling. Even worse, I'd lost Kevin, which

Frustration ate at me. I glared at the convention goers, wondering if the PI manual had a rule on how long I had to wait. I'd memorized a nearby display. A net full of tiny starfish, a small book with a conch shell on the cover, and a miniature beach bucket, all promoting the benefits of working in Latin America.

"Who are they kidding?" I muttered.

The shifting waves of people gave a glimpse of a dress with a bright Hawaiian print. The woman wearing it walked next to the slim form. A child? Who would bring a child to a Vegas conference?

I basked in a glow of self-righteousness. I'd left Marcus, my eleven-year-old, Korean, foster son in the care of my friend and apartment manager.

The tide of humanity ebbed again. The gaudy muumuu was wearing pink, fuzzy slippers.

My self-righteous glow wavered. My heart sank. She couldn't. She wouldn't. I didn't want to know, but could there be two old ladies in the world who'd wear those slippers in public?

The crowd parted like the Red Sea. My son's black eyes glittered in excitement as he put a hand on Mrs. Colchester's arm. His straight black hair and golden coloring contrasted with her pale, parchment-like skin. The seventy-plus, white-haired woman shuffled forward doing a slow but determined two-step. Not even her firm grip on my son mollified me.

They were supposed to be in Langsdale, a pricey resort town of twenty-five-thousand souls a fast two-and-a-half-hour drive north of Vegas.

Silly me, I'd expected one of them would act like an adult.

If the client showed up now, followed by villains, my son and Mrs. C would be caught in the line of fire.

A glance showed a few forty-ish men around. None headed my way. Instead, a crowd gathered at the mouth of the corridor directly behind Marcus and Mrs. C. My gaze returned to the boy and the old woman. Her ever-present, gardenia scent wafted into my nostrils.

"Thank, heavens, we found you." Mrs. C's shrill British accent rose above the background noise. She leaned in close enough to whisper. "Your contact is dead."

The scolding died on my lips.

"He's been murdered." The older woman's tone under-scored the final word as if personally offended. She jerked her head in the direction of the growing excitement behind her. "Far hall. Body in a side alcove."

I sucked in air as my mind refocused on business. "What makes you think it's my guy?"

"You're in Vegas, luv. Play the odds." Mrs. C's voice held a thread of disdain. The same tone she'd adopted when she'd insisted this case wouldn't be as simple as it sounded. "Middle-aged white male. Brown hair. Pink tie. Brown leather briefcase handcuffed to his wrist."

She sniffed and looked down her nose. "Bit amateurish that."

Though she denied any history with cops or criminals, her terse report had the earmarks of a professional.

My hope withered. "Sounds like Harrison."

Had he been meeting someone else? Had he been caught by his pursuers?

"What are you doing in Vegas? What are you doing in this hotel?" Questioning Mrs. C gave me time to think. Besides, no way was I letting her off the hook. "How did you just *happen* to walk by the body?"

"Kevin's with the dead guy." Marcus grabbed my arm. His

brow furrowed. "We saw him through the crowd, but we couldn't keep up with him. He went into the hall marked 'Employees Only'."

The floor dipped beneath my feet.

"By the time we peeked into the alcove, hotel security was on the scene." Marcus's grip tightened. "His hand is covered with blood."

Fear burned through my stomach like a hot coal. "Whose hand?"

"Kevin's." My son jerked my arm. "He's in trouble."

The older woman folded her hands beneath her sagging breasts. She cocked her head toward the far hall. "A bobby is on the scene. Plainclothes."

I did *not* like the way this was shaping up. Kevin just happens to follow an old acquaintance into a murder scene with a cop nearby? A setup seemed an easy guess, except no one could have known Kevin was in town. "I'll talk to them. Crawford's time as a Vegas cop should buy some goodwill."

Marcus stepped forward. "I'll come, too."

"You. Two. Stay. Here." I set him firmly on his heels, then reinforced the words with a steady stare at my erstwhile sitter. "We can't afford any mistakes if this is murder."

"Absolutely right." Sounding like Churchill during the blitz, the old woman settled a firm hand on my son's shoulder. "We have to stand together. Give the authorities an inch, and they're bound to get the wrong man."

"Right." Marcus's early years as a street urchin had left him with a strong penchant to blame authorities or run from them. Sometimes both.

Though I usually try to dissuade his mistrust of those in power, I grabbed any excuse to keep these two from interfering. I bent to meet his eyes. "I'm counting on you."

"Don't worry." He leaned close enough to whisper. "I'll keep an eye on her."

Sad fact was, I couldn't say which of them I trusted less. My smile felt forced, but he seemed satisfied. I turned and walked away. After two steps, I glanced behind me. They were still in place. No telling how long that would last, but I had little choice.

Cutting across the current wasn't as difficult as it would have been moments before. Though the ringing of slots could still be heard, the crime scene was drawing a crowd worthy of a chorus line. A security officer was visible at the mouth of the hall. A dozen feet behind him, Kevin faced a man in a dark suit. To the right was an opening to another hall.

Casino security was stretched thin by the growing crowd. I marched up to a gap on the left side, shouldering aside a woman with a camera.

A chunky security guard thrust an arm in my direction.

Without slowing, I flashed my private investigator license. "Crawford sent me."

My certainty gave him pause. I strode by before he realized he didn't know Crawford. Moving at a steady clip, I approached Kevin and the detective. Only a few steps into the hall, and I had a clear view of the alcove.

The corpse of a man was slumped against the wall. He looked to be a very old forty-three, the brown hair was heavy with gray but otherwise Mrs. C's description was spot on. The only details lacking were the blood on Harrison's crisp, white shirt and the knife sticking in his chest.

Once past the body, I eyed Kevin. He flashed me a warning look over the head of the man facing him. The guy finished snapping pictures of Kevin's right hand, covered with blood. Then the detective pocketed his phone and clasped his hands behind his back.

Mrs. C's plainclothes cop was five-ten with a squat, square build. Feet set wide to balance his broad shoulders.

Head thrown back, so the light reflected off the bald spot in the middle of his light brown hair.

Recognition washed over me. Fred Pierce. The one detective in Vegas who hated me. Okay, maybe not the only one. Pierce had no use for Kevin either.

I'd hoped Mrs. C might be wrong and the guy would be casino security, but my bad luck was running hot.

Pierce had to have been in the building to get here so quickly. The suspicion of a setup flared again. I raised my chin.

Sucking in a deep breath, I looked for an angle worth playing and came up empty. Pierce was too young to have known Crawford and too old to be impressed by my boss's reputation. Then, there was the guy's animosity. I clenched my jaw and warned my tongue to play nice.

"Belden." Pierce spat out my name without turning around. "I should have known. Where there's one of you, the other follows, especially with a corpse on the floor."

"Too bad it's not yours." And there went my resolve.

Humor flashed through Kevin's sapphire eyes then he zeroed in on Pierce. "I told you. When I tried to help the man, he grabbed my hand. Then he died."

I walked to Kevin's side, then swiveled to face the detective. With a firm hold on my self-control, I tried again. "Kevin has nothing to do with this man. We're in town on vacation."

Pierce leveled a hard stare at me. "It's never that simple with you two. You attract trouble. Tell me the truth, and I'll see what I can do."

"I'd sooner cut cards with the devil." My mouth can't help itself. "If you'd take one minute to check your facts, you'd know Kevin and I have been in town less than an hour. You'd also know he has no motive to kill your victim."

Pierce's sneer was too common to cause concern.

However, the triumph in his eyes was worrisome. The guy swung back to Kevin. "Once a criminal, always a criminal."

Kevin's blue eyes flashed with the right amount of indignation. "I've never been convicted of a crime."

The disclaimer set off a purple flush in Pierce's neck that rose like molten lava to his face. Steam would pour out of his ears any second. "You've never been caught because your family is too slippery. You're all guilty."

Looking down from his six-foot-two-inch height, Kevin remained impassive. "I haven't been in contact with my family in almost a decade. I'm a partner in sub-contracting business."

He was telling the truth, but he could have lied as convincingly. He'd been raised by the trickiest con artists to hit Vegas in decades.

Pierce's lips stretched wide. His bared white teeth reminded me of a lion ready to gut an antelope. He rocked on his heels. "Is it a coincidence I was staked out in this hotel?"

Kevin said nothing.

The seconds stretched out as I waited for the lion to quit toying with his prey and go for the kill.

The heavy-boned man leaned into Kevin's face. "A *coincidence* that the woman who entered this hall on the heels of the victim was your twin sister?"

2

17 Down; 6 Letters;
Clue: Away from the correct path
Answer: Astray

I bit back a gasp. Pierce had been tailing Kevin's sister? Who just happened to walk past Kevin's field of vision?

Coincidences were piling up faster than clues.

Fortunately, the detective didn't spare me a glance, and Kevin had learned control from masters of the art.

"Coincidence is a hard sell." Kevin's stoic expression tightened. "While I hate to believe my family would frame me, we all know they've done it before."

"You should remember, Pierce." I relished the chance to attack the detective. It made for a good distraction. "Ten years ago, you refused to believe Kevin had been framed. He and I had to find the killer. Perhaps you should consider the possibility this time."

He ignored me. He'd never forgiven me solving his homicide case.

"You and your sister hooked up again. Your con went bad, and you killed the guy." Pierce kept his glare aimed at Kevin. "You were in league with her then. You're in league with her now."

Considering that the Feilen clan ran cons across the globe, the odds that she was here, now, were astronomical.

"I've told you what I know." Kevin's unruffled tone was in sharp contrast to the police detective's hostility. "When I walked into the hall, it was empty. A few steps in I saw the alcove. That's when I found the victim. He was dying. The surveillance cameras will back me up."

The detective's smug expression wasn't reassuring. "This is the convention area, not the casino. There are blind spots in this building, and we're in one of them."

I held in a groan. That figured.

Kevin's sister had given both her brother and Pierce the slip. No easy task. Unless she knew she was being followed. By both of them. My anger meter shot to red-hot at the possibility that she'd set up her brother.

I'd never met the woman, and already I didn't like her.

Pierce's narrowed eyes weighed every nuance of Kevin's tone and expression.

"Here are the facts." Pierce thrust his broad shoulders forward. "I got you, a dead body, and the murder weapon."

"Which doesn't have my prints on it."

I hid my relief that Kevin hadn't committed the error made by every suspect in the history of police television dramas.

The detective stabbed a finger in Kevin's face. "You're plastered with the victim's blood."

"Which I explained." The first hint of impatience crept

into Kevin's voice. He held out his arm. "When I went to help the guy, he grabbed my arm and my hand."

Four smeared trails of blood, dried to black on his tanned skin, gave evidence of the dying man's final moment.

"The guy mumbled something I couldn't make out, then died." Kevin paused. "You barreled in before I could call 9-1-1."

"I'm done talking. Give me your contact information and where you're staying in town." Pierce flipped his notebook to a clean page and handed it to Kevin. The detective smiled, a Cheshire Cat with fangs. "The pictures of your bloodstained arm and the samples of the blood are evidence. When I get the noose ready, I'll string you up. Until then, don't leave town."

Then, he shot me a steady look. "You either."

"It would be rude to leave without solving your case for you – again." I loaded on the syrupy tone to mask my growing concern.

"Get 'em out of here," Pierce growled at a nearby security guard who escorted us past the makeshift barricade.

Once beyond the gawkers, I took in air not tainted by the smell of death. I stopped in my tracks. "I forgot to tell him the victim's name. Did you give him the scoop? Smuggling antiquities. Stolen files."

Kevin eyed me with a deceptively innocent expression. "I told him I never saw the guy before."

When I turned in Pierce's direction, Kevin took my arm and steered me away. "He'll figure it out."

"I like your attitude," I said, happily conceding the point. "What did you give as your reason for being in town?"

"The truth. I came to Vegas for some alone time with my girl."

His leer earned him a lingering smile. "How's that working out for you?"

He sauntered along with his easy, athletic stride. "I'm hoping things improve."

"Don't bank on it." I've always found the best way to break bad news is to blurt it out. "We're going to need more than two beds. Maybe a suite. We have company."

His brow furrowed.

I cocked a finger and pointed up ahead. I watched his puzzlement morph from recognition to resignation. I shared his pain. "I don't know how you feel about bunking with Marcus, but I am not sharing a bed with Mrs. C."

"The best-laid plans… " He exhaled slowly, then clicked his tongue. "Too bad you insisted on going halvsies. A bigger suite is going to cut into your profit margin."

"Don't remind me. This romantic weekend is going down in flames." I saw no chance of salvaging our getaway. Mrs. C couldn't be trusted to return to Langsdale on her own, or she wouldn't have brought my son here in the first place. Maybe I could find someone to stand guard over both of them. "At least they're still where I left them. I suppose that's a good thing."

A smile softened his narrowed gaze.

He knew I was kidding. Sort of. "Quit being so nice."

He shrugged. "If you can't duck the blows, roll with the punches."

I rolled my eyes. "Is this from Grandma Feilen's Grifting Philosophy 101?"

By now we were within a few feet of the miscreants. Marcus's face lit up when he saw Kevin. My first impulse was to confront Mrs. C on why she had come, but I didn't want my irritation to spill over onto Marcus. After all, *she* was the one who'd been in charge.

"Bit of a dustup, eh?" Mrs. C's wrinkled face folded into a sympathetic expression along her laugh lines. "No bother, we'll put things right."

Kevin responded with a gallant nod. "Decided to take a trip, Mrs. Colchester?"

She drew herself up to her limited height. "We've come to help, of course."

"I appreciate the offer." A ribbon of steel cut through Kevin's words. "But there's no reason for the rest of you to stay. I'm the one in trouble."

Marcus's eyes sparkled. "Are we involved in another murder?"

"No." Was what came out of my mouth, but "yes" was what I feared. "Kevin was just in the area."

"I'll explain later, sport," Kevin ruffled Marcus's hair. "Right now, you need to go home. All of you."

He turned to me as he underlined the last sentence.

Shock coursed through me. "Pierce told us both to stay in town."

"He wants me, not you," Kevin said. "I won't drag you into a murder investigation."

"And people say chivalry is dead." After a lifetime of fighting my own battles, his gallantry still thrills me. I rested my hand on his arm. "You and I have been involved with murder twice in the past few months. At this point, being a suspect is merely an inconvenience. Besides, you wouldn't be here but for me. It was my client who got murdered."

"We got your back, Kev." Marcus insisted. "Right, Mrs. Colchester?"

"Certainly, dear." Busy patting her pockets, she answered with a distracted air. "I seem to have misplaced me favorite set of knitting needles."

"One man's been murdered." As if he hadn't heard, Kevin's worried gaze remained on me. "This could get dangerous fast."

"Don't worry, luv." Mrs. C's muffled tone rose from the depths of her cavernous purse. "We'll save you."

"How could you refuse such an offer?" I asked in a flat tone. Eyeing the other woman's continued search, I turned so only Kevin could hear me. "I understand why you might want to go solo, but you're stuck with us."

Worry darkened his eyes.

I shared his fear of involving an old woman and a boy in a murder investigation. However, they couldn't be trusted to make their way home without supervision, and the thought of turning them loose on an unsuspecting Las Vegas gave me the willies. "I can call in reinforcements."

"Rabi." Kevin mouthed the name silently.

"I hate to thrust Marcus and Mrs. C on him," I admitted. "But after twenty some years in Special Ops, the man at least stands a fighting chance against them."

"We aren't leaving you." Marcus forced himself between Kevin and me. My son's undersized frame looked even smaller compared to Kevin. Wounded pride lanced through the boy's fierce tone. Until I took him in, living on the streets was all he knew. Our patchwork family was literally all Marcus had to call his own. "We're in this together."

Understanding softened Kevin's gaze. He put an arm around the boy's shoulders. "I wouldn't have anyone else on my team."

"Admit it." I shot Kevin a teasing look. "You need us."

"Absolutely." Mrs. C gave up the search with a resigned expression. "One for all and all that rot."

The rally cry of the Musketeers sounded odd framed in a British accent, but the sentiment was solid.

"Besides," Marcus chimed in, "you can't have all the fun."

Kevin met his gaze, then jerked a thumb toward the main hotel lobby. "How about you and I check on a bigger room?"

Marcus plastered himself at Kevin's side.

I eyed Kevin's lean, muscular form as he walked away - sighed - then turned to the old lady by my side. "Why did you come to Vegas? You agreed to watch Marcus in Langsdale."

"I got to thinking." Her gaze roamed over the two-storied blue atrium rising above us. She slowly shuffled her pink slippers down the busy casino corridor. I was forced to follow. "I haven't been to Vegas in decades. Not since I was –"

"You could have come to Vegas at any time." My irritation boiled over. "I left Marcus with you so he'd be safe."

Mrs. C showed no sign of having heard. She tapped her finger on her lips. A faint chorus of ringing slot machines served as a perfect frame for her trip down memory lane.

"Was I here in fifty-two? Or was *I* fifty-two? Lud, how the years fly. I remember," she snapped her fingers, "I made a huge score at the Golden Nugget on me fifty-second birthday."

I sucked in another breath, but dollar signs temporarily derailed my annoyance. "How much did you hit?"

She slowed, then stopped completely, forcing the convention's suit-coated business professionals to flow around us like we were rocks in a stream. The old woman leaned forward with a conspiratorial air. "I hit for five thousand, four hundred, eighty-six on one machine."

"Five thousand dollars?" An impressive jackpot. Despite the circumstances, I perked up. When she shook her head, my rising enthusiasm slowed but didn't die. "Quarters? Still decent. I'd take it in a hot minute."

"Pennies," she announced in a grand tone, her triumph undimmed.

My envy vanished as I moved the decimal point. "Fifty-four dollars?"

"Over five-thousand credits." She put a hand on her scrawny chest, eyes focused firmly on the past.

For me, the moment was over. I walked after Kevin and

Marcus, both long gone from view. I slowed my usual fast pace to Mrs. C's shuffling step. Small, over-priced boutiques, upscale restaurants, and fancy bakeries lined the corridor connecting the meeting rooms to the hotel and casino.

"We need to get you and Marcus clothes since you'll be staying the night." I shuddered at how much even one outfit for the boy would cost in this tourist mecca.

"We packed before we came." The Duchess of Wales couldn't have sounded more offended. "One does need proper attire for a weekend in Vegas."

Frozen in shock, I watched the old lady trundle ahead of me. "You were planning to stay all along? What are you supposed to be? Chaperones?"

My yell drew a frown from a portly man with beady eyes.

"Mind your own business." I shot him a dagger-filled glare as Mrs. C sailed down the corridor. Selective deafness is a handy tool in the hands of a master, but when she put herself not only between me and my profits but between Kevin and me, she was outclassed.

"Stop right there." I stormed after her. "How did you get here so quickly? You and Marcus had to be packing before Kevin and I hit the Langsdale city limits. We only left you a few hours ago, and you don't drive."

She pulled herself up to her five-foot-six-inch height. "I happen to have a friend who delivers various goods to Vegas. We rode with him."

I clenched my teeth. "You rarely leave your apartment. How do you cultivate more contacts than MI-6?"

Her expression remained placid despite my cutting tone. "I wasn't born yesterday, luv."

Despite the provocation, I refused to take a cheap shot. Instead, I stuck to the issue. "Your delivery man explains how, not why."

"Ooohh, dear. I didn't want to say anything in front of the

boys, but… " She finally had the grace to look embarrassed. She put a red-taloned hand on my arm. "I knew you'd need my help."

Taken aback, I stared at her. "What?"

She patted my arm. "You always do."

My jaw dropped. I was, for one of the few times in my life, speechless.

"My forethought has proven correct. This looks like quite the affair, but don't worry." She set sail down the hall again. Her muumuu flapped around her ankles as her shrill tone mixed with the ringing slot machines. "I'm here for you."

Recovering from my shock, I hurried after her. "I'm not paying you one cent for babysitting."

3

1 Across; 7 Letters;
Clue: An event causing sudden damage or distress
Answer: Mirror

Forty minutes later, I was lounging in an overstuffed sofa in a mammoth suite courteous of Kevin's skills-- gambling, conniving, and personal.

Cool aqua walls and shimmering silver artwork carried out the Aquarius Hotel's ocean theme. In the furniture department, the place had decorated for comfort, and I appreciated the effort. No way could I have afforded this place. Though I'd have to pry Marcus out of here with a crowbar when we left, I decided to embrace the moment.

Kevin sat in a nearby chair positioned at a right angle to the sofa. I had a perfect view of his toned muscles beneath his tight t-shirt.

Whether he felt my gaze or heard my sigh, his eyes met

mine. He flipped a pair of dice into the air, then rolled them over his knuckles with practiced ease.

Our gazes caught and held. The connection that passed between us was one of the things I valued most about our friendship. It was also one of the things I feared losing if, like my past relationships, our romance imploded. Yet, after waiting so long to dip my toe in the water, I wasn't even going to get my freshly painted toes damp this weekend.

While Kevin kept his eyes locked on mine, he let the dice fly. They clattered across the coffee table, stopping on a six and a one.

I gave my guy an apologetic smile. "This isn't the way I planned to spend our first evening away."

"Yeah." Marcus vaulted over the back of the sofa to land at my side. The aroma of convenience store beef-stick surrounded him. "This is way better."

Kevin's mouth melted into a smoldering grin as he swept up the dice.

Mrs. C entered and settled into an overstuffed chair. Her knitting needles, freed from the clutches of her bag, started clicking before the seat was warm. "So nice to relax after our busy morning."

Marcus wiggled his cell phone at me. "I texted Uncle Nick we were in town."

A glow of satisfaction filled me at Marcus's thoughtfulness. "That was nice of you."

He shrugged. "He had to be warned in case you need to be bailed out of jail again."

I mentally removed the gold star from his good conduct chart. My eighty-one-year-old uncle was more likely to hit on Mrs. C than ride to my rescue. "I was questioned by the police last time, not arrested."

"There's always next time." Marcus's tone rang with hope.

"That's the attitude for Sin City." Kevin shot him a jaunty smile. "Play the odds."

"Don't encourage the boy," I warned as Kevin threw a four and a three. "Are those trick dice?"

His disgusted expression held a touch of "you-know-better" as he tossed a five and a two.

I shook my head. This was the man who broke even at the tables? "How do you do that?"

"A wasted childhood." Kevin swept the dice off the table. "That's how I got part of the room comped."

I grinned. The only thing casinos love more than big-time gamblers are big-time losers. I eyed the gorgeous suite again. "You're my hero."

The dimpled smile popped, which did make my heart flutter like a schoolgirl with her first crush.

"Belden," Kevin chuckled. "You're so predictable."

"At least I've solved my first mystery of the weekend." Okay, so I was the only one who'd wondered at his failure to win even one dollar. "You been keeping in practice?"

"Some things you never forget." He tossed the cubes carelessly into a decorative bowl, hitting a six and a one. "Seeing Safina brought back old memories."

"Not surprising." I ached at the sadness in his eyes at the mention of his twin. Over the years, he'd spoken of his family several times. Often enough to fill in the blanks of a con-always-comes-first childhood. "You worked together all your lives, more so than most siblings or even twins."

"That didn't make any difference in the end. We were born on opposite sides of the planet." His short laugh had a rueful note. "She looked down on mundanes. I envied them."

Marcus wrinkled his nose. "What's a mundane?"

Kevin snorted. "Marks. Rubes. Anyone not in the biz."

Despite growing up in a family of thieves, Kevin wasn't a

hardcore cynic like me. The gulf between us seemed wider in moments like this one.

Looking older than his eleven years, Marcus studied Kevin. "Sometimes, you have to steal to eat."

Neither my street-smart son nor my ex-grifter boyfriend had had much of a childhood.

Kevin met the young boy's gaze in understanding. "Safina once said I was born on the wrong side of the Looking Glass."

"Like *Alice in Wonderland*," he explained to Marcus's puzzled expression. "In the rabbit hole, life is upside down."

"Like on the streets." My son glanced at me. "The rules are way different, but living with you is cool. You're not boring."

Kevin's laughter lightened the mood. "That's for sure."

"Great," I muttered. "That can be my epitaph."

"Have you talked to your sister since you left?" Marcus, who didn't remember a family life, was constantly curious about other people's family ties.

"She tried, at first. I ignored her e-mails." Kevin's melancholy expression gave only a hint of how difficult the struggle had been. "I didn't want to get dragged into the business."

After knowing him only a couple of weeks, I hadn't wanted him to leave. I could only imagine the gaping hole Kevin's absence left in his sister's life. I'd been so worried that he missed his family and the exciting life they led that I never brought it up.

"It takes courage to start a new life." Mrs. C's subdued voice sounded over the click of knitting needles.

I waited, unsure how many undercurrents this conversation could hold, but she didn't expand on her comment. Though tempted to pursue any opening into the old woman's shadowed past, I decided to follow up on Marcus's comment about Safina. "Why did you follow her?"

"I didn't think. I reacted." Kevin's mellow voice held a note of surprise. "She was walking like an arrow aimed at a bull's-eye. I took off. I didn't even spot Pierce."

I sighed in mock disappointment. "The straight life is making you soft."

"It does that." Marcus nodded sagely. "But hanging with T.R. should have kept you on your toes."

"I know." Kevin agreed with a bit too much enthusiasm. "Tracy has as many run-ins with the cops as my family."

Sad, but probably true. "Must be that karma wheel getting back at me for a previous life."

The PI gig is the problem. If not for the cases, I wouldn't be involved with crimes. But the money keeps me afloat, even if I have landed as a suspect more than once in the past few months.

"Did you see your sister with Harrison?" I wasn't sure if he'd held anything back from Pierce. Kevin was a master at answering questions honestly without disclosing information.

"I told Pierce the truth." Kevin's slight smile faded quickly. "By the time I walked into the hall, Safina was gone. Harrison was dying."

"Too bad he mumbled when he died." Marcus sounded personally aggrieved at the victim's selfishness. "We need a clue."

"I may not have been entirely truthful about that part."

Kevin's admission buoyed my spirits.

Marcus perked up as well. "What'd he say?"

I tried to be more casual, but I felt myself leaning forward. "Yeah, what did he say?"

Kevin's gaze flicked from me to my son. "From this angle, the family resemblance between you two is amazing."

Since Marcus's ancestors hailed from Korea and mine were from the rolling hills of Kentucky, any similarity was in spirit only. But that was all that mattered. Kevin knew nothing could have pleased Marcus more.

Marcus's grin flashed. The boy's constant quest to prove he belonged with me had just gained another point. "It's in the blood."

I rewarded the love of my life with a look of gratitude, then shifted to business mode. "Back to point. Did Harrison mention Safina?"

"Not directly." The denial sprang from Kevin's lips. "Harrison looked at me, grabbed my wrist, and said 'Con. Shill.'"

Air hissed out between my teeth.

"If the Feilens are involved, we have a huge problem." Stating the obvious is one of my gifts. Kevin's family holds no love for me since they blame me for his departure. "Did you recognize Harrison? Old friend? Old enemy? Past scam?"

Kevin stretched his long legs out in front of him. His gaze grew thoughtful. "I've never seen him before."

His certainty was backed up by a memory imbued with a lifetime of lessons.

"Your sister had to know he was in that hall." Caution honed on the streets had taught Marcus not to overlook details. "Would she set you up?"

"She couldn't know I'd be in the building," Kevin answered.

"Or the city." I studied the situation from all angles. "I made the reservation yesterday, and the room is in my name."

A heavy silence fell, punctuated by the click of knitting needles.

"Don't worry." Marcus waved a carefree hand in Kevin's direction. "We'll figure it out."

"Never doubted it." Kevin cocked his head to one side. "Safina knew about your meeting--she decoyed him into that hall. Short brown wig. The boot cut jeans you live in. Four-inch platforms for added height."

Marcus swung toward me. "She was meeting Harrison in your place."

Shock sucked the air out of my lungs. I fell against the sofa. "How could she have known?"

"Your man was compromised," Mrs. C grabbed a strand of yarn and pulled with all the strength in her chicken-like arm. "Easy enough to listen in on a cell phone. Child's play, really."

I heaved a heavy sigh. "That means our opponents are several steps ahead of us in the game."

An oppressive aura cast a pall over the room.

"Time to call Crawford." I'd avoided it long enough. "Maybe I can get him to pony up for the other half of the room."

A moment later, my boss's greeting rolled over the phone line like a gravel truck. "What?"

Sometimes I hate caller ID. "Bad news."

A few minutes later, he had the facts.

"Why do clients end up dead around you?"

I pulled the phone away from my ear to avoid hearing loss.

"She's a murder magnet," Marcus yelled.

"The kid's right." Crawford's disgruntled tone put my back up. "You're better than a hitman. The client is dead. The files are gone, and one of you is a person of interest in a murder investigation. All in the first hour."

"This is not my fault." The fact that he spoke the truth only fueled my ire. "The smugglers must have caught onto his game and killed him."

Marcus had his cheek plastered against the phone. His warm breath fanned my fingers. I slid my gaze sideways and stared into his black eyes. "How about some breathing room?"

"I don't want to miss any details." His nose was almost touching mine. "You're old. You might forget."

"I don't need you reminding me of my age. I have a mother for that." I touched my finger to his forehead and pushed him away. "Besides, people in the hall can hear Crawford."

Marcus retreated exactly ten inches then held steady. Straining forward, he eyed me like a starving vulture.

I returned to the conversation with my boss. "Did Harrison name his contact or the business that was involved with smuggling in the stolen artifacts?"

"No, and it doesn't matter." The finality in Crawford's tone signaled a death knell for the case. "The evidence is ashes by now, and murder is a matter for the police."

Crawford's motto: no money, no investigation. Altruism doesn't pay bills. The man has operatives to pay, me among them. So, normally, I'd mark the case closed and lay by the pool. Unfortunately, Kevin being a suspect turned what should have been a breezy decision into a do-or-die matter.

"What about the retainer?" My boss's bluster didn't fool me. Family and friends counted big time with the old fart. He wouldn't leave Kevin hanging. I hoped. "You have to earn the money he gave you."

Crawford's snort of derision sounded in my ear. "You want to save your boy toy. A few weeks ago, you'd have taken the fee and run. Now your head's on holiday."

"That's not the issue." Not completely. "Kevin's my friend… and yours. Whether you fulfill your contract to the victim or not, I'm staying."

"Quit whining." This time Crawford's unexpected bellow made me jump. "I'll cover one day on the case. I'll pay half the cost of the suite. No room service."

A moan sounded at my side.

Marcus's face twisted into a mask of anguish. He buried his head in the cushion with a wail any banshee would envy.

"I heard that," Crawford said. "Eat at the buffets like normal people."

"Deal." I snatched at the offer before he could withdraw it. "I'll report tomorrow, and we'll renegotiate."

I hung up on him in mid-yell.

"Score one for the home team." I did a little dance on the sofa. "Hotel's paid in full for one night."

Marcus popped up. "If you're not paying for the room, that means -- "

"No room service." My gaze held his, steady and firm. Crawford's expense account was business. I wasn't about to part with my own money for luxuries. "Don't push your luck. You shouldn't even be in town."

My son aimed a pleading look at Kevin.

"Give it up," Kevin said. "You know Tracy and money."

I gave my guy a big grin. "I could come out of this case with more profit than I'd planned."

"And solve a murder." Marcus sat up. Pushing aside his disappointment, he became businesslike. "The guy was a lawyer. We should check his office."

"Good idea." We'd be treading on Pierce's toes, but it couldn't be helped. Since Kevin had no contact with his sister, the victim was our only lead.

"The police will check his files for suspects," Kevin added. "But it's a start."

Marcus started to stand. "I'll get my shoes."

I blocked him with an arm to the chest. "You're not going."

His excited grin melted. He lifted his chin. "I'm part of the team."

I handed him the laptop. "You're in charge of research."

Kevin leaned forward, resting his elbows on his knees. "We need everything you can find on Reginald Harrison. Reputation. Court cases. Background."

The knitting needles stilled. Mrs. Colchester's face lit up. "I have an acquaintance who works at the courthouse who could help."

"Perfect," Kevin said. "You two check on antiquities smuggling in the area. Recent cases. Local arrests. Harrison's involvement. Everything you can find."

The boy straightened his shoulders. "You can count on me."

"As soon as Rabi arrives," I grabbed my purse, "you can go sightseeing or find child-friendly attractions in the area."

"Those are for kids," Marcus whined.

"You *are* a kid," I reminded him.

"Wait. How are you paying Rabi? Not with cash." Marcus narrowed his eyes, then grimaced. "You're not going to bake cookies again."

"No cookies," I said.

"Cake?" Kevin frowned.

Mrs. C clicked her tongue. "The fire department ruined the curtains the last time you attempted to bake."

I wrapped my wounded dignity around me. "I promised him pizza. Takeout."

The relief in the room was palpable.

"Kevin and I will check in later." I scowled at Marcus and Mrs. C equally. "Rabi knows a guy with a two-engine plane. He'll be here within the hour. He had better find you both in this suite."

Mrs. C looked up from her knitting. Befuddlement clouded her pale, green eyes. "Well, dear, wherever would we go?"

The Taj-Mahal? The Great Pyramid?

With this pair, who knew?

4

33 Across; 8 Letters;
Clue: The personality of an individual
Answer: Identity

Reginald Harrison's office was in a solid building in an upscale area. The wide sidewalk was lined with large planters filled with small, sculpted evergreen bushes. Palm trees edged the parking lot. On the third floor, a carpeted hall framed by bright walls led to the attorney's office. Nameplates on the closed doors in the empty corridor listed a chiropractor, a doctor, and another lawyer.

Kevin pointed toward the nameplate on the last door in the hall. "The late Reginald Harrison."

The silence made me itchy. Something felt wrong. "No cop car outside. No uniform in the hall."

Kevin's quick stride betrayed his uncertainty. "Pierce is too good not to interview Harrison's staff, check his cases."

"Maybe he's been and gone, taking the files with him."

The conversation reminded me of the times Kevin and I had done this before, including the day we'd first met. Pierce had been at that murder scene as well, and he'd been just as belligerent. My mouth quirked up in a smile. "Somehow checking on a murder seems the perfect way to spend our first weekend away."

"It must be fate." Kevin's rich laughter brightened the atmosphere. "Murder brought us together."

I caught a whiff of his woodsy cologne mixed with the ocean breeze scent of hotel soap. "I hope death doesn't follow us forever."

Kevin looked surprised. "Not death, justice."

"That's a comforting spin." It wasn't the first time I'd noticed Kevin's proclivity to emphasize how the scales of justice balanced out. Perhaps as a result of the injustice he'd witnessed in his past.

I settled into an easy rhythm beside him, fighting the urge to grab his hand. I was thirty-five, working a murder investigation. My mind should be on business, not crushing like some hormone raging teen on a high-school quarterback. "If Pierce is here, he'll blow a cork when we walk in."

Kevin twined his fingers with mine. "You'll cut him down to size."

Glad he'd given into the impulse I'd fought; I tightened my hand around his calloused palm. My phone buzzed with an incoming message. The text brought me a measure of relief. "The cavalry has arrived. Rabi's at the suite."

"Las Vegas is safe."

"I'm glad his friend could fly him here so quickly. I owe him for coming on such short notice."

Kevin pushed a strand of hair behind my ear. "Rabi could say no. He just never does to you Beldens."

"They're at a pizza buffet." I read from another text.

"Marcus says… Mrs. C found crumpets? I don't even know what a crumpet is, but leave it to the alleged Brit."

The sudden appearance of the woman's accent last fall had driven my curiosity into a frenzy. Nailing down her past should have been easy, but the trail was as slippery as the woman herself when it came to straight answers.

"Any headway on her history?" Kevin was always amused at my lack of progress in uncovering the woman's past.

"None so far. Rest assured, I'm diving into her shady background as soon as we get you off the hook."

"I like your confidence in clearing me."

I pocketed my phone as we reached Harrison's office. I barely had time to wonder if the place was locked when Kevin turned the knob and opened the door.

A square-faced secretary, with a heavy sprinkling of gray in her dark hair, looked up from her computer. A stack of files sat next to a statue of Lady Justice, complete with balancing scales. Candy weighted down one side while pearl-hued seashells sat on the other. A smattering of knick-knacks lined the front of her computer.

No cops. No tears. No way could Kevin and I have outraced the announcement of Harrison's death.

The woman's dry-eyed indifference changed to a gleam as her gaze lingered on Kevin. "May I help you?"

Her reaction to Kevin didn't surprise me. Her composure did.

I outpaced Kevin as we walked to her desk. I, at least, had a PI license to flash. Kevin didn't even have that thin excuse. Shoving aside my confusion, I gave her my best wide-eyed innocent smile.

Life lesson number four, stick with the truth as long as you can. It's easier to remember when situations go south. "My name is Tracy Belden. I have a business meeting with Mr. Reginald Harrison."

Had, actually. Which he'd missed, having been murdered.

One painted eyebrow rose enough to question the validity of my statement. "Mr. Harrison is finishing with his twelve-thirty appointment."

I hid my astonishment behind my cool mask. While my brain stalled, my mouth took off. "Our meeting was for this morning. He never showed."

"That's impossible." The woman - Alice Winter, according to the nameplate - eyed me with a hint of condescension. "Mr. Harrison was in court for an early case. After that, he spoke at a convention. He returned thirty minutes ago."

My mind scurried in circles.

"I make all of Mr. Harrison's appointments. I didn't make one for you." Her starched tone matched her stiff jacket collar. "You're mistaken."

Mistaken? On the day? The time? Or… the man?

I was beginning to think the latter. Either Harrison wasn't dead, or this woman's acting talents were wasted. More annoyed with each passing second, I raised a brow. "Perhaps Mr. Harrison arranged the meeting himself. It's a personal matter."

Her eyes widened.

Just because you don't have a personal life, I wanted to say, doesn't mean your boss doesn't, er… didn't.

The click of a doorknob interrupted our little war of words. The door to the inner office opened.

"Thank you for coming." A man's deep voice resonated into the waiting area.

I found myself holding my breath.

He stepped into the doorframe, body and face in profile, speaking to someone in his office that I couldn't see.

My jaw dropped.

Though not an exact twin to the dead man, the particulars matched. White. Brown hair.

This Reginald Harrison was a couple of inches shorter than Kevin's six-two height. Also, stockier, with less muscle. I couldn't tell if his frame matched the dead man. It's hard to compare height and weight with a corpse. *This* guy looked forty-three. The corpse had appeared to be older, but I'd written that off to a hard life.

Kevin stepped close enough for his arm to graze my back. His chin brushed my hair. "What. Is. Going. On?"

I shook my head. "I got nothin'."

The victim had used Reginald Harrison's name. Surely not to fool me. I hadn't known either man. Which meant a third party must have been at the Aquarius. Someone who, like me, had never met the real Harrison and would have believed the victim's story.

Too bad I hadn't stayed at the crime scene long enough for Pierce to check the victim's wallet. Then, I'd have known the dead man wasn't Harrison. I'd also know the victim's real name.

Now I was several steps behind the detective.

That was annoying.

"Why did the dead guy give Harrison's name to Crawford?" I barely breathed the words. My brain was too full of questions to hold them in any longer.

"To lead us here?" Kevin muttered after a heartbeat. "He must have known… "

He was being followed. As I mentally completed the statement, I gave an infinitesimal nod. The murder victim had been playing a dangerous hand.

"Aces and eights." As if he'd read my mind, Kevin's words followed my thoughts. "Deadman's hand."

The victim had died trying to bring antiquities smugglers to justice, and the path had led me here. To find the real smuggler?

I had to admire a guy who'd found a way to finger the real

Harrison from beyond the grave. I grimaced as a growing sense of obligation to the murdered man took hold in my gut. I didn't want any ties to this case beyond clearing Kevin.

"No wonder Pierce isn't here," I muttered. "We never gave him Harrison's name."

The lawyer continued listening intently to the person in his office. "I'll see to it at once."

I raised my chin, planning which attack... er, greeting would get me into his inner office.

A young blond woman stepped into the doorframe. I calculated five-five without the heels. Curves in all the right places. Even in profile, her chocolate brown eyes had a fragile air. Full lips set in a round face. Long blond curls fell over her shoulders.

I didn't like her or her wounded bird aura. So not my style.

Kevin drew in a sharp breath. He rested his hand on my waist. Alice Winter may have assumed it was a random gesture. I knew better. It was a signal, alerting me. I studied the blonde with added intensity.

Turning away from Harrison, she walked into the waiting area. Her limpid gaze stopped on Kevin, then the script changed. After an instant dismissal, her gaze continued to me. Her attention stopped for a hesitation so brief I might have missed it but for the hardness that turned the chocolate orbs to daggers.

An air of professionalism returned as her attention focused on the secretary. "Thank you for everything, Alice. You're always so kind."

The older woman responded, but I didn't process the words.

The blonde walked toward the outer door. Eyes forward, she didn't spare another glance for Kevin or me.

My radar flared like a star gone nova.

No one ignores the Adonis at my side. Men. Women. Straight. Gay. Whether the person is interested or annoyed at possible competition, aesthetics demand a second look. In the ten years I've known him, this blonde was the first person who'd appeared indifferent.

Then, the angel focuses on me?

No way.

I could think of only one person who might respond in that manner. Kevin's twin sister, who I knew to be a brown-eyed blond. Safina Drummond was the name I knew her by. The one she used most often, just as Kevin had chosen his name after his break with his family.

The glimpse I'd caught at the convention center had been from behind, and her hair had been short and brown.

Ten years ago, when I'd met Kevin, she'd been out of town. A rare separation for the twins, which surely made it easier for my guy to leave the family fold. Hair and eye color can be disguised in an instant. However, her round face and her height - two details that are hard and fast - matched Kevin's description.

Anger hardened in my veins like ice. Safina had led her brother into a hall that contained a dying man. Then, almost certainly knowing she was being followed by a cop, she'd abandoned him.

Her presence in Harrison's office added weight to my suspicions. Kevin's too casual expression, coupled with my experience at reading him, confirmed Safina was in this crazy scheme up to her pretty blond curls.

The outer door clicked shut. Harrison studied Kevin and me with a polite gaze.

I walked forward before Ms. Winter could speak.

"Mr. Harrison, I'm Tracy Belden with Crawford Investigations out of Langsdale. We had a meeting today at eleven." Putting my business card in his outstretched hand, I stopped a bare two inches from the tips of his Italian leather loafers. When he retreated, I leaned forward and lowered my voice. "You were murdered before we could talk."

His eyes widened. His mouth gaped, but no sound came out.

"The young woman who just left was there as well." I continued in a low tone. I wanted to say she may have killed you. Then, I studied the man's hazel eyes, already narrowed in thought. Why had the dead man wanted me here? Was Harrison in this scheme with Kevin's sister? Was he a mark or a murderer?

I locked gazes with him. Then, I slipped past the stunned lawyer into the inner office.

Kevin strode forward. His physical presence forced the lawyer to retreat. "Let's sit. We have a lot to discuss."

The ring of benevolent command drew the attorney from his stupor. Kevin's air of command had swayed stronger men. The attorney told his assistant to hold his calls, then walked to his desk as Kevin shut the door.

Kevin and I sat in matching leather chairs. Harrison faced us behind a sensible oak desk. Abstract prints priced in the low five figures graced the walls. Living in a resort town that promotes high-end art auctions and contains numerous galleries has given me a knowledge of art prices.

The man facing me dressed for success. The building and office marked him as successful.

Harrison looked down his patrician nose, first at me, then Kevin. His attention settled on me. "You'd better explain your comments regarding my client. Not to mention your outlandish statement about my alleged death."

"Murder," I corrected. "You were murdered. At least, a man calling himself Reginald Harrison was killed this morning."

I watched as the stone I'd thrown hit him between the eyes. Holding his gaze, I leaned back and crossed my legs.

Kevin gestured across the desk with a long arm. "There was blood all over the tie."

Harrison nervously fingered the silk noose hanging around his neck. Blood leached out of his face.

"I found him as he lay dying," Kevin added.

The other man swept a hand across his brow. His dark hair contrasted with his grayish skin tone. "I don't understand. Who are you two?"

"I told you my name, Tracy Belden. This is my partner, Kevin Tanner. I work for Crawford Investigations." No need to mention Kevin was my partner in our handyman business. Instead, I nodded at my PI business card on the desk.

Not a flicker of recognition stirred in Harrison's expression. He took a deep breath, recovering some of the color in his face. "I've never heard of you or your company."

Considering the man was a lawyer who played to juries, I reserved judgment on his denial.

"The woman who just left," I waited for him to meet my gaze. "Why was she here?"

He drew himself up. "She's a client. Her business is none of your concern."

Kevin leaned forward, resting an elbow on his knee. "I followed her into the hall where I discovered the murder victim."

Surprise splashed over the lawyer's face.

I watched the guy closely. "She may have thought the victim was the real Reginald Harrison."

"That's preposterous." He dismissed my theory with a wave of his hand. "The young woman and I have met several times. Who was the man? How did you know him?"

I gave a bare outline of the call to Crawford and the

planned meeting. I gave no details on what crime the victim had evidence on.

The furrows on Harrison's brow deepened with each detail. "What did the documents pertain to?"

"Since you're not the correct Reginald Harrison," I said in a professional tone, "that information would fall under client confidentiality."

The attorney's lips thinned. Evidently, he didn't appreciate my lawyer-speak.

"Why would this man pretend to be me?" he asked.

Despite his evident confusion, I kept him firmly on my suspect list. "I'd say he wanted to lead us to your doorstep in case the worst happened. Which it did. Which, a suspicious person might believe, leaves you holding a smoking gun."

His gaze darted to his desktop as if he'd find the explanation written in neon green.

An enigmatic emotion flashed over Kevin's handsome features. "Unless he was your partner."

"I hadn't thought of that angle." Admiration colored my tone. "Are you missing one of your associates?"

A calculated expression settled in the lawyer's eyes. "I don't know what game you're playing, but it's time you left."

"Thrown out after five minutes?" Amusement underlay Kevin's comment. He cast a sideways glance in my direction. "That's a new record for you."

"Murder's hardly a game, Mr. Harrison." I remained seated, stalling for time. "If you doubt what I've told you, call the police. Ask for Detective Pierce."

If he was going to throw me out so soon, why let me in at all? Had he been fishing to find out how much I knew? There had to be more to this. My brain retraced what had gotten me through the door.

Safina. After I mentioned she was at the scene, Harrison let us in the office. When the conversation turned to the victim, then to Harrison, it was game over. He was protecting Safina, or who he believed her to be. I had to discover what identity Kevin's sister had given the lawyer.

For that, I needed Kevin's help. If my plan had any hope of success, our familiar connection needed to burn at full wattage.

I shot Kevin a "do you believe this guy" look. Hardening my expression, I held his gaze for several heartbeats. An answering gleam sparked in his eyes.

Letting my impatience show, I faced Harrison. "A man is dead. You expect me to believe your client didn't mention she was at the scene? The police will follow us to your office. They'll need to know her *identity* to track her movements."

The last statement was aimed at Kevin. We'd been in enough schemes that we could usually pick up on each other's unspoken agendas. Usually.

"I will cooperate with the police." The lawyer rose. "Your time, however, is up."

"I'm out of here." Right on cue, Kevin rose to his feet. "I'm not getting in trouble for you again."

"Take her with you," Harrison commanded.

"You let her in." Kevin walked toward the door, playing his part to perfection. "You throw her out. And good luck with that."

"One more minute," I pleaded to Kevin's back.

"No." He tossed the refusal over his shoulder, then slammed the door behind him.

I threw myself against the chair. "What a jerk."

The lawyer stared at me as if I'd grown a second heard. He stabbed a finger in my direction. "Why are you still here? Follow your friend."

Except I needed to buy time. I was betting either those sapphire eyes would melt Alice Winter's heart or his con-game wiles would weasel the information we needed out of the secretary. I didn't care which tactic worked, as long as he succeeded.

Harrison aimed a laser-like stare at me. "I've asked you to leave."

"Fine. I'll go." I stood and turned toward the door. Relief melted some of the tension from Harrison's face. Boy, was he naïve. I stopped and planted my feet. "One more question."

His body stiffened. Silly man, he'd actually believed I would leave so easily.

"Your speaking engagement this morning was at the Aquarius." I studied him closely. His expression could have been carved from ice. "Did you plan to give your client an alibi for the crime? Or was it the other way around? What went wrong?"

"I'm not discussing this with you." He ground out the words through a stiff jaw. He stepped around his desk. "Do you want to be thrown out bodily?"

From the look in his eyes and his tight fists, he looked willing to do the deed himself.

"Mr. Harrison, I'm trying to help you." I pulled out a conciliatory tone. "The murder victim used your name. He may have masqueraded as you for weeks, making who knows how many enemies. You should call the police. You're in danger."

"I can manage my own affairs, Ms. Belden." The purple flush subsided slightly from his face, but his expression remained stern. He stepped around the desk with surprising speed. His hand closed around my upper arm, but I twisted out of his grasp.

"Last chance, Belden." Kevin's raised voice sounded through the closed door. "I'm leaving."

That was my cue. I threw my hands up in surrender. "I tried. You have my card. If you need my help, call."

His muttered response had something to do with "hell"

and "freezing". I couldn't make out all the words, but I'm pretty sure I caught the sentiment.

The hard thump of Harrison's footsteps followed me out of his office. My feet did a stutter-step at the sight of the secretary's empty desk.

That hadn't been part of my plan.

"Ms. Winter… " Harrison's stern tone faded at the sight of her absence. He'd obviously expected the woman to be at her desk.

My gaze sought Kevin. Standing in the outer doorway, he thrummed his fingers in evident impatience. Only our long association helped me recognize the excitement buried beneath his annoyed expression.

He shoved away from the doorjamb. "'Bout time."

I lengthened my stride. Once in the hall with the door safely closed, I grabbed his arm. "First things first. What was your sister doing with the real Harrison? That was your sister, right? Why was she here? A con? A scam? What's up? I'm right, aren't I? It's her. "

Kevin waited patiently through my tirade of unanswerable questions. "Safina Drummond in the flesh. Why? No idea."

I stared down the corridor, trying to sort out the facts. "What about Alice Winter? What did you do? Where did she go?"

"She was AWOL when I came out." He glanced over his shoulder before continuing. "Her computer was locked."

"Drat." My feet practically flew down the empty corridor. Nerves? A plan? I wasn't sure. I couldn't slow down. "Something lit a fire under her, and I missed it."

"She took off in a hurry." He eyed me as he spoke but he

kept pace with me. "Left a drawer open and a handful of folders on her desk."

"Score one for the home team." At least Harrison was old school and still kept paper files. Filled with impatience, I hurried toward the stairs. "Tell me you recognized a name."

"Since you ask so nicely." His smile widened as he stopped with his hand on the doorknob. "Clarissa Hogard, one of Safina's aliases, is listed as a rep for Westercamp Imports."

"I've never heard of that company."

Kevin shot me a knowing look. "It may not exist outside of a website and that folder. I memorized names, along with addresses and phone numbers."

"Now we have a lead for the troops to investigate." Ignoring the elevator, I opened the door to the stairs. I pinned him against the doorjamb, enjoying the warmth of his body next to mine. "We make a good team."

"Nice to hear you admit that." He wrapped one arm around me, lifted me off my feet for a quick kiss, then swung me through the open door, and deposited me on the top stair.

I grabbed his hand and ran down the steps. "Let's go."

Though his long legs kept up easily, Kevin frowned. "Got another meeting I don't know about?"

I threw up my hands, unable to explain the sense of urgency that drove me. Despite the sunny day, I felt dark clouds moving in, carrying with them a sense of doom.

So why was I rushing out to meet my fate?

5

9 Down; 10 Letters;
Clue: Commit to a course of action
Answer: Double Down

When Kevin and I stepped from the stairwell into the first-floor corridor, his arm settled comfortably, naturally, around my waist. Anchored by his presence, my mind picked at Alice Winter's unexpected departure.

"The woman obviously knew more than she let on." Frustration at having missed something crucial bled into my voice. "She shot from calm secretary to ballistic missile in the minutes it took Harrison to throw us out."

"What's this *us* business?" Kevin's outrage sounded sincere. "You're the one who ticked him off."

I bumped my hip against his, throwing us both off stride.

"Something lit a fire under Winter." His tone turned thoughtful. "I don't see what, unless she listened at the door."

"Doesn't sound like the uptight Ms. Winter I met."

Though the puzzle gnawed at me, I had no answers. Time to concentrate on our next step. Our leads had expanded beyond the "ransack Harrison's office" option that had topped my list when I arrived.

I hooked two fingers through a belt-loop on Kevin's jeans. "Marcus can check out Westercamp Imports, Safina's supposed employer. By now, he should have the basics on Harrison."

"If he needed an in, I'm sure Mrs. C was able to put him in touch with a well-placed friend." Laughter flowed through Kevin's voice. "That woman has more contacts than a CIA operative,"

Sunlight from the main lobby overflowed into the spacious side hall. Outside, a comfortable seventy-five degrees blew in off the desert. Though it was mid-November, the building's AC unit filled the entryway with cool air.

Yet I was sweating bullets trying to find a pattern in the seemingly random clues. "Interesting to find Safina connected to both the dead and the living Harrison. Once we get to the hotel, we can work on tracking her down."

"Our resources will be better served digging into her alleged company." Kevin flipped the keyring out of his pocket. "Safina will find us."

"That's what worries me." I prefer to keep danger away from my son. "I could carry through with my earlier threat to send Marcus sightseeing."

Kevin's laughter rang through the quiet hall of the office building. "Keeping that boy and Mrs. C on the straight and narrow will consume a lot of time and energy. Feeding them leads will ensure we know what they're doing."

"Most of the time." Best to keep friends close, and the totally untrustworthy closer. Besides, our resources had to be aimed at removing Kevin from the list of suspects.

Having made my decision, the tension in my shoulders eased.

Kevin shot me a glance. "Got a plan?"

"Not even close," I admitted ruefully. "Too many threads don't connect."

"Too many coincidences." A somber expression descended on his face. "I thought I left duplicity behind."

I gave an unladylike snort. "I thought I'd left my ex-hubby behind until wifey-number-two got murdered and I got blamed. Evidently some parts of our lives need to be dealt with more than once."

"You could still go home."

"No one is leaving." I cut him off. "Marcus is having the time of his life. He's determined to clear you."

"Glad I could fill his weekend. And yours." He studied me with a thoughtful expression. "Why can't you admit you enjoy investigating as much as Marcus does?"

Was he crazy? "I'm only in this to save your butt."

"And get paid."

"That, too," I put a hand on his arm. "For you, I'd investigate for free."

He paused in opening the door. His expression softened. "That is the most romantic thing anyone has ever said to me."

Considering his family had put money before everything but breathing, I didn't have a lot of competition. Still, I felt my cheeks flush under his intense gaze. My fingertips swept across his arm as I walked by. "True love."

Wrapping the emotion around me, I walked outside. The warm air, hotter than usual for November, matched the heat in my veins. I shifted my gaze away from the sun's brilliance and scanned the quiet parking lot. A woman's stiff profile in the car on the end of the first row grabbed my attention.

A wooden-faced Alice Winter sat in the driver's seat of a dented four-door Chevy. The driver's window was lowered.

I crossed the sidewalk in long, quick strides. The thud of my footsteps was the only sound other than the creaking of the pine branches. No thrum of a car engine carried on the air.

"Ms. Winter?" My raised voice sounded loud in the still air. Though I was only six feet away, her gaze remained locked straight ahead. She didn't even blink. "Alice?"

No response. No movement.

A stone fell in my stomach. My steps slowed. She couldn't be dead. I'd traded words with her not ten minutes ago. By the time I was three feet away, I could make out the rouge on her cheek. That's when the aura of death started to crawl across my skin.

The urge to call her name again was almost overpowering.

Part of me wanted to believe that this time she'd respond.

I scanned the parking lot again. Half-a-dozen cars. No other people. Careful not to touch the door, I squatted by the open window and felt for a pulse in her neck.

The stone in my gut turned to ice.

Kevin's shoes scuffed the concrete behind me.

I spoke without turning. "No pulse."

She'd been right in front of me. Yet, I'd been blind to her involvement. At least consciously. My subconscious had picked up some detail. It had driven me to hurry out here, but too late.

Why had she left?

Fury filled me. At myself. At her killer.

I stood quickly. "If I'd thought to ask the right questions, she might still be alive."

My hands shook as I pulled out my phone to call the police. Before I could punch a single number, Kevin's arms surrounded me.

His hands covered mine as he drew me close. "It's not your fault."

My inner spring uncoiled. Neither regret nor guilt would help Alice. I needed to find her killer. "The murderer had to be close. They must have come and gone while we were inside."

I stepped out of his comforting embrace. Silence seemed to rise from the warm concrete. Though the rumble of a thoroughfare carried on the air, this out-of-the-way neighborhood had little traffic. "Could the killer have followed us?"

"No one followed us." A hint of annoyance mixed with the certainty in his tone.

I should have known. He'd been checking for tails when he could barely walk.

"Only one car left this lot since we drove in," he said. "I assume that was my sister's ride."

"You memorized the cars again?" The weird skills his con artist family taught never failed to amaze me.

"There weren't many." Kevin raked the building with a narrowed gaze. "The murderer could be closer to home."

"Everyone's a suspect," I repeated the cliché as I followed his gaze to the office building. "Everyone in there, too. Except Harrison."

Kevin, hearing the disgust in my tone, folded his arms across his chest. "You really thought it would be easy?"

My gaze lingered on the muscles beneath the tight t-shirt while my brain sought for answers. "Harrison was at the location of both murders."

"So were you and I," he reminded me.

And his sister, I silently added.

"Pierce is going to love this. Two murders in one morning." I gazed at the woman's form in the quiet car. "I suppose we should call this in?"

"As opposed to fleeing the scene?" His subtle sarcasm made the point. "That would put us in prison before sundown."

"All right." I dragged out the words like a seven-year-old agreeing to chores. This would so not look good. I bent to look through the car window. "I'd love to check out her cell phone. See who she called in the past ten minutes. Her purse is on the seat."

Kevin thumbed a number into his cell, then put it to his ear. He shot me a flat stare then jerked his head toward the building. "Lots of possible witnesses."

I eyed the purse longingly. "I wasn't actually going to do it."

"Sure, you weren't." His eyes shifted to his phone; his focus followed as he spoke to the 9-1-1 dispatcher. "I need to report a death."

I studied the facade of the building. Two offices faced this side on each of three floors. Blinds carefully drawn. No movement in any of them.

"Someone would see me," I muttered. "I bet none of them saw Alice's killer."

"Yes," Kevin spoke into his phone. "We're in front of the building, next to the vehicle. We'll wait."

"We don't have any choice now," I said as he pocketed his phone.

"That's why we're waiting," he explained with a smile.

My impatience with protocol always amused him.

I pointed to the third-floor windows on the right. "Harrison's office?"

"No." Kevin's response was instantaneous.

"Has to be." I mentally retraced our path inside the building. We'd only made one turn. Unfortunately, directions are not my friends. "You sure?"

"Harrison is at the rear of the building."

I scowled at the unfairness. "Alice may have called the killer or stopped in an office and spoken to him or her. We have to account for everyone in there. Four offices on each of three floors."

"The boy detective can hunt down a list of tenants."

The sun reflected off the concrete. Blinking against the bright glare, I refocused on Alice's Chevy. I reviewed the sequence of events. "She comes out, starts the car. Then lowers the window to talk to someone and turns off the car while they talk."

"The keys aren't in the ignition." Kevin's puzzled expression matched his tone. "They're not on the floor or in her hand. They might have rolled under the seat."

"The killer could have taken her car keys." Which would make this case weirder. "I'm not giving Harrison a pass, not after the first victim's alias pointed us in the lawyer's direction. Only you get the benefit of a doubt."

"Thanks."

"You think Pierce would share the records from Alice's office phone with me?" I asked, knowing the answer.

"You never give up." Surprise colored his response, as if my stubborn streak was a new development. "Even if he liked you, which he doesn't, the police frown on detectives giving information to a known associate of the chief suspect."

I gave another snort. "I never liked rules."

"And you wonder where Marcus gets his attitude."

"I only skirt stupid rules." Niggling guilt added a defensive edge to my response. I was supposed to be sanding away Marcus's rough edges, helping him adapt to society. "I always tell him to stay on the straight and narrow."

"He's too good a profiler not to know how you really feel," Kevin said. "Don't worry. He was a rule breaker long before he met you. That's why you two make such a good team."

I walked over to my guy. My hand trailed up his arm as I leaned my cheek against his shoulder. "We all make a good team."

His hand covered mine. "Even Mrs. Colchester?"

I sighed in resignation. "Her, too."

The gears in my mind shifted to Alice's murder. "How long was she alone in the outer office?"

"Four minutes, thirty-six seconds," Kevin answered without hesitation. "From the time I closed the door to when I walked out."

Yeah, weird skill number three, from con games one-oh-one. Exact timing is crucial to success. You can't constantly watch the time. It makes the mark nervous. So, you tick off the time on your own internal clock.

Marcus never tired of testing Kevin's skill. For the record, ninety-eight percent of the time, Kevin nails the elapsed time within three seconds.

"Four and a half minutes," I repeated. "She had to be moving as soon as we shut the door. What set her off?"

"She didn't react to your name. No shift in her eyes. No tension." He snapped his fingers. "You mentioned Crawford when you introduced yourself to Harrison. Our backs were to her. We didn't see her reaction."

"If Alice recognized Crawford's name, then she knew the dead guy."

"The first victim evidently didn't tell her he was using Harrison's name. He also didn't tell her your name." Kevin's mouth thinned. The muscles in his arm tensed. "Everyone on the team should know the entire plan, beginning to end."

The Feilen family are renowned grifters. Often suspected. Rarely caught. Never convicted. Every scam planned with excruciating exactness. Kevin had been raised in a climate of perfection.

Sympathy for Alice had me searching for an excuse for her perceived failure. The dead woman's eerie death-stare drew my gaze like a magnet. "Maybe she called the killer. Someone she thought she could trust."

Kevin's narrowed gaze studied the woman's profile. "And she was betrayed."

Sirens sounded in the distance.

I frowned in their direction. "It never takes the police this long to arrive when *I* break into places."

"The person in question is dead." Kevin pointed out. "And I promised we'd stay put."

A plan brewed. "I hope they send Pierce."

"Eager to see your buddy again?"

"I can't keep calling my former client Dead Harrison." My lack of knowledge made my tone sharp. "I need to find out his real identity."

Kevin, always active, spun his keyring on his finger. "Pierce has no idea we don't know the dead guy's real name. He'll blurt it out."

After a quick nod, my mind jumped tracks. "How do you think Alice was killed? Poison? Injection? Whoever it was got close."

"It was someone she knew." A thread of worry sounded in Kevin's tone.

"Safina fits." I figured I might as well say what we were both thinking. "But she was known in this building. Killing Alice here would be a huge risk. Safer to meet her elsewhere."

Kevin's shoulders relaxed. His look of tempered gratitude made me glad I'd noted the flaws in that scenario.

Two police cars jetted around the corner and made a beeline for the parking lot. Pierce's unmarked car led the way. Lights flashed as the mini parade pulled into the lot.

"I'm betting Dead Harrison tried to scam one too many people." I gave my guy a teasing glance. "Not everyone is the Kevin Tanner of con artists."

"A good con is when no one realizes they've been had." Kevin had exited most games with other marks believing he was also a victim. "I'll bet Dead Harrison talked to the wrong person. A lot of people have trouble keeping their mouths shut."

"Some people are better at that than others," I spoke in a self-righteous tone as Kevin - the clam - stifled a laugh.

Pierce's slow, penetrating stare raked over us as he pulled up and parked.

I wiggled my fingers in greeting, tossing him a jaunty smile.

"You're not supposed to taunt cops," Kevin warned in a low voice.

"I don't harass police as a rule." I was already anticipating crossing swords with the detective's pre-conceived conclusions. "Is it my fault Pierce makes it such fun?"

The detective's self-righteous attitude was so annoying, he almost asked to be harassed. Besides, I couldn't really be blamed. It was all in the line of duty. Right?

6

12 Down; 7 Letters;
Clue: Requite. Return on an investment
Answer: Payback

J.D. Darlington. Attorney-at-law. Getting the victim's name was almost too easy." I crowed as we pulled away from Harrison's office building. "I'd much rather fence with a surly detective than find dead bodies."

Kevin laughed deep in his throat. "Somebody's drunk on a drop of success."

"Too bad that's all I accomplished." Finding a second body had confirmed the detective's theory that Kevin and I were in on the murders. "It's not fair that we gave Harrison an alibi for Alice's murder. We're still on the suspect list."

"We had time." He took my scowl in stride. "We had opportunity."

"Blah. Blah. Blah." I waved a hand in the air. "Fairness sucks when it works against me."

He drove down residential streets, a side of Sin City most tourists never see. Having lived and worked in Vegas years ago, I can tell anyone that behind the lights, glitz, and neon, the garbage on the curb and peeling paint is the same as Anywhere, USA.

"We need background on Darlington." I hated the idea of starting from ground zero. "Did he work for the smugglers? Was he involved with Safina? Alice Winter?"

"Don't forget Crawford." Kevin returned my puzzled look with a sharp glance. "The victim didn't call a Langsdale PI by chance."

I chewed on my lip. "Every fact we learn adds a new complication."

Kevin's classic 1967 pearly white Cadillac, otherwise known as the Great White Beast, climbed a wide, blind curve. The city streets fell away, replaced by a blanket of blue above a panorama of rolling dunes. Cactus and scrub stretched to the horizon. In the distance, purple mountains circled the desert like links in a chain. The stark beauty couldn't have been more different from my Kentucky roots, but it was no less entrancing.

"Harrison and Darlington were lawyers in the same town. They must have crossed paths." I took out my cell phone. "What are the odds I can do a search on Darlington on this thing?"

Kevin's hand covered the phone and pushed it down without taking his eyes off the road. "Stay away from the Internet, and no one will get hurt, including the phone."

I clicked my tongue. "A child could do a search on a cell phone."

"Then let's leave complicated tasks to professionals, like Marcus."

I drew myself up as much as possible in the soft, leather seats of the Caddy. "I've done this before."

"And cracked the screen in the process."

"The Internet is supposed to be super-fast." I shook the phone at him. "It wasn't moving. Then it jumped places I didn't want to go."

Kevin's gaze slid sideways. "Searching will make Marcus feel useful."

I rolled my eyes at his transparent maneuver, then jiggled the phone. "How about if I dial numbers and call another human being?"

His brow wrinkled. "I suppose that's safe."

"If Darlington chose Crawford for a reason, Bossman should know the deceased."

The *Hawaii Five-0* music filled the car before I could hit my speed dial. I groaned. "It's Crawford."

"You were planning to call him anyway."

"He's calling to tell me the dead guy is Darlington." I shook the ringing phone. "That's *my* revelation."

"You don't know that's why he's calling."

Another ring sounded. "It's my luck."

Kevin pointed at the phone. "Answer it."

With a heavy sigh, I thumbed the speaker button. "Hi, Crawford. You're on speaker with Kevin and me."

"J.D. Darlington."

"Is our client's real name," I interjected, shaking a fist in frustration. "I was calling you with the info."

"What do I pay you for?" A harsher edge than usual punctuated Crawford's deep voice. "I'm up to speed, and I'm not even there."

I glared at the phone. "I've been busy."

"Doing what?"

"Interviewing Reginald Harrison, Esquire. Who isn't dead."

Kevin fought to hide a grin. "And finding a second murder victim."

Crawford groaned. "Why do you always complicate cases?"

"Hey." I brought the phone up to eye level as if Crawford could see me. "How about we blame the murderer this time? What's up? You sound grouchy, even for you."

"What did you learn from Harrison?" Crawford asked, ignoring my question.

Kevin kept his eyes on the road and an overly innocent expression on his face.

"The guy's hiding something." I stalled with this unimpressive tidbit, unwilling to admit I had few revelations. "I'm digging into his connection with Darlington. Kevin's sister was leaving Harrison's office as we arrived. She's using an alias as a rep for a possibly bogus company."

"She was at both murder sites." Crawford's low whistle came over the line. "What else?"

"He didn't let much slip," I paused, "before he threw me out."

A bark of laughter exploded from the phone. "Another record still intact."

I bristled. Was it my fault people refused to cooperate? "You taught me everything I know about the detective biz."

Kevin rubbed his brow. "That's a frightening thought."

"No, you don't." Crawford's rough voice filled the car. "You aren't blaming me."

"What do you know about Darlington?" I asked. "His corpse looked older than Harrison's forty-three years. He must have been practicing law when you were on the force in Vegas. Why did he choose you for this setup?"

A growl that sounded like an angry grizzly roared out over the phone line.

When nothing else followed, I pushed. "Old history, I take it?"

"Darlington was scum before he passed the bar exam on

his third attempt," Crawford said. "Figures he'd end his life on a lie."

I grimaced. There went my paycheck. Crawford wouldn't step on the cops' toes to pursue a murder case for a man he'd disliked.

Kevin shot me a look of sympathy. He took one hand off the wheel and rubbed two fingers and his thumb together. Money.

Good-bye, suite. Hello, cheap hotel. Marcus would be crushed. I wasn't too happy, either.

"What about the case?" Prepared for certain dismissal, I lined up a speech about duty, honor, earning the retainer. The whole bit.

"It means we have to find out who murdered the rat bastard."

"He paid you a sizeable retainer. You owe him – " My brain finally got past Crawford's grudging tone and digested his words. I was left with my mouth hanging open.

Kevin gave me a questioning look, then slowly shook his head.

"Wait a minute," I hit rewind. My mouth always did work faster than my brain. "You *want* me to investigate?"

Turning the big Caddy with one hand, Kevin followed a curve away from the desert's stark beauty into a street lined with strip malls.

"Crawford," Kevin's gaze darted to the phone before settling on the road. "Why spend time and money for a man you never liked?"

"Stupidity," came the answer. "My own."

"You're going to have to narrow that down." This was too good to pass up. "I could be guessing all day."

"Very funny." His disgruntled tone only added to my curiosity. Seconds ticked by before he spoke again. "When I was a rookie, a local grocer was killed. The detective pinned the murder on a sixteen-year-old kid. I was young and cocky and wouldn't let it go. Told the detective and the DA their case was crap."

I mouthed a silent "Wow" at Kevin. Breaking ranks in the police force is not done lightly.

"Don't ask me why, but Darlington took the case." A heavy exhale came over the line. "During the trial, I cleared the kid."

I wasn't tracking the problem. "Then why don't you sound happy?"

"Darlington helped." Crawford spat out the words.

Obviously, the sticking point.

"Even worse, the rat saved my career."

"How?"

"He filed a complaint demanding I be fired."

I stared at the phone. "You lost me on that last curve."

"Reverse logic," Kevin explained. "Working with a scumbag attorney like Darlington would have left Crawford tainted. The complaint forced the police to close ranks to protect one of their own."

"Bingo," Crawford said.

"I get it." Being in debt to someone he viewed as a lowlife would stick in my boss's craw. His decision came down to duty and honor, the hinges Crawford's world swings on.

I did a silent cheer in the car. My pay meter was back on.

"Darlington knew I wouldn't take his money if he gave me his real name. Now I have to find his killer."

"That's what you get for being a good guy." I always admired the bossman for that, though I'd never say it out loud. "On to important matters."

"I'm not paying for the Aquarius." He read my mind. "I'll give you a stipend. Move to a cheaper place or pay the difference."

"Marcus will be disappointed." He wouldn't be the only

one. I gave Kevin my best puppy-dog gaze. If he continued to get the price knocked down by winning big then losing large, I'd be all to the good.

After a sideways glance, Kevin stared at the long Vegas road. His dimple peeked out. Then, my own, personal card sharp gave a thumbs-up. "Least I can do for the Belden Detectives."

"What is?" Crawford asked.

"Nothing. I'll take the stipend." What happens in Vegas, stays in Vegas. Back to business. "Did Darlington and Harrison work together? Step on each other's toes?"

"I never heard of Harrison before. He didn't work criminal cases when I was on the force," Crawford said.

I thought for a moment. "What else do you know about Darlington?"

"I've been gone a dozen years," Crawford said. "He always had his hands dirty, but he never got caught."

Great. Crawford's tie to the victim amounted to ancient history. That meant more leg work. "You're not much help."

"That's - why - I - pay - you." He spaced out the words as if talking to a six-year-old. "Wrap this up while I can still pocket some of the guy's money."

As I drew a breath to retort, a click sounded in my ear. I glared at the phone. "I hate it when he hangs up on me."

Kevin snorted. "One of you is always hanging up on the other one."

"'Wrap it up,' he says." I had more complications with each passing hour. "We've barely scratched the surface."

"We have a lot of clues," Kevin offered in a hopeful tone. "They're just not connected yet."

"Maybe Marcus found something juicy on Harrison." I was hungry, tired, and frustrated. A tangled murder was not how I'd planned to spend my day. "Did I mention I think better on a full stomach?"

"Did you notice we're not headed to the strip?"

Small businesses, pint-sized motels, and neon signs on every building announced lucky slots inside.

"You're kidding, right?" I had no *idea* where we were located. "For all I know, the Aquarius is around the next corner."

"You'd have seen the bigger hotels on the strip." Kevin threw out one hand in a sweeping gesture. "Where do you wish to dine, my lady? The four corners of Las Vegas are yours for the asking. Wine. Pheasant. Pate de foie gras."

I wrinkled my nose in disgust. Give me a burger anytime. I opened my mouth to say as much.

"Or… " Kevin held up one finger, stopping me before I uttered a word. "A greasy cheeseburger nirvana. Complete with crispy fries and a shake thick enough to hold a spoon upright."

"That's why I love you." A rumble from my stomach echoed the sentiment. "You know the way to a woman's heart."

He shot me a sideways glance. "Doesn't take a genius with you, Belden."

Warmth filled me. We matched so well. No pretense. No need to impress. The theme music from the latest *Sherlock* show erupted from my cell phone. "The boy detective."

"Probably looking for an update." A mischievous twinkle lit Kevin's eyes. "Or he and the troops need bailing out."

"Don't say that. My stomach can't stand any delays." However, like a good mother, I answered the call. "Hello?"

"T.R.?"

Interference scratched out the voice. "Marcus?"

Just when I thought I'd lost the call, a blast of static made me wince.

"– you'll nev – " More static shredded Marcus's high-pitched voice.

"He sounds scared." My heart picked up speed. "Marcus?"

The line cleared.

"T.R." Marcus emphasized my nickname. "– was - killed –"

"What? Who was killed?" Fear swept through my veins like wildfire. Mrs. C? Rabi? Please, God, not one of ours. "Marcus?"

My voice rose in panic. Silence answered me.

The call dropped.

---

7

11 Across; 8 Letters;
Clue: Recollections of days past
Answer: Memories

I gripped the phone to stop my hand from shaking. "Who was killed?"

"Calm down." With his gaze locked on the road, Kevin reached over and put his hand on my arm. "You shoot straight to panic when you think Marcus is in trouble."

"Because he usually *is* in trouble." I gave a strained laugh. "He said someone was killed, and we have a killer who's racked up two victims."

"Marcus may know about Winter's death." Kevin pointed out.

The terror in my gut loosened its grip. "True."

While the old woman and my boy might court trouble, Rabi was caution itself. Even as I told myself they were safe, I punched my son's speed dial with extra force. One ring. "It went to voice mail."

"He's probably calling you back." Kevin squeezed my arm in a comforting gesture. Warmth spread through my veins, calming my jangled nerves. "Disconnect and text him. Or be patient."

"Not my strong suit." I tried to remain calm, but my body remained tense. Then the *Sherlock* theme sounded. "Marcus?" Thankfully, my voice sounded calm.

"Harrison wasn't killed." My son spoke without preamble. "A guy named Darlington was the victim."

Relief flowed through me. Then I realized I'd been beaten to the punch again. First my boss. Now my son. "How did you find out the dead guy's identity?"

Kevin jerked his head at the phone. "Put it on speaker, so I can hear."

I punched the key. "You're on speaker. Kevin is here. Who told you about Darlington?"

"Hey, Kev." Marcus's loud greeting echoed in the car. "Mrs. Colchester knows a guy with the Vegas police. He's in records or something. The victim is J.D. Darlington. A lawyer. I got all kinds of stuff on him. Harrison, too, before I found out he wasn't dead. Bet you guys were surprised."

"To say the least." Especially considering Safina's appearance and Winter's murder. "Harrison's definitely connected. We need to compare notes, but I'm eating first."

"Good. I'm hungry," Marcus said. "Rabi wouldn't let us go to the smuggler's lair. Where are you eating?"

The smuggler's comment intrigued me, but no way could I follow Marcus's jackrabbit topics on an empty stomach. "How can you be hungry? You ate pizza and crumpets an hour ago."

"That's forever to a growing boy." Kevin waved aside my

comment. "We're headed to the Penny Lane Café. A dive outside the city limits. Tell Rabi to head south."

"We'll find it," Marcus promised. "We're meeting them – "

His voice broke off. Quiet descended.

"That boy should have come with a warning label." I sat back, consciously relaxing my muscles. "I could have had a heart attack. On an empty stomach, too."

"A double tragedy." Kevin slanted a laughing glance my way before focusing on his favorite sport, driving the Caddy. The vehicle rocketed down the street at jetliner speed.

"I wonder what he meant by going to the smuggler's lair." I watched the glitzy, gaudy city of Las Vegas fly by in a blur and felt out of my depth. "This trip was supposed to be easy. Collect some files and be done."

Kevin glanced my way. "Too late for easy. At least Rabi nixed one of Marcus and Mrs. C's crazy plans. Some of us don't catch on quick enough."

He clicked his tongue. "The thing is, the schemes don't always sound crazy."

I had to chuckle. I'd been caught a few times myself.

"I go to Vegas for a weekend away," Kevin's strong hands handled the steering wheel with ease. "First thing you know, a dead body turns up. Before I can blink, I'm on a watch list as a suspect in a murder investigation."

I narrowed my gaze. "None of that was my fault."

"That's what Marcus says. Every. Time." Kevin looked me over before returning his attention to the streaming traffic. "Are you sure you two aren't related? Switched at birth?"

A chuckle forced its way out of my lips. Kevin could always lighten my mood.

As we headed for the outskirts of Las Vegas, my curiosity kicked around the smuggler's comment. "What information do you think he and Mrs. C uncovered?"

Kevin shrugged. "A possible ex-MI-6 agent and a street rat? No telling. You want to call him?"

"I can wait."

"Since when?" He laughed out loud. "You have a chronic need to know."

"No, I don't."

"Plus, you like to be in charge."

That made me sound bossy, which was so not... Okay, maybe it was a teeny bit on target, but still...

"That is so not... completely true." My improper English made my feeble defense sound even more pathetic.

"It makes you a good detective." Kevin focused on maneuvering the oversized car into a slim opening then shooting away from a potential traffic jam. "Your curiosity keeps you digging until you figure out the puzzle."

I do love solving puzzles, and the one for this case was looking to be a doozy. "That part is true."

Former con artists, I've come to realize, make better profilers than FBI agents.

"Too bad you have to wait ten whole minutes for answers." He turned off the highway, smoothly merging onto city streets. His expression melted into one of mourning. "I don't know how you'll survive."

I fought a smile, then deliberately turned my head toward the mix of small businesses and residential neighborhoods flashing past. "My time with you and Marcus has taught me patience."

Kevin pulled into a parking lot split with a spider's web of cracks. The full light of the desert sun highlighted a faded, chipped sign for the Penny Lane Café. Two cars, equally faded, sat in the corner of the lot. The building itself was a small brick affair. From the outside, it looked deserted.

Kevin parked facing the door, turned off the car, then waited with an expectant look on his face.

"I'm not saying a word."

He just sat and grinned.

He didn't have long to wait before my willpower collapsed. "This hole-in-the-wall looks like a place I'd frequent, not you."

Mind you, it wasn't the neighborhood or the rundown atmosphere. It was the contrast between the dive and the confident, urbane posture Kevin had been raised to present, a state he exuded naturally.

It's not clothes that make the man, it's attitude. Even dressed in a t-shirt and jeans, Kevin could have walked into any boardroom in the country and taken charge. He oozed confidence.

"Safina and I used to come here after every score in Vegas." The distant haze of memory clouded his gaze as he stared at the decrepit café. A smile teased his lips. "Those were the only times we were truly on our own."

How could I have forgotten? He'd referenced this place more than once during his stories over the years. Freedom - in one, crumbling brick pile. I raised a brow. "Good food?"

His finger skimmed lightly over my forearm. "Would I mess with you and a meal?"

"Good enough." I got out, slamming the heavy car door with a satisfying thud. We rounded the car together. He veered closer as we fell in step and our fingers entwined.

"Alone at last." I teased. While my eyes scanned the surrounding area, my mind fidgeted. Each new fact knotted the murders deeper into my brain. Even if Kevin weren't involved, it would be hard to walk away without finding answers. Not that it mattered.

Kevin needed saving.

Safina needed saving.

I stopped in my tracks. Why would Kevin's sister need saving? She was one of the movers in this scam.

Wasn't she?

Kevin's outstretched arm pulled me forward.

I tucked the thought away as Safina joined Darlington and Winter as another unwelcome obligation. Each additional weight dragged me in deeper and deeper.

Inside the diner, whitewashed brick, aided by a few windows, added light to a dim interior. Faded posters of Sinatra and the Rat Pack hung next to Elvis and a panorama of acts from yesteryear. Photos showed the Golden Nugget's marquee along with a place called the Thunderbird Hotel. This was "old" Vegas, without the glitz and glamor.

Despite the mid-afternoon hour, half-a-dozen old souls sat scattered at the tables. They looked to be from the same time warp as the building. The ever-present clicking of slots harmonized with piped-in big band music. I remembered this rundown aura from the days I lived in Sin City, fresh from Kentucky.

An intoxicating aroma of onions, grease, and melted cheese suffused the air. I bumped Kevin's arm. "My kind of place."

He shrugged. "I know my gal."

"Sit anywhere." An old woman's dry voice spoke from somewhere in the region of the grill, partially masked behind the counter.

Kevin steered me toward one of only two large, round tables. This one nestled in the rear corner, farthest from the door.

Though I tend to sit against the wall, a trait picked up from Crawford and his twenty-five years on the force, I left that for Rabi. Though the man had never been a cop, caution was etched in his bones. I slid into the wooden chair next to Kevin. It was by the counter and still afforded a view of the door and most of the room.

Two glasses of water slammed on the table. The woman's thin hands were deeply tanned and looked like old leather.

"What'll you have?" she barked.

I didn't bother looking at the menu or craning my neck to see our waitress. "Cheeseburger with grilled onions, fries, and a chocolate shake."

"You?" The dry voice prompted before I'd finished. "The usual? Reuben, onion rings, iced tea?"

"Ye-ah." Kevin did a slow double take as he answered. He put his arm across my chair. "Thanks."

Her shoes were clipping across the linoleum before his gratitude hit the air.

Shock lanced through me. Couldn't be... but that was Kevin's go to order nine times out of ten. "Is she– "

"Same waitress." His eyes reflected the same surprise I felt. "There can't be two of her."

It was eerie. I got the strange impression she would know my order if I walked in ten years from now. My curiosity disappeared five minutes later. The perfume of hot fries wafted off my plate and ordered my stomach to stand at attention.

"Mmmmm." I groaned around a bite of beef and cheese. "I may have to move to a hotel in this neighborhood."

"I can't see Marcus leaving the suite." Kevin barked out a laugh as he lifted his sandwich. "You and he can duke out that issue. They should be here any second."

As if his words conjured them, the door flung open. Marcus led the charge with more light and life than this place had seen in decades. Ripples of energy spread through the grease-laden air fed by an eleven-year-old whirlwind. He pointed at us from the doorway.

"There they are." He yelled over his shoulder at Mrs. C and Rabi, directly behind him and staring right at us. His black, straight hair gleamed with its own light. His grin was infectious.

I smiled with food stuck in my cheek and wiggled my fingers in greeting.

Mrs. C shuffled along in pink muffs while bestowing a benign smile on the astonished regulars.

Jack Rabi strode in, a tall, cadaver-thin, African-American man with shoulder-length, perfectly waved hair. With ebony skin covered by an ashen hue, the man has less meat on his tall frame than a skeleton. He carried himself with a cool aloofness. His eyes, as black as Marcus's, swept the room, missed nothing.

Retired from Special Ops after over two decades, he used to pick up packages for my now former full-time job. Soon after moving in, Marcus had adopted him as a surrogate uncle. No one would harm Marcus and live to tell the tale while Rabi was around.

Though his blue linen shirt had few hiding places to mask a gun, I knew he carried one.

Once everyone settled, I gave Marcus a quick hug and a kiss on the cheek before the waitress returned. A gnarled old stick of a woman, she had one pencil stuck through a scraggly, gray bun and pulled another pencil from behind her ear. With orders in place and drinks delivered, calm returned.

Kevin nodded at the other man. "Hey, Rabi."

Rabi stretched a bare smile that faded quickly. "Hear you stepped in it again."

Kevin spread out his hands. "That's nothing new with Belden in the picture."

"Rabi." I smiled a heartfelt welcome. The man's solid presence never failed to calm my worries. Perhaps because he met every situation - calm, calamity, or crisis - with the same neutral expression that returned my greeting. "I don't know how, but we found trouble."

I outlined the trip to Harrison's office from Safina's appearance to Ms. Winter's demise. "She was behind the wheel. No keys in the ignition. No blood anywhere that I could see from outside the vehicle."

I shot Kevin an accusing look.

"Yeah, we're not in enough trouble," Kevin said sarcastically. "We need your fingerprints inside the car or a witness to see you messing with a dead woman's body."

He was right, but the cause of her death baffled me.

Mrs. C pursed her lips together. "Poor lady."

"A second murder." Marcus gave a silent whistle. "The killer's running scared."

Which only increased the stakes. Kevin and Rabi exchanged a telling look. The older man, sitting ramrod straight, dipped his chin. With the increased danger, I was doubly glad for his presence.

Kevin pointed a finger at Marcus. "I'll give you a list of names and numbers from the file in Harrison's office for the Westercamp Corporation. It may be real. It may be a front. One of Safina's aliases is listed as a consultant."

At Marcus's nod, Kevin jerked his head in my direction. "She was going to start an Internet search. I thought it best to wait for a professional."

Marcus's dark eyes twinkled above a serious expression. "She's so cute when she tries."

"Listen, fella." I aimed a French fry and a mock glare at my pint-sized detective. "Don't get smart with me, or I'll cut off your Internet access."

"Go ahead. I know every Wi-Fi password in five hundred yards of our apartment." He narrowed his eyes as he fought a losing battle against a grin. "And my cell phone has a hotspot."

He shot forward and bit off the fry. However, neither

food nor drink would distract Marcus from a case. He slid his gaze from one side then to the other.

"Guess what?" His mouth barely moved. His voice could hardly have carried beyond our table.

My little Sherlock. I bit back a smile.

Marcus kept his face a somber mask. "I found something weirder than murder."

I couldn't stop my groan. "Please, no more surprises. I can't take it."

But inside I couldn't wait to hear him out.

8

7 Down; 5 Letters;
Clue: Illuminate
Answer: Light

I met Marcus's shining gaze and caved instantly. "What's weirder than murder?"

Marcus's smug expression said more than any words could how much the boy loved having a secret to tell.

I snatched one of my fries from his fingers and inched my plate away, earning a frown.

"You ate an hour ago," I said in my own defense.

"Here." Kevin handed him an onion ring. "Hit the high points."

Marcus grabbed the prize as if he still had to steal to eat. He bit into one side of the onion ring.

"Harrison was in court at eight o'clock. First case of the day." Marcus rattled off the facts like a machine-gun. "The defendant was a no-show. Ivan Graham, arrested for assault in a bar fight last weekend. Thing is – "

He broke off. The pause stretched enough to peak the tension, then the little showman delivered. "This was Harrison's first criminal case in like forever, fifteen years at least."

Forever isn't what it used to be. While the waitress delivered the food for the other three, I squirmed in my chair until she left. "Why hasn't he been in court in fifteen years?"

"I'll get to that." Marcus grabbed his cue. "Ivan Graham and Harrison both work for Westercamp Corporation. The place Safina is contracted with. It's legit. An international import-export company. They've been in business for forty years. The company flies produce and spices in from South American and Latin American countries."

I bit my lip while I thought back on Crawford's briefing. "Harrison… er, Darlington said the files pertained to artifacts being smuggled out of Latin and Central America, then sold to private collectors for big money. He had the goods on the bribery and the routes."

"Good front," Rabi spoke softly. "Been in that area a few times back in the day. Too much land for anyone to secure. Locals learn of the archeological digs and take what they can find when the sites are deserted."

The man had been silent for so long, I'd almost forgotten him. For a guy with his size and presence, he had an uncanny ability to hide in plain sight.

Kevin jerked forward, jarring me out of my comfortable position. "The file I found in Harrison's office lists Safina as a public relations contractor for Westercamp. She'd be able to keep an eye on the flights in and out."

"The principals are all tied in a little circle." I swirled a fry through the ketchup. "Do Harrison and Ivan Graham work closely together?"

"Nope. Ivan works in the computer department. It's at the headquarters outside the Vegas city limits, close to a small airport." My son delivered the facts in a clear tone. "Harrison works at his office. He does civil cases, represents businesses. Boring stuff. Westercamp Corporation is his biggest client."

"Why would the company pull in one of their business attorneys to defend a computer geek on a minor charge?" I tossed the question around without finding an angle.

No one offered an answer.

"They must have a reason." Kevin settled in his chair, a thoughtful expression on his face. "International connections. An airport. Perfect setup. Safina's after an artifact."

"The Feilens must have a buyer ready." I took a long drink of my chocolate malt. "What about the dead guy, Darlington? How does he tie in?"

Marcus folded his arms across his chest and gave us the eagle eye. "If you people want the facts, quit interrupting."

"Yeah." I nudged Kevin in the ribs. The moments are rare when I can pretend to be self-righteous. I grabbed this one and ran. "Behave yourself."

Kevin slid me a sideways look. "Don't even start."

"Go on," I prompted Marcus. "We'll be quiet."

The boy rolled his eyes. He balanced precariously in the edge of his chair as he began another report. "J.D. Darlington was a shyster, an ambulance chaser."

"Crawford knew Darlington," Kevin interjected. "Said the guy was a bottom feeder."

"The cops didn't like him because he got his lowlife clients off." Coming from the streets, the boy's sympathies were solidly with castoffs. "He made deals with the DA, had clients snitch to get lower sentences. Whatever worked."

Marcus had lived most of his life on the bottom rung. Skirting the system to survive was something he understood.

Kevin thrummed the table with his fingers.

A secret gleamed in Marcus's eyes. "Darlington's son, Shawn, has worked as a paralegal in Harrison's office for two years while going to law school. He took classes with Ivan. They're friends."

"Interesting." My pulse picked up speed. Part of the puzzle was coming together. "Son Shawn would have access to Harrison's files."

Kevin's arm encircled my shoulders. "Shawn discovers evidence of smuggling and gives the files to J.D., who calls Crawford."

Mrs. C's eyes peeked over the rim of her cup as she sipped her Earl Grey tea. She dabbed at her lips with a napkin. "Someone caught on and killed the poor man. What about the son?"

Marcus typed away on his phone, a present from Rabi. The boy's eyes darted over the screen. His expression sobered. "Shawn Darlington died in a one-car accident last night. His identity was released this morning."

I sat back in a feeble attempt to distance myself from this latest blow. However, the hooks of the oppressive announcement had already sunk into my gut.

Mrs. C's grimace at the news multiplied her wrinkles. "Three murders."

Rabi's hand engulfed his coffee cup. He gave an infinitesimal shake of his head. "No proof of murder."

I took refuge against the discussion by resting against Kevin's warmth. This morass of crime was not what I'd envisioned for our time in Las Vegas.

Kevin's hand tightened around my shoulders. "We'll have to see what we can find out about the accident."

I let out a long breath, fighting to find my voice. "Father and son dead. But why Winter? Did she know about the smuggling or the files? Why would Shawn involve her?"

Asking unanswerable questions is only one of my many skills.

"We need to make progress before the killer strikes

again." I fought to shake off the weight of another death. "Or before Detective Pierce dredges up enough circumstantial evidence to arrest Kevin or, worse, me."

My quip drew smiles. I was only half-joking. It's hard to investigate from a jail cell. I've tried.

"Ivan Graham is our best lead," Marcus spoke with the certainty of youth. "We have to find him before the killer does. He may have only hours to live."

I would have liked to dismiss the comment as melodrama, but at the rate we were losing leads, the boy had a point. If Ivan knew anything useful, his time in this desert town could be running out.

"You and Kevin better stay behind." A mischievous gleam lit Marcus's gaze. "We need this one alive. You just find dead people."

Kevin pointed at me. "It's her."

"If your Mr. Ivan has anything under his hat, he's most likely left town." Mrs. C delivered the helpful tidbit with a sigh of defeat.

I frowned at her doomsday attitude. "He didn't go anywhere."

"Guys like him don't leave their hood." Marcus threw his street smarts into the fray. "They don't know anything else."

A pang lanced through my heart at the casual certainty in my son's tone. The same bleak future had faced my precious, little, trouble making PI most of his life.

Though Rabi's expression remained neutral, the man's black eyes burned with a protective fire as he studied the orphaned street angel who'd brought us together.

"What are you scowling about?" Marcus frowned at me. "I agreed with you."

"Yes, you did." I grabbed his hand. "Because we're both geniuses."

His concern melted into a smile.

Kevin squeezed my arm. "All right, geniuses. Where do we find our man?"

Marcus pulled his hand from mine and put up first one finger, then another. "Hangouts. Friends. Crash pads."

Rabi set his elbows on the table. He almost smiled. "Arrest record."

The man's low drawl added an ironclad certainty to the argument.

"Let me make a call." Mrs. C smacked her mug on the table. "Quite a bit of information might be gleaned from the young man's run-in with the bobbies."

Cautious hope took hold in my gut.

"We need facts." Kevin's gaze lingered on the door before refocusing on our table. "With two, possibly three murders in one day, the police will be under pressure to bring in a suspect."

When I covered his hand with mine, his sapphire eyes focused on me. His protective nature still weighed on him.

"Don't start," I warned. "We're stronger together."

"She's right." Marcus half-stood. "Without us, the cops will railroad you."

"The police are trying to find the real killer." The boy's certainty forced me to defend the legal system. "Kevin and I were in the wrong place at the wrong time."

"Twice," Mrs. C muttered as she clicked off her phone.

Marcus waved his hand. Whether he meant to dismiss my opinion of the police or banish Kevin's worry was an open question. "If anyone can dig up this Ivan guy, we can."

"Absolutely," Kevin agreed with the dubious pronouncement with a straight face. "Let's do it."

9

31 Down; 8 Letters;
Clue: Meet face-to-face with argumentative intent
Answer: Confront

Kevin and I exited the Penny Lane Café into a shock of sunlight. The others were ahead of us, walking toward the cars. I blocked Kevin's path, forcing him to stop. "You kept glancing at the door. Were you expecting Safina?"

Now that we were outside, his shoulders were more relaxed. "After seeing her at Harrison's, I thought she might show."

"You didn't expose her identity to Harrison."

"She's my sister. We worked together until I was eighteen." Big brother loyalty rang in his voice. Nostalgia lit his eyes. "It's like undercover cops. I couldn't break her cover."

I chuckled at the comparison. "I'm tucking that away to use on Crawford the next time we discuss how much cops and criminals have in common."

Kevin leaned close. "I want to be there."

"No locking lips." Marcus's yell cut across the empty lot. "Focus on business."

Kevin held up our joined hands as we resumed walking. "Is holding hands allowed?"

Marcus slapped a hand to his forehead. "We're trying to save you from being locked up. What's more important?"

While Rabi and Mrs. C looked on with amused expressions, Kevin scrunched his face up. "Let me think about it."

The boy dictator crossed his arms across his chest.

The uplifting strains of the *Rocky* theme erupted from Mrs. Colchester's purse, saving Kevin from making a choice.

"That will be Shep. The dear man was a boxer in his day."

I leaned against Kevin, prepared to wait out a lengthy explanation.

"Strength and stamina were there." She confirmed with her head half-buried in the duffle bag purse that was her constant companion. "Decent speed, but one can't bob-and-weave forever. Poor boy simply couldn't take a hit. Glass jaw, don't you know?"

I shook my head in mock sympathy, partly for poor, dear Shep, partly for the rest of us. "I take it, he's your police contact in Vegas?"

"He took a job with the county." She balanced the bag on the hood of the Caddy as the phone trilled on. "Works in a civilian capacity with the bobbies. I asked him to keep an ear out for updates on the murder as well as news on Ivan Graham."

Kevin eyed her as she continued to dig for the phone. "Need help?"

"Here it is." The ringing grew louder. She pulled the phone out like a buried treasure from a chasm.

"Hello, Shep." Her eyes grew distant, then her expression became animated. "Really?"

Marcus stood on tiptoe and leaned toward her.

I rolled my eyes. "You can't hear what – "

"Shhhh." He flapped a hand at me without shifting his stance.

Kevin reached out and pulled me into a close embrace. "This may be our only chance. The guard is distracted."

I smiled and put my arms around his neck.

After another moment of the older woman's Ah's and Oh's, she hung up.

"That was Shep," she repeated. "He's got Ivan Graham's arrest records as well as additional documentation. He assures me it's worth reviewing in person."

"At the police station?" Marcus caught his breath. Police stations were his amusement parks of choice. When he saw Kevin and me, his expression became stern. "You were *hugging* her."

Kevin leaned his cheek against my hair. "I couldn't help myself."

The ringtone of an old rotary phone sounded from Kevin's cell. He released me to take it out of his pocket.

Marcus narrowed his gaze. "Who's calling you?"

"I have other friends." Kevin's defensive tone was light-hearted, but he frowned at the readout. "Vegas area code."

"Don't answer," Marcus whispered. "Could be the cops trying to find your location."

I gave an unladylike snort. "They don't need to track our cell phones as long as we drive the Great White Beast."

Kevin swept a thumb across the screen. "Hello?"

Silence fell as everyone hovered to hear his side of the conversation, which amounted to nothing. Nada. A moment passed. Still nothing. Now I knew how Marcus felt.

Kevin's puzzled expression deepened. "Isn't speaking with me a conflict of interest?"

My curiosity reached a fever pitch. A conflict of interest wouldn't pertain to the police.

"You must be confident of your information to risk a meeting." Kevin's gaze cut to me. After a slight pause, he continued. "I'd say we should definitely get together."

Despite his smooth tone, his eyes held a look of caution.

"Who is it?" I mouthed silently, while my hands fisted in frustration.

Kevin's gaze shifted. "I'd have to ask Ms. Belden. However, I'm certain she'd be interested in speaking with the Las Vegas District Attorney."

Ripples of shock spread through my body. I felt my jaw drop. The only thing I knew about the local DA was that she was female. Possibly crazy or drunk - or both - to risk meeting with a murder suspect.

"Whoa." Marcus slapped the Caddy's hood. "I did *not* see that coming."

Kevin's gaze locked on mine. "Where and when?"

I bounced from foot to foot. If the man had had the slightest consideration, he'd have put the conversation on speaker.

"One hour," Kevin said with a note of finality. "We'll be there."

The moment he ended the call, I pounced on him like a striking cobra. "What does she want? Why is she involved? What does she know?"

"The DA's a woman?" Marcus asked. "What's her name?"

I gritted my teeth. Random questions like these were one reason our information swaps took so long.

"Her name is Elena Young," Kevin said with more patience than I felt.

"Cracking down on crime is the campaign slogan she's built her reputation on." Mrs. C was a faithful watcher of twenty-four-hour news channels. No disaster, tragedy, or political campaign escaped her notice. "The woman is running for Congress. She's got a strong lead."

Kevin glanced around the still empty lot. "No name on her phone, she probably used a disposable. She claims Darlington's murder is part of a case involving police corruption."

I picked my jaw off the pavement and gathered my wits. "You mentioned she had information. What was that about?"

Kevin threw his cell in the air, then made it disappear with a flip of his wrist. "She says an informant swears I'm innocent."

Hope bloomed in the desert air. Then I came to my senses and cut off that thinking with a ruthless stroke.

The DA meeting a murder suspect? The situation was far too iffy for anything but a large dose of caution.

"If the police are crooked, she can't go to Pierce." Marcus leaned against the Caddy. "If she trusts the witness, the DA knows you're not a killer."

Mrs. C's gaze remained on Kevin. "Prosecuting a high-profile murder case would be just the ticket to give her an unbeatable lead going into the election."

The older woman was spot on. The players in this case had their own agendas. The sun, bright and unyielding in the clear sky, cast no light on the case. While myriad objections swirled in my brain, I said the first thing that hit my lips. "This meeting's a gamble either way. One thing is certain, it won't last long once she discovers we know nothing."

Marcus tilted his head, showing a flush on his golden-hued skin. "We know lots. Once we find Ivan, we'll know more."

"You're right." I sought to lock onto his youthful confidence rather than my own "doom is around the corner" philosophy. Besides, how could we resist a chance for inside information? "What does she have to gain? She already has access to police reports."

Kevin's poker face was firmly in place, but wariness glowed like embers in his eyes. "She mentioned her confidence in my PI friend's abilities."

I almost lost control of my jaw again. "She thinks I can crack multiple murders involving possible police corruption?"

Though I'd had a couple of successful cases recently, this was only my fourth or fifth solo investigation.

Marcus threw his fists up in the air. "That is so cool!"

"No pressure." Humor replaced Kevin's guarded expression. "We meet in an hour. Sunset Park on a nature trail."

Mrs. C gave a dainty sniff. "A secret meeting would give her deniability if she ends up charging you with murder."

I wasn't so sure, not in an era where every phone was both camera and recorder.

Marcus squinted against the sun. "Mrs. Colchester, Rabi, and I will meet with Shep and get the low-down on Ivan."

Mrs. C's bright eyes sharpened. Her gray hair and parchment-like skin framed an expression akin to a five-year-old promised a treat. "We'll have a nice coze with Shep. His project involves cold cases."

"Cool." Marcus's gaze fired with a matching enthusiasm, then he paused. "Clearing Kevin is priority."

"You and Mrs. Colchester are good at getting facts." Rabi delivered the compliment with an admiring gaze.

Marcus, his straight black hair gleaming in the sun, snapped to a military-like posture before his expression melted to a frown. "Aren't you coming with us?"

Kevin's gaze caught Rabi's in a moment of unspoken agreement. "Rabi will provide cover for Tracy and me."

Marcus's eyes narrowed, then he nodded. "Never hurts to have backup."

"Absolutely." A serious note weighed down the older woman's tone. "Probably nothing more than a barrister trying to get a leg up on her career. However, with three deaths, it won't do to underestimate the opposition."

Her words cast a chill on the desert air.

I waded in, eager to end the conversation. "Where is Shep's office? Does Rabi have time to drop you off?"

"Shep is on this side of town," Mrs. C confirmed. "Just a bit east of I-15."

"The old southern branch?" Kevin asked. "Ten minutes. No problem."

No doubt he knew the position of every police substation in the area.

"Quite right, dear boy." The older woman hoisted her bag onto her shoulder like a private would a rifle. "Marcus and I will do our part. We'll report later."

"Find out all you can," Kevin said, slapping Marcus on the shoulder before turning to Rabi. "You know the layout of Sunset Park? The trail is on southern edge with higher ground on both sides."

The older man nodded. "Twenty minutes. In position."

I shoved my hands in my jeans to hide their shaking. My stomach was doing the jitterbug.

Two murders in broad daylight. A suspicious accident. The DA nosing around.

If things had been less unsettled, I would have urged Rabi to stay with the other two. But that was foolish. They were going to the police station. What could happen?

By the time Rabi's rented sedan disappeared, my bout with nerves was almost a thing of ten minutes ago.

"Now we have time to waste until we meet the Vegas's DA." I pointed at Kevin across the top of the Caddy. "I hope you know an ice-cream place in the neighborhood."

Kevin leaned his arm on the open door on the driver's side. "You just polished off a chocolate shake."

"Marcus drank half," I reminded him. "Besides, that was lunch. This is dessert."

Kevin gave me a warm look, then his gaze shifted behind me. His expression froze.

The low thrum of an engine rolled into the rundown parking lot. A low-slung sports car pulled up and screeched to a halt.

A young woman rose out of the depths. She wore a sleeveless, neon pink dress that looked painted on, plus a wide-brimmed hat of the same color. Her auburn hair was cut in a sleek bob that curled at her jawline. Oversized sunglasses hid most of her face. With a designer bag on her shoulder and bracelets jangling on her wrist, she looked like a New York model who'd lost her way.

She sauntered over and stood dead center in front of the car, a thundercloud on six-inch stilettos. Pushing the sunglasses to the end of her nose, she eyed Kevin over the rims. The ends of her mouth lifted. "Hey, bro."

10

23 Across; 11 Letters;
Clue: Betray or cheat an associate
Answer: Double Cross

S tanding by the open door on the driver's side, Kevin's hand hovered millimeters above the top of the car.

As his gaze swept over Safina's third persona of the day, I remembered his comment about being on the other side of the looking glass. For a moment, reality shifted and I wondered if, in another universe, he might have stayed with his family. In that universe, he would have been standing by her side.

My breath caught. Did Safina think she could pull Kevin back to his old way of life? The thought had haunted me in the first years after we'd met. How could I live without him?

As the thought swept in on a dark cloud, his fingers landed on the Caddy, anchoring him to my world, my life, my side. Well, me and the Great White Beast. I breathed a silent thanks and blamed my insecurity on love. A fierce possessiveness rose inside me. Kevin was part of *my* life, *my* future.

"I figured you'd come," was all he said.

The tight line of Safina's jaw relaxed. A long, slow breath escaped her lips as an air of coming home moved through her expression. Her reaction reminded me of hugging base in a childhood game. A player on base can't be eliminated. But, as Darlington and Winter had learned, in this game, there was no safe place.

"Nice ride." Safina pointed at the car with a hot pink lacquered fingernail the exact shade of her outfit.

For sheer effect, it was hard not to be impressed. I could have scoured my entire wardrobe without finding a dress, hat, and shoes that matched. And that's discounting the nails and the lipstick completely.

The hope of getting some insight into the two murders alleviated my disappointment at watching my promised Rocky Road ice-cream cone melt away.

Kevin leaned his arm on the open car door. "What's the game? Murder isn't usually part of the script."

Her gaze slid to me, then she took off her hat. With practiced grace, she plopped it on the hood and shook out her auburn wig.

I dialed back my annoyance. Maybe I should give her a break. Maybe she was here to help. Maybe she wanted to switch to our side. "Hi, I'm Trac--"

"I need to speak with my brother. Alone."

I felt my half-hearted smile stiffen. "Wouldn't this morning, before the police found him with a dead body, have been a better time for conversation? Or maybe at Harrison's office?"

Her cool expression held. Only the slightest of sneers gave any indication my dart had struck.

Oops. New record for snarky beating out nice.

I have the best of intentions. They just don't last.

She lifted her chin, then turned to Kevin. "What are you doing in Vegas?"

The underlying censure made me wonder if they'd divided up the state and he'd crossed a line.

He simply shrugged. "Tracy and I came for the weekend."

His calm tone was in sharp contrast to his sister's tight delivery.

Safina's expression turned skeptical.

In light of what had happened, I have to say I wouldn't have believed him either.

Kevin shut the car door and rounded the front of the vehicle. His expression hard. His jaw set. "Why were you meeting Tracy's client at the convention center this morning?"

Her green contacts met his gaze with a guileless expression a cherub would have envied.

A grudging admiration for her chutzpah wiggled its way under my shields.

"A retrieval." She blinked those big eyes. "I came in a week ago as a contractor for Westercamp in case we needed someone on the inside. I'm signed up to help at a booth at an expo on Sunday. I planned to be gone by then; now I'll have to show up. This was supposed to be quick. In and out."

That was the same line Crawford had fed me. Easy money. Look where that had landed me. "What went wrong?"

She looked down her straight, little nose and sniffed. "Everything."

I nodded before I could stop myself. The question was - had she resorted to murder when things went south?

With a toss of her auburn wig, she continued. "When the seller stalled, I got worried. Then, he admitted someone got into his files and took the item. He wants the files. I want the goods. The family is waiting in the Riviera. We have several buyers lined up."

"In the end, the scales balance." Kevin's stern words held no sympathy for her plan gone wrong. "Maybe your tab came due."

Except Kevin was the one who'd been caught with the body. The one suspected of murder.

She raised her chin. "I don't have time to discuss my morals."

I bit my lip. Do. Not. Say. A. Word.

We were short on time anyway. There was simply no way to cover that much material.

"You have to move the item." She pressed a hand against the Caddy's hood. Her skin showed white around the nails. "I can take it off your hands. Today would be best. Gram and Shark are waiting for Fedor and me to deliver it. We have several buyers in play."

I tapped my knuckles on the Caddy's hood sharp enough to send a metallic clang ringing through the air. "What item are you looking for?"

The only thing I knew of were stolen files. If there was more, I needed to know, and I've never been shy about asking.

Safina aimed her best sneer my way. "The golden Mayan codex, of course. Did you really think your pathetic little test would trip me up?"

I covered my shock by holding onto a neutral expression with both hands. Inside, my mind was stuttering. I couldn't believe she'd given me a straight answer. And what an answer. Crawford hadn't mentioned a Mayan codex. Gold or otherwise. Darlington was a whistleblower. I'd never dreamt an ancient artifact was involved.

Kevin paused a beat, then leisurely folded his arms across his chest. "Maybe I don't have the codex or the files."

She searched his seemingly unconcerned expression. A frown puckered her brows. "I never could read you."

Nice to know it wasn't just me.

"You're the only one who *could* have the files." Safina's mew of impatience cracked her mask. "Darlington had them when he was killed. I didn't take them. They're not among his possessions in police custody."

Her certainty left no room for argument. Her expectant gaze focused on her brother.

Why was she sharing this information? Why had she given me a direct answer about the codex? Did she think Kevin would reciprocate?

"How could anyone believe Kevin took documents off the body?" I was baffled. "Pierce arrived within seconds. Kevin couldn't have hidden bulky folders."

She gave me a look dripping with disdain. "This isn't the nineteen-seventies. We're talking about a thumb drive."

I fought to hide my chagrin. I knew that. My boss had told me as much, but my brain had been planning a getaway with Kevin. Kicking myself for the oversight, I shot her a sneer and wished I hadn't let my romantic weekend distract me. I skipped the recriminations to focus on what was happening now.

Kevin had said Darlington gripped his hand before dying. Images of my man manipulating dice, cards, and coins flashed through my mind. Pierce frisking Kevin meant nothing.

Kevin's expression remained unchanged. "What about Pierce?"

Safina didn't so much as flick an eyebrow, yet the tension flickered and coiled like a serpent. "The cop didn't have time to pocket anything after he… "

We stood in a silent tableau as a desert wind swept in to rustle the leaves of the palm trees. The breeze did nothing to cool the air. Instead, the heat seemed to rise to a boiling point.

"After he stabbed Darlington." Her words rushed out on a lungful of air. Her tone held a cutting edge of anger that I couldn't decipher.

I cocked my head to one side. "You saw Pierce stab Darlington?"

Between the spitting sand and her accusing the lead detective of murder, I couldn't have drawn a full breath if I'd tried. Pierce was an arrogant pain in the neck. But a killer?

This day was chock full of surprises.

"I lost sight of him." She bit off the words. Her flushed cheeks gave an outward sign of her disgust at such a basic failure. Her smooth mask returned with the speed of a flipped switch.

I floundered for a response. She, and possibly Kevin, might view the lapse as unforgivable, but I was used to falling. After a setback, I pick myself up off the ground and start again.

Safina's shoulders relaxed an iota as she turned away from her brother's unyielding gaze. "Pierce was behind me. I know *that*. I looked over my shoulder. Didn't see him. I thought he'd lost ground. Then, I see his twenty-year-old navy jacket up ahead. That rolling foot patrol walk. I can spot a cop."

She tossed the comment over her shoulder to Kevin. The tone harkened back to their childhood.

Grifting lesson number two, no doubt.

She aimed her lacquered nail at my chest like a rocket launcher. "He was hot-footing it for Darlington. I doubled my pace. No crooked cop is going to cheat me out of my payday. When I got to the hall, Pierce was rushing toward the exit. I looked into the alcove and saw the knife in Darlington's chest. Pierce had his back to me, but I could tell he'd been careful not to get splattered."

Which explained how the detective arrived at the scene moments later free of blood stains.

She flicked a hand in front of her face as if brushing away an insect. "Pierce bolted to the far corner of the hall without turning around."

The images painted a compelling scene.

What's the worst kind of murderer? A bad cop.

Who's the best witness? A trained con artist.

"What did you do?" Kevin's tone made it obvious he knew where her priorities lay.

She settled back on her stilettos. "I asked Darlington where to find the codex. Then I checked him for the thumb drive."

Her callous attitude made me shudder. "How about calling for help?"

She rolled her eyes. "He was dying. I started to check his pockets then I heard footsteps, so I ran."

She and Kevin couldn't possibly have the same blood in their veins. "How do we know you don't have the thumb drive?"

She graced me with a smile that would have lit a Vegas marquee. "If I had the files, I'd hunt down the codex and be on a plane to the Riviera."

Okay, that was naive on my part.

Safina's fingers trailed along the hood as she stepped in Kevin's direction. "I won't let you take the fall for murder, but I can't go to the police. Who would believe my version?"

I don't care if what she said was true; I refused to let her off the hook. "You could still tell the truth if you remember what that means."

She narrowed her green eyes at me. "I gave you the facts. You're Wonder Woman. You clear him."

We locked gazes.

"I will." Though I had no idea how. Not having answers had never stopped me before. No reason to let being clueless interfere now.

Safina aimed a direct gaze at Kevin. "Tell me the location of the codex, or give me the thumb drive. Darlington and his son surely recorded the new hiding place. Then, this could all go away."

Breath hissed through my teeth. Who was she trying to convince? Could enough money make two murders disappear? I hated to think it was true, but my cynical side said it could happen.

Kevin hooked his thumbs in his jeans. "I'll stick with Wonder Woman."

His sister's gaze slid to me.

I had no trouble keeping my expression neutral. Not only had I been fabricating stories since grade school, but my PI experience had also honed my skills. Besides, I was absolutely clueless as to the thumb drive's whereabouts.

Safina whisked her hat off the hood. "Just remember, I tried to help."

A moment later, the roar of her Corvette was a memory. I sat next to Kevin in the Caddy while the AC wafted over me. Too bad I was steaming on the inside.

"Belden, you're not going to redeem Safina, but your penchant for tilting at windmills is one of the reasons I love you."

Inwardly thrilled, I raised a brow, pretending to misunderstand. "Are you saying I remind you of an old, Spanish man?"

"Not even a little bit." He stroked my chin with one finger then kissed me.

Shivers shot all the way to my toes.

The kiss ended far too quickly.

His mouth was still close to mine when he spoke. "Wanna go see what the DA has to say?"

"Absolutely." Although more kissing didn't sound bad. An adage I'd read somewhere popped into my mind: Being an adult means doing not what you want to do, but what you have to do.

Who was I kidding? I couldn't wait for the next episode in this drama.

Think about it. Why would a DA, even if she suspected the lead detective was dirty, turn to a possible suspect and a part-time PI?

As Mrs. C said earlier, this is Las Vegas. Play the odds. What's more likely…

That she needed help?

Or that she was setting us up?

17 Down; 4 Letters;
Clue: The movement of air
Answer: Wind

A cop as the killer.

A grifter as the only witness.

A DA who doesn't trust the police.

I wasn't sure this case could get much worse. I stood a couple of feet away from Kevin and Elena Young in the shade of a large oak in Sunset Park. Without a whisper of a breeze to stir the seventy-degree air, nervous sweat trickled down my neck.

A wood-covered bluff rose thirty yards from where we stood. A rocky promontory sat at a right angle to the gentle rise. Either was a perfect spot for any number of people to hide. Knowing Rabi was up there somewhere was my only cause for comfort.

The DA had outlined her position with a plainspoken

efficiency I admired. Her silver blond hair softened her square face while a compelling passion fired her help-me-help-you appeal. Give her a podium and a camera, and she was a shoo-in for Congress.

Her last comment about rounding up crooked cops had me ready to toss Safina's testimony against Pierce into the ring. However, Kevin, an old hand at playing his cards close to his chest, said, "What about Pierce as the possible murderer? He was on the scene."

"I'm aware of that." Young never shifted her gaze from Kevin's face. She seemed to weigh every word she uttered. "I believe several people are taking money from the smugglers. To make a case I need proof. Contacts. Payoffs. Amounts."

At this point, I was less concerned with the smuggling than homing in on who could clear Kevin of Darlington's murder. "Can your witness identify the killer?"

"I never said my contact witnessed J.D. Darlington's murder." Her hard eyes stared into mine to drive the point home. "My informant simply confirmed Kevin didn't strike the fatal blow."

My Spidey senses tingled at her odd choice of words. How could her contact *know* Kevin was innocent unless they saw the murder? Safina hadn't gone to Young with her story, and there were only so many people in that hall when the blow was struck. If the informant wasn't Kevin's sister, who could it be?

Though Kevin didn't move a muscle, his attention zeroed in on the other woman. "It would save time if we knew the identity of your contact. If we run into them during our investigation, we could work together."

"There have already been two murders and one suspicious death." Young's hand sliced through the air. "I refuse to endanger people who trust me by giving out a name."

I couldn't fault her logic or her caution.

"Darlington gave you no information?" Young wasted no time turning the questions back to Kevin. She hadn't been able to hide her disappointment, bordering on disbelief, at our lack of anything concrete to offer. "He said nothing before he died?"

Con. Shill.

The dead man's last words implicated Safina in a con game, which would tie her to the murder.

I was willing to throw her to the wolves, but I knew my chivalrous knight wouldn't.

Kevin fisted his hands. For anyone who didn't know his iron control, his frustration appeared to match Young's. "If I had evidence that would clear me and ensure the safety of my friends, I'd hand it over."

I loved the way he answered questions without giving anything away. Even if he had the thumb drive, it wouldn't clear him of murder.

Young's no-nonsense hazel eyes swept over me in my Girl Friday role. "Hard evidence is the only thing that will clear you both and cement my case."

I kept my "well, duh" response to myself. I knew that much and I didn't have a law degree. The thumb drive was the MacGuffin, as Marcus called it, that everyone sought. Though, I had to wonder how many people were aware there was a missing golden artifact. That upped the stakes.

Young's tone signaled the wrap-it-up phase. She pulled a slip of paper out of her pocket and tapped it against her short nail. "The cell number on this card is untraceable. If you learn anything, call me. I'll help any way I can."

Young held out the card.

Kevin reached for it.

At the moment of exchange, a contrary wind whisked the paper out of her hand. Moving as one, they bent and grabbed for it.

Firecrackers popped from the rocky promontory.

The DA jumped. In other circumstances, her stunned expression might have been laughable. She ducked, stumbling in the grass.

Time seemed to stretch out as shock raced through my veins.

Kevin's hand closed on the paper. He pivoted toward me.

A thrumming sound zinged through the air.

The sound repeated, clarified into the sharp report of gunfire.

Young's shocked gaze searched the wood-covered hill. "Two shooters?"

A divot of dirt kicked up several feet on the other side of Kevin and Young.

More gunfire sounded in the distance.

Fear galloped through my blood, but I couldn't move.

Young spun on her heel and bolted for her car. The roar of her revving engine and tires spinning on gravel sounded over the blood rushing in my ears.

In the nanoseconds since the gunfire, my body remained locked in place.

Still crouched over, Kevin's muscled arm slammed into my gut. He turned me around in one fluid motion. Before I knew my feet were moving, the broad trunk of the oak tree was racing toward me.

By the time I drew in air, rough bark poked through my shirt.

The sound of the DA's car faded as it sped down the path and out of sight.

Though the tree stood between us and the direction of the gunfire, Kevin shielded me with his body.

"Alone at last," I spoke the words in a breathless tone. My heart thudded in time with his until all I could hear were the beats sounding in my ears. I fought to ratchet my brain into working order, but it kept focusing on the card fluttering in the wind.

Silence fell. A scrawny, gray squirrel scurried through the dry underbrush and up a nearby tree.

Kevin's phone erupted.

A rush of adrenaline fired my jangled nerves.

Three notes sounded of *The Good, the Bad and the Ugly*. Rabi's ringtone. Theme music from some old western movie Marcus had downloaded for all of us. The guys thought it was hilarious.

Like the love affair with cars, I never got the joke.

The scattered thoughts zipped through my mind as I sighed in relief. Our own personal cavalry coming to the rescue.

Kevin had the phone to his ear. "Yeah?"

His step back gave me more room but left me feeling exposed. Crazy, I know. Unless the squirrel pulled out a semi-automatic.

I glanced at the branches overhead, just in case.

Kevin palmed his keys, then peered around the tree.

I ducked under his arm and checked as well. No one in sight. Young was long gone.

"Moving in ten." Kevin's gaze met mine as he spoke into the phone. He hung up. "The guy withdrew when Rabi returned fire. Rabi will cover us."

A sense of calm descended over me. "Say when."

Kevin's calloused hand grasped mine. "Now."

My feet flew across the grass.

Halfway to the car.

No firecrackers.

My feet slammed against the hardpacked ground. I skidded to a stop by the Caddy.

No shots.

In the car. Slam the door. Take off.

No car racer on the planet can touch Kevin behind the wheel. Before my heart resumed its normal rhythm, we left the park behind. The safe cocoon of city traffic surrounded us. My mind was still processing what had happened when he turned into the parking lot of a mid-sized motel and shut off the ignition.

My breath rushed out in a whoosh, like the errant breeze that had sent the DA's card kiting to the ground.

But for that gust of wind, I might have lost Kevin.

My fingers dug into his arm. Warm. Solid. Real. I followed the thought to him and pulled him into an embrace.

His strong arms crushed me to him so close I could feel his heart. Still beating.

Thanks, God.

"That was more exciting than I'd planned." His breath fanned my skin.

I planted a kiss on his cheek.

His jaw slid away from mine. He looked into my eyes then kissed me on the lips. A slow, lingering kiss that drove away all other thoughts.

We pulled back. Our breaths mingled.

My lips smiled against his. "How about we stay here and make out?"

His grin widened. "I've got a better venue planned for our time alone."

He gave me a quick, tight embrace, then his arms relaxed. "Time to get back on the job, Belden."

I reluctantly rolled away. "I always seem to be on the job."

I stepped out of the car, spread my arms, and welcomed the late afternoon sun. Amazing how almost getting shot had elevated my appreciation of even the most mundane moments.

Rabi was parked next to us. He leaned against his car, eyes scanning all directions.

I appreciated his discretion, happy for the few minutes of privacy.

Kevin gave the other man a grateful nod. "Nice backup."

Rabi shook his head, a disgusted expression on his face. "I couldn't get a bead on him in the heavy underbrush."

"You scared him enough to make him miss." I shivered in the desert heat at the memory of the close call. "That's good enough for me."

"I had the sun at my back." Rabi's tone slighted the shooter's choice.

"Still," I said. "That's a distance."

The sides of his mouth tilted up. He walked to the driver's window of his car and pulled out a pair of full-size binoculars.

A long, drawn out groan escaped my parted lips. "Does everyone have a pair of those but me?"

"Don't compare yourself with others." Kevin rubbed my shoulder. "You're the one who has a Trixie Belden Junior Detective Card, direct from Marcus's printer."

"That's so true," I said in a mollified tone, still eyeing the binoculars. "Those look like the pair Mrs. C uses to scout out the neighborhood."

A smirk flashed across Rabi's face.

That's when it hit me. "Those are hers?"

He nodded. "She had them in her purse."

I groaned. "Why am I not surprised?"

Rabi jerked his head toward the car. "Got a flashlight, too."

"Of course, all PI's need flashlights." I quoted the boy detective while my nerves regrouped.

Marcus was constantly tossing out rules of his own invention or ones gleaned from classic detective stories. I had a trunk full of so-called necessities in my car at home.

"I'm doubling your fee." I was more grateful than I could say, but Rabi wasn't long on words. "Two pizza parties."

Kevin snorted. "Isn't that a bit self-serving since you're probably going to be invited to the parties?"

"Why do you think I chose pizza? Besides, Rabi doesn't have to invite me, or you for that matter." The banter helped quell my nerves. "I'm sure he has other friends."

Kevin snorted. "He won't get away without inviting Marcus."

"Did you see the shooter?" I asked Rabi, unable to contain my questions any longer.

"A glint off the barrel." The smile that had tugged at Rabi's mouth faded. Steel hardened his tone. His eyes were dark in thought. "Shot from cover. Sniper style."

"Who was he aiming at?" I met Rabi's gaze. I'd replayed the scene in an endless loop, but it happened so fast.

"Target?" The lean man stared into the distance. "Either."

Kevin's eyes narrowed. "I'm betting on the DA. I'm a suspect in both murders. Too good a scapegoat to kill this early in the game. At least he wasn't aiming at you."

The tightness around Kevin's eyes eased.

I'd been standing four feet away from Kevin and Young's tête-à-tête. A ten-year-old with a BB gun could have nailed me.

"That leaves the DA." Rabi didn't sound broken up. He didn't have pizza riding on her safety.

"Makes sense." I kept my cheers silent. I didn't want to be unfeeling, but if I wasn't a target, it followed that Marcus, Mrs. C, and Rabi were also safe. Hopefully.

The pieces of the puzzle, like the questions for my crossword puzzle, lay scattered in my mind. It was far too early to make sense of this case.

"The shooter saw us with Young." Kevin cast me a

worried glance. His jaw was set. "We need to be more careful."

I knew what he was thinking. "Don't start that again. No one's leaving."

"I can't go." A somber tone deepened Rabi's voice. "Pizza's on the line."

I laughed at his intensity, then slipped an arm around Kevin's waist. "Whoever's behind this won't stop at the city limits."

Rabi nodded in my direction. "Woman's right."

"That's why I have the junior detective card." The quip rolled off my tongue, but my brain turned to more immediate matters. "The only way to be safe is to put the guilty people behind bars."

Kevin scanned the area. "Ms. Young's secret investigation isn't as well hidden as she thought."

That unwelcome realization had hit me while hiding behind the oak. "Somebody knew where and when we were meeting."

Rabi lowered his eyelids to half-mast and shook his head. "The shooter set up early. Otherwise I'd have seen him arrive."

Kevin crossed his arms across his chest. "They must have listened on Young's end. It's the only way the guy had time to arrive before any of us."

I analyzed the angles. "Tapping Young's cell would have been child's play for a crooked cop."

Kevin nudged Rabi. "Marcus bought a microphone on an infomercial last year that lets him listen in from thirty or forty feet."

Rabi's rare laughter rang out. "He does have the collection."

Every penny the boy earned went toward more gadgets.

My son definitely had me outclassed in the PI gig. "Either cops or smugglers would be as well-equipped."

"Our usual luck is holding," Kevin spoke in a sardonic tone. "Our only ally is the target of a killer, and she can't report the attack to the police without exposing her investigation."

"She had to know the dangers of chasing dirty cops." I felt bad for the woman, but she'd have to take her own precautions. I had my own problems. "We need a lead on the smugglers."

"Until we nail them, we play it doubly cautious." Kevin's electric blue gaze included Rabi in the warning.

Moments like this showed the two men were in easy sync with each other.

"Are we going to be taking watch overnight?" I tried to hide my trepidation by replacing my grimace with a stiff upper lip, a la the British. "I'm ready to take a shift."

I pumped my fist to prove I was serious.

The corners of Kevin's oh-so-cute mouth turned up. "You're the brains of this outfit. You need your rest."

"You sure?" I tried to hide my relief. Really, I did. "I promise I won't fall asleep."

This time.

Rabi winked. "We'll cover it."

"If you insist." I could afford to sound disappointed. I was off the hook. "For now, we need some facts about Darlington's role in the smuggling biz."

My phone trilled. None of my programmed contacts. "I'm going to stop answering this thing."

But I did. "Hello?"

"This is Officer Naughton with the Las Vegas Police Department. Is this Tracy Belden? Do you know a Mrs. Colchester?" When I answered affirmatively to both questions, the female voice continued in a curt tone. "You need to retrieve her and the boy."

"I understood they were visiting a volunteer at a local precinct." I eyed the guys. "Is there a problem?"

"We've had rival gangs that were less disruptive." She bit off the words. "You have to get them. Now."

Kevin had evidently caught the gist of the conversation. He jerked a thumb at the car. "It's a ten-minute ride. No problem."

I covered the phone. "What's the worse the cops would do? Arrest them? At least we'd know where they were."

Kevin gave me a flat stare. "Belden."

"Marcus loves to be fingerprinted," I reminded him in a wheedling tone, including Rabi. "It gives him a chance to point out the flaws in their technique."

Kevin jabbed a finger at my phone. "Ten minutes."

"Killjoy." I put the phone to my mouth. "We'll be right there."

I disconnected, then shot him a killer look. "Nobody would've gotten hurt."

Kevin started toward the car. "We don't need to piss off the police. Pierce is already looking at me for two murders."

"These are my tax dollars at work?" I tossed my hands in the air. "I have to rescue the police?"

Kevin glanced over his shoulder. "You don't live in Vegas."

"I live in Nevada," I said. "Besides, it's the principle."

"Get in the car." Kevin turned to Rabi. "You coming?"

The other man's eyes took on an enigmatic expression. "I'll check in later."

Wondering what contacts Rabi had in Vegas, I climbed into the luxurious leather seats of the Caddy. "Let's go see what our pair of rogues have dug up."

Once in the car, Kevin turned to me. "Do I get a pizza party for being shot at?"

I put on my best professional face. "You don't get paid when you're the problem."

Kevin started the car. "This morning I was a potential boyfriend. Now I'm a problem."

"You're also the client." I paused a beat. "The only one still alive."

"Let's keep it that way. After all, we have plans…"

3 Across; 9 Letters;
Clue: A narrow escape
Answer: Close Call

I walked into the police substation, a small brick affair, wondering what chaos Marcus and Mrs. C had wrought. Other than the Caddy, the parking lot held three cars. No one else came or went as Kevin and I arrived.

Inside, molded orange plastic chairs hugged the walls of a square waiting room. Opposite the door, a four-foot counter was topped by ceiling-high plexiglass. The low ringing of phones was punctuated by the soft clatter of computer keys.

I wondered what would happen if I reported the sniper attack. But I couldn't do that without compromising the DA. Better to stick with finding my son and Mrs. C.

A woman and man clad in tan LVPD uniforms scrutinized Kevin. Trained observers. Professionals. So why was I rescuing them from an old woman and a boy? I fought to hold onto my usual mask for police encounters - clueless but friendly. Unfortunately, jumpy nerves, fueled by residual fear trampled good intentions.

"I received a phone call regarding my son." A brusque edge hardened my tone.

The two exchanged a sheepish, almost guilty glance. Their relief was almost palpable.

"That boy of yours is something." The man, Cooper by his nametag, shook his head. A rueful tone filtered past his tough expression. "He was chattering so fast we barely caught your name and number."

"What's the issue?" Kevin stepped forward. He spoke in a mesmerizing, oh-so-reasonable tone. "They were invited here to visit one of your people."

"That would be Shep." Naughton, the female officer, tore her gaze away from Kevin's eyes long enough to respond. "His project, to scan cold cases into the computer, was axed three years ago. He's a volunteer now, but he's easily diverted. You have to get the boy and the woman out of here before they drag him off-point."

Shep sounded like a male version of Mrs. C. My worry receded, but I refused to let them off the hook. "You scared me half to death so I could solve your problem?"

Okay, so my wayward troupe *was* the problem. Hopefully, if I talked fast and moved faster, no one would trip me up with that detail.

My peripheral vision caught Kevin's glance in my direction. I didn't need to turn my head to see the amusement in his eyes. I never can fool him.

I crossed my arms over my chest, holding onto my attitude by a thread. "Where are they?"

Hope sprang into both sets of eyes. In choreography worthy of the Olympics, they pointed to their left. Two elevators faced the small lobby from a dead-end hall.

"Take the elevator to the basement. The first right turn leads to Records." The woman's voice was warm with relief. "Good luck."

"I'm going to need luck," I muttered as I walked to the elevator and punched the button. Despite my grousing, excitement bubbled in my veins like champagne on steroids. "I wonder if they have a lead?"

"We'll soon find out." Kevin put his arm around my shoulders and urged me into the open elevator. "My grandma always said: Work the case, get the goods, get out."

"Great, I'm getting advice from a geriatric grifter."

If the lobby had been quiet, the basement was tomb-like. Rippled tile on the floor matched walls of cinder blocks covered with peeling white paint. The place was a dungeon dressed up for company.

Equipment. Lab. Evidence. I checked the doors as I passed. All locked. "Where is everyone?"

"It's a substation, and it's two o'clock on Friday afternoon." Kevin pulled on our linked hands, maneuvering me away from the doors. "Quit trying to break into police labs."

"I'm just checking."

"Here it is. Records." Kevin gestured to the last door on the right and opened it with a turn of the knob.

We walked into a room the size of a gnome's house. The gnome in question, Shep I assumed, sat behind a metal desk that had been old before my birth. As he perched on an antique office chair, his round belly abutted the front of the desk. His gray hair ringed a bald scalp where a pair of wire-framed glasses stared at the ceiling.

"He has cookies," Marcus said by way of greeting. He waved a chocolate chip confection as proof. "You won't believe what we found."

I spared him a smile. No blood, bandages, or handcuffs. Relieved, I checked the rest of my surroundings.

"Hello, ducks." Mrs. C raised a china teacup in greeting. She was ensconced in a wood framed chair with ragged upholstery. "Tea? Chamomile? Earl Grey? Quite the selection."

I felt like I was in the tea party scene in *Alice in Wonderland*.

"Coffee?" The gnome gestured at a two-drawer metal file cabinet covered with offerings. Without waiting for an answer, he pointed a stubby finger at me, notched crooked on the first bone. "Or straight to business?"

I took one step forward. The move covered half the distance to the gnome. "What have you found?"

"Business." A satisfied glimmer shone out of his watchful eyes. He darted a glance at Marcus. "You were right."

The boy grabbed another cookie. "I win the bet."

Kevin hooked a chair with his foot and sat by Marcus. He filched a Macadamia nut cookie. "I'll skip the tea, too."

"Let's move along." I hooked two fingers in my front pockets, too on edge to sit in these confined quarters. "You are... "

"Shepfield Miller. Call me Shep." He stabbed a finger at his chest. "I'd have called, but cell phones can't be trusted."

"Anyone can listen in," Marcus piped up around a mouthful of cookie. "You don't even need a search warrant."

"Smart lad that." Shep sat back, having fueled both paranoia and ego. "Landlines are much more secure."

"Now that we've established the need for caution, what have you learned?" I prompted, hoping for solid answers.

Marcus did an excellent imitation of a Mexican jumping bean. "Harrison has worked for Westercamp for sixteen years. His lifestyle shot up seven years ago. Shep also has the goods on Ivan from the arrest record."

"Ivan Graham, Harrison's client this morning, was arrested on charges of disturbing the peace. Guess who his drinking companion was all evening?" Though the old man paused, no one got a chance to guess. "Shawn Darlington, Harrison's paralegal."

Talk about a tangled web. "Sounds like Ivan is definitely connected. Good job."

Marcus's chest shot out at my admiring tone. "Mrs. Colchester was a giant help."

"Oh, tish-tosh." She gave an airy wave. "I did little enough. A few hints. A few contacts. It was nothing."

Her artful disclaimer brought a smile to my lips.

"However," she looked over her coffee mug to wink at Marcus, "it's a good thing we came."

I held in a sigh. I wouldn't be able to check out a cheating husband without these two tagging along. Still, I couldn't help but smile.

Though I hadn't forgotten her comment from this morning about me always needing help, the news put me in a good mood. They'd actually scored information. All Kevin and I had accomplished was nearly getting him and the DA - our only ally - killed.

I sat back on my heels. "I think I'll take that coffee and cookie now."

"What did the DA say?" Marcus grabbed another cookie with a quick sleight of hand. "What does she know?"

A quick update, including not only a ban on more cookies for him, but news of the thumb drive, the missing artifact, and the gunman was followed by my son's silent whistle. "A sniper. You two could have been shot. Good thing Rabi was watching your back. You need to be careful. Someone is running scared."

"That would be me." I pointed my oatmeal raisin cookie at him. "We need to be cautious while we dig for answers."

Marcus sipped apple cider out of a plastic bottle. "Where do we start?"

I leaned against a four-drawer filing cabinet. Strands of the crisscrossing clues seemed to glimmer in the air. "Sounds like Harrison is smuggling ancient artifacts into the country and selling them on the black market. Shawn was in a perfect position to uncover the information. He downloaded the files on the smuggling and gave them to his sneaky, lawyer father, D.J. Darlington."

"Evidently, neither of the gentlemen were sneaky enough. They're both dead." Mrs. C click her tongue. Sympathy filled her tone. "Poor, dears."

Marcus's brow wrinkled. "We studied the Mayans last month in school. A codex is like a book. All but four of them were destroyed by the Spanish. If a new one was found, it would be worth a gazillion dollars. But why does your family want it, Kevin? Do they usually sell stuff?"

"Not just once." Kevin spun a spoon around on his finger. "Private collectors can't display the illegal artwork they acquire. So, a piece, known to be missing, can be copied and sold multiple times. That's what the thieves did when the Mona Lisa was stolen decades ago. That golden codex is a huge payout."

By the time he finished, I had several answers for my crossword puzzle and a new appreciation for the Feilen family's schemes.

"Ivan's our best lead." Kevin tossed a piece of cookie in the air and caught it in his mouth. He always had to be moving when he was thinking. "The guy was Shawn's drinking buddy. He has to know something."

"Ivan has no reason to cooperate with us." I washed down a bite of sugar and oatmeal with a surprisingly rich brew. "Unless we convince him he's next on the hit parade."

"Or trick him into giving us information." Kevin broke off a piece of white chocolate to munch. "We'll need details on his background to make that work."

Shep slapped his desk with more effect than noise. "Your young man helped with the research. Tell them, Marcus."

Marcus straightened in his seat, settling into his reporter stance. "Ivan Graham has worked for Westercamp for twelve years, originally as a delivery guy. He put himself through college, where he shared several computing classes with Shawn Darlington. Ivan's current job is in the computing department. The police report lists his address. We should check it out."

I froze, the coffee poised at my lips. "Sounds promising."

"Locating him will be easy." Kevin dusted the crumbs off his hands. "We need him to talk."

"Cops got nothing on T.R.'s interrogation." Marcus gave an emphatic nod that sent his straight, shining black hair flying around his face. "She just keeps talking until they crack."

I marked that in the compliment column, though I wasn't sure it qualified. After a short wrap up session, we headed to the hotel.

Fast forward to the Aquarius elevator rising toward the suite. It was late Friday afternoon, my first day in Vegas. Regretting the lack of the romantic dinner I'd envisioned, I leaned against Kevin. His strong arm around my waist held me upright. Once the doors opened, I stepped onto the deep pile carpet with a sense of relief. The day had been packed with more violence and twists than I could have imagined. Refuge, in the shape of my lush suite, waited down the hall.

For the past several hours, one of the pots simmering on my mental burner had been to ensure that my gang made it back safely. My goal was half a hotel corridor away from being accomplished.

Marcus popped out of the elevator with a spring in his step. "We should head out now. Ivan could be dead by morning."

Where did the boy get his energy? "He's not in danger."

"That we know of." Marcus shot back.

"We need a foolproof plan before we approach our mark," Kevin spoke in a no-nonsense tone that even my adventure crazed son could never budge.

Mrs. C shuffled behind us. "Me poor muffs need a sit-down. They're flat as pancakes, they are. I'll have to get out me reserve pair."

The day was catching up with me as well. "We need to plan a strategy… for dinner."

"Where'd Rabi go? When's he coming back?" Marcus bounced around the hall without waiting for an answer. "I'll get the door. Then we can decide on supper."

Kevin shook his head. "You definitely ended up with the right child. We just ate."

I aimed a tired smile at Kevin, already thinking of a long, hot, soaky bath.

Marcus's small-for-his-age frame bolted forward at twice the speed of sound, rattling on about lists and suspects.

The door to our suite opened.

A dark form stepped out inches from my son. Short. Square. Black clothes. A stocking cap covered his face. He glanced our way.

My heart leaped to my throat.

"Hey." Outrage rang in Marcus's tone. "That's our room."

The intruder bolted down the corridor in the opposite direction.

As I bunched my muscles, Kevin was already flying down the hall at a dead run. He caught Marcus's arm.

The boy struggled to escape. "We gotta get him."

My handsome knight wrapped his arm around my son's smaller body and skidded to a stop, pulling him into a protective hug.

I felt as if I were running through molasses. My mind felt even slower, like a movie at half speed.

The culprit reached the end of the corridor, pivoted, and vanished around the far corner.

"Go after him, Kevin." Marcus's arms wind-milled. "You can catch him."

Kevin kept a firm grip on the struggling child. "No one's chasing anybody."

As I caught up to them, time snapped to normal speed. I threw my arms around Kevin, squeezing my son between us. My heart thudded in my chest.

I let my fear explode all over Marcus. "What are you thinking, running after a burglar? We're dealing with dangerous people. You could have been hurt."

Marcus, looking chagrined, dug his sneakered toe into the carpet. "I didn't think."

He sounded exactly like me when I was his age. Or it could have been me last month. I bent and met his gaze. "The people we're up against have a lot to lose. You have to be more careful, or I'm seriously sending you home."

Kevin put a hand on the boy's hair. "Detectives have to be smart enough not to rush into situations."

The two guys exchanged a serious look; then their smiles broke the tension.

My eyes gazed at the door to our suite, which had swung closed. Trepidation seized my lungs.

The worn toe of Marcus's sneaker kicked the door open.

Kevin stepped in front of us both. He kept the door open with the back of his hand.

The boy peered around Kevin. "We've been ransacked."

I looked over Kevin's shoulder. Chaos met my gaze. Seat cushions cut open. Tabletops cleared of adornment. Vases broken. Clothes everywhere.

Kevin and I exchanged looks.

Marcus looked up at us. His golden-hued skin was a shade lighter than Kevin's tanned hand still holding his shoulder.

"Thumb drive," was all the boy said. "Or the codex."

It was what we were all thinking.

"Safina warned me," Kevin said in a somber tone. "The rest of the players think I've got the files and the gold."

"You think someone is still here?" Marcus leaned forward as far as Kevin's grasp allowed. "Let's find out."

"Let's not." Kevin grabbed his collar and pulled him back. The door slammed shut. "Hotel security and the police can earn their paychecks."

A long, slow exhale pulled my attention from the disaster that had been our suite.

Mrs. C leaned against the wall a few feet from the door. "Does this mean I won't get me afternoon lie down?"

"Back to the elevator," Kevin commanded.

Mrs. C's expression crumpled. "I'm certain the intruders are gone."

I put a hand under her arm. "Lean on me."

Kevin had his phone out. "What's the hotel's main number?"

I rattled off the number without thinking. While directions and cooking are mysteries I've failed to conquer, phone numbers, math, and puzzles have never deserted me. After spending an hour loitering in the convention center and reading hotel literature, I had the extension for every department at my beck and call.

A sniper and an intruder in the same day. And what do I have in my arsenal?

A phone directory.

13

8 Across; 8 Letters;
Clue: Deadlock between two opponents
Answer: Standoff

I f you want to be secure in Vegas, be a chip on a gambling table. Casino surveillance can spot a fly on a blackjack card at a hundred yards.

Standing inside the shambles of my demolished hotel room, I had no such confidence our intruder would be so easily identified. A stocking mask in the desert was my first clue. Pierce arriving right after hotel security was my second.

Rabi's return alleviated some of the chill coursing through my veins. His dark gaze marked each man and woman in the crime scene unit then dismissed them.

Pierce met his gaze and held.

Despite my opinion of the detective, his response showed a measure of inner strength. Which, if he was our killer, was not a good thing.

Rabi's gaze shifted to me, then Kevin. In motion all the while, another stride allowed him a view of the bedroom where Marcus and Mrs. C waited. Only then did he scan the chaos littering the floor.

"Took his time," Rabi muttered, as he strode into the bedroom.

Marcus greeted him with an excited yell, chattering about our latest adventure.

I studied the chaos with a keener eye. My nerves had been too lit up for me to digest the obvious. Such as how much time it takes to search each room, pull out drawers, dig into possible hiding places.

With so many of us in the suite, how could the intruder be certain we wouldn't return? Obviously, he hadn't known, since we'd almost tripped over him.

My list of suspects included a police detective, a lawyer, and a known pair of grifters, Safina, the only supposed witness to the murder, and Fedor, whoever he was. While I considered various possibilities, Pierce probed Kevin's defenses, looking for a weakness.

"What if the boy had walked in a moment sooner?" Pierce's question cut into me like a scalpel opening a wound. "The guy could have killed him with his bare hands."

My gut clenched as the detective paused to let my worst fear take root. I fought to keep my stricken feelings under wraps.

Show no weakness was a creed I'd heard on several fronts – Kevin, Marcus, Rabi, and Crawford – and observed on several occasions.

While I fought to control my emotions, Kevin's expression showed no cracks. His eyes locked onto the detective's face, searching no doubt, for a sign of the other man's true motives.

"The old woman?" Pierce dug the knife deeper. "One hard shove could break her neck. Think of them."

I heard a threat hidden behind the detective's supposed concern. My fury raged all the more because I'd fought with my conscience against those very dangers. I still struggled.

"Tell me what happened with Darlington." Pierce edged closer to Kevin. "If I can close the case, this violence will end."

How can you guarantee that? I shouted silently. Unless you're the author of the attacks. Okay, for fairness's sake, the man might be playing a police game. How could I know?

Kevin remained silent, refusing to be coerced into a response. His subtle method of waiting for answers was sometimes far superior for gaining information than my slash and burn mode of attack.

Silence is a powerful weapon. As the stillness lengthens, people feel a need to fill the moment, usually revealing more than intended.

Pierce cracked first. "You know what the intruder sought."

Kevin's expression changed to one of confused inno-cence. "I assume you mean the documents Darlington had on him. The ones he was supposed to deliver to Tracy."

The detective's hawk-like gaze didn't waver.

Kevin paused a beat, then shrugged. "I told you. I never saw the files. When I found him, his briefcase was open and empty. You should know. You arrived before I stood up."

The other man studied him for a long minute. "We're not talking about paper files."

I fought an impulse to wade into the fight. Insults and smart remarks tend to tick off people. Go figure. But the interaction between the two men wasn't that kind of fight. It was a chess match, and Kevin was doing fine.

The discipline he had developed over a lifetime came into

play as Pierce fished for information. A puzzled frown touched Kevin's handsome features.

I admired his control. When I look confused, it's because I actually am clueless.

Pierce exhaled when Kevin didn't respond to his comment about the lack of paper files. "Darlington downloaded the information onto a thumb drive. He had it on him when he died."

"A thumb drive?" Kevin spread his hands, taking in the destroyed room. "The guy who tossed our room thought he could find something that small in here?"

He gestured at the room's expanse, strewn with broken items, any of them larger than the piece of equipment being sought.

Kevin shook his head. "Who would be dumb enough to think brute force would work over brains to find a tiny piece of electronics?"

Pierce's gaze narrowed. If he were responsible for the attack, the words were a slap in his face. If not, the detective was no doubt analyzing Kevin's sincerity.

It was a delicate match.

Pierce shifted his bulk to square off against Kevin. "You were palming dice at five. You could have concealed a thumb drive even if I had frisked you."

True. I stopped myself from nodding just in time.

"I've been all over the city today." Kevin's exasperated tone spoke volumes. "If I ever had a USB drive, which I did not, I wouldn't have left it where I was staying."

"Where would you stash it?" Pierce asked. "If you were a criminal?"

Kevin shrugged. "I don't need a hiding place. However… "

Everyone in the room paused, momentarily forsaking the illusion that we weren't hanging on every word the two men uttered.

The detective froze like a dog on point, waiting for the former grifter to misstep.

Kevin's blue eyes narrowed. "If the thumb drive had been on Darlington's body, the coroner would have found it. He didn't. That leaves the police detective who checked his pockets as the most likely person to have palmed it."

Said detective clenched his jaw, no doubt to contain his red-faced fury which looked ready to blow.

A suspicious glint appeared in Kevin's gaze. "If you have the files, this interrogation is for show."

Like a flipped switch, Pierce's fury abated. Realizing he'd been played, he answered Kevin's verbal attack with a smirk. "I have no reason to keep the files secret. I'm not trying to make money by threats, blackmail, and extortion."

The slow rhythm of his words built to a crescendo.

Pieces of the puzzle that I'd seen and heard over the past several hours coalesced into an epiphany. Okay, a semi-epiphany. Or maybe, just a flashlight in a dark room.

None of the players involved had the thumb drive or the golden codex. Pierce, if guilty, would have passed the files to his bosses. Harrison or Safina would have sold them.

None of that had happened. Which was why everyone believed Kevin possessed the incriminating information and, possibly, the location of the stolen artifact.

I know, for a PI with a growing rep, I'm kind of slow sometimes. Epiphanies need to smack me upside the head. This one finally had. Despite being watched, Shawn or his father had managed to ditch the prizes before either of them were killed.

But where?

"You know what your problem is?" Pierce's words pulled me out of my speculation. He leaned in close to Kevin. "You and your amateur sleuth are behind the curve."

"Get it straight, Pierce." I'd be the first to admit I didn't have all the answers. However, calling me an amateur was rude. I might not be the brightest bulb in Vegas, but I was getting paid for this gig. "I'm a professional."

"Crawford must be desperate." He dismissed my bravado with a shrug. "You have no idea what's going on."

Hard to argue with the truth, but that wasn't about to stop me. "Neither do you. You're wasting time sniffing around us. We're the victims, not the perpetrators."

His features tightened. His hard jaw clenched.

I continued. "You don't have a clue about the location of the missing files or the murderer. Unless you see him when you look in a mirror."

The silence in the suite was broken by the muffled sound of movements.

I smirked in turn. "Or are you sniffing around, waiting for me to lead you to the truth like last time when Kevin was suspected of murder?"

The detective's jaw turned white.

For the record, I don't taunt animals, but harassing Pierce was too easy. Besides, I hated having him point out what few facts I had in my pocket.

A tight smile broke the detective's expression. His ability to control his anger was worrisome. As a fifteen-year veteran of the force, his intelligence had never been in doubt. Whether as a cop or a criminal, he was an opponent to be watched.

"You play a dangerous game." His words slid through gritted teeth.

His earlier comment regarding Marcus and Mrs. C's safety coiled in my gut. Beside that fear, anything else ran a distant second. I raised one shoulder in a seeming indifferent shrug. "Comes with the turf."

The tightness in my muscles tied me in knots. I wanted to

take a deep breath, roll my shoulders, but I couldn't let him see me sweat.

"We're done here," a nameless voice said.

The announcement gave both Pierce and me a way out.

Ripples of movement spread through the suite as the crime scene team packed their equipment, then headed for the door.

"You're going to need someone in your corner, or you'll be eaten alive." The detective stabbed a stubby finger at Kevin but stopped short of touching him. "I'll see you when the next body turns up. Hopefully, the corpse won't be one of your friends."

"Whoever who has the thumb drive is deliberately letting me and my friends take the brunt of the suspicion and the attacks." Kevin stared down the other man. A threat glittered in his sapphire stare. "If any of them get hurt, the person responsible will never be found."

"You can end this at any time." Pierce strode toward the door. "Want your friends safe? Call me when you're ready to confess."

With that parting shot, he crossed the threshold into the hall.

The room itself seemed to breathe easier.

I took a deep breath, then released it to a slow count, seeing how long I could make it last.

"Ms. Belden." The oily sounding voice brought my defenses up to full strength. "We need to discuss your future at our establishment."

Ankle deep in the ruins of my hotel room, the condescending tone set a match to the lava inside me. This was one hotel bureaucrat who had stepped into the wrong room at the wrong moment.

14

19 Down; 4 Letters;
Clue: Exchange one thing for another
Answer: Swap

With the volcano inside me coming to a boil, I met Kevin's amused gaze. He mouthed a silent, "Go, get him," as I turned toward the door.

A pale, ghoul of a man with short, silver blond hair faced me with a sorrowful expression.

"We've all had a long day." The man continued in a smooth voice. "However, after your involvement with a murder this morning and a break-in this afternoon, I fear we must discuss you seeking accommodations elsewhere for the remainder of your stay."

"*We've* had a long day?" A boiling irritation rippled across my raw emotions. I approached him with slow, measured steps. "How bad could your last eight hours have been?"

My peripheral vision caught Marcus's dark-haired body bolt from the bedroom where Rabi had kept him contained during the police presence.

Kevin captured the boy before he could enter the fray, leaving me free to concentrate on Mr. Ghoul.

The man raised his chin. "This unfortunate break-in is not your first involvement with violence today."

"I'm aware of that." I raised a brow. "I've come face-to-face with two dead bodies. My boyfriend was shot at. My son came within yards of a burglar who might well be a murderer."

The hotel rep cleared his throat. He looked over his shoulder as if expecting backup. Finding none, he continued. "In light of this latest event and the possibility of future danger, the management feels it is in everyone's interest if you seek rooms in another establishment."

Hit the streets. You are outta here.

"I hesitated to say anything while the police were here," I put my hand on my chest. I even managed a little sniffle, "but I'm relieved to be able to address this thread of violence."

The guy blinked rapidly. A wrinkle appeared between his brows.

I love to see ghouls squirm.

"I'm not blaming you personally," I assured him, watching surprise flutter across his face. "However, all signs indicate your establishment isn't safe."

Outrage rose from his Italian leather wingtips to his pointy, little nose. He straightened to his full five-foot-eight-inch height.

I didn't even pause for breath. The lava boiling beneath the surface had to vent. "As you've said, you had a murder in your convention center - – "

"We most certainly do not - – "

"A bloodstained killer no one saw because your security cameras are focused on the gambling tables. There are none in the service hall of the convention center. If those facts appeared on the front page of your local paper, the public might be led to believe you care more for profits than the safety of your patrons."

Horror crossed his thin, pale features. "That is not – "

"I'm certain nothing could be further from the truth." My hand waved as if to drive away any thought of such a possibility. "Unfortunately, the public is easily swayed. Facebook. Twitter. Instagram."

The man was going gray, gasping for air. "I– I – "

I met his gaze with a sympathetic expression. "I shudder to think what would happen if someone painted these events in all the lurid details."

His wide eyes gazed at me with a stricken expression, as if, heaven forbid, I would follow through on the steps I'd just described. A smear campaign. Imagine.

He studied me through narrowed eyes. He looked ready to pull out a cross and a stake from his jacket pocket.

"Two visits from the police in one day. A murder. A break-in. A child repeatedly endangered." I waved a hand at Marcus, whose stricken, fear-filled gaze did me proud. I had to pause a moment to maintain the proper tone. I schooled my expression to sorrow.

The rep eyed my son as if picturing his undersized frame on the front page of the local rag.

I leaped in before the man could find his voice. "Today's events could be twisted to make your fine establishment look, I hate to say it, dangerous. In these times, when everyone is seeking tourist dollars, there's no telling what mileage your rivals will make of these facts."

I patted his arm in sympathy.

He inched away, eyeing my hand like it was a snake ready to bite. "Perhaps I - "

"I don't believe you can be blamed for what has happened." I assured him. "Any more than my party could be held liable for the violence others have visited on your convention center and one of your suites."

A sweep of my arm took in the debris littering the rooms.

The desperate look of a hunted animal glittered in his eyes.

When you've got the opponent on the ropes, go for the knockout. "I'd be horrified if these unfortunate events were used against your fine establishment."

"As would I, madam." The man came up for air, sucking in a lung full that drove the ashen hue from his skin. "I'm thankful none of you, as our guests, were injured in either altercation."

"As am I," I assured him, unhesitatingly using his own words.

I glanced at Kevin, who stood with a comforting arm around the shoulders of a stricken-looking Marcus. My little shyster sniffled. The street rat who never cried looked ready to burst into tears.

I'd have to congratulate the boy later. His undersized frame had never been so advantageous. I pressed my lips together.

Mrs. C had co-opted the one upright chair and now sat amidst the debris field like a queen on her throne.

Rabi leaned against the doorjamb leading to the bedroom. Arms folded over his chest, he appeared oblivious to the conversation.

Certainly, the twinkle in his eye couldn't be one of amusement.

The official representative, whose name had escaped me if he'd ever mentioned it, cleared his throat. His studied gaze roamed over my face. His resigned expression held what may have been a spark of admiration. After all, we were both professionals. He'd been beaten fair and square.

He gave a nod of defeat. "Perhaps we can alleviate your pain and inconvenience."

Most of an hour later, I leaned against the locked door of another suite. It had taken an amazing amount of time to find our clothes among the mess. They'd been scattered with as much thoroughness as the hotel's knick-knacks. Evidently the culprit thought we had no imagination when it came to hiding places.

Now, safely alone with my little troop, I danced in place. "Comped for the whole weekend."

"T.R., you're the best." Marcus circled to the main room, having completed a running tour of our new digs. He plopped on the sofa. "I think this one is a little smaller. Can we complain?"

"Lesson number nine. Don't push your luck." Kevin cut him off with a slashing gesture before pointing at me. "You are completely shameless. You had that man buffaloed from word one. I was about to switch sides."

I slanted him a mock glare. "You wouldn't dare."

"Never." He couldn't conceal his grin as he put his arms around me. "I like being on the winning team."

"And fighting for the forces of good." Marcus intoned in perfect comic book tones.

Kevin spun me around as he turned to face the boy-child. "The forces of good can use all the help they can get."

I stepped out of his arms and walked over to sit beside my son. With a comforting arm around his shoulders, I allowed myself a relieved sigh that Pierce's vision of my little boy-child running into the culprit hadn't come true. The last two hours caught up with me, leaving me aching with exhaustion. "That was close."

"If only I'd been quicker." Marcus shook a fist in the air. "I'd have caught him."

Shock rippled through me. Anger, fueled by fear, followed. "That was not what I meant, and you know it, young man."

The boy had the grace to look abashed.

I didn't give him time to respond. "The great PIs, like Holmes or Poirot, don't rush into situations. They're cautious and thorough. You could have been hurt."

Marcus scrunched up his face.

Kevin put a hand on his shoulder, waiting until the boy met his gaze. "Any of us could have been injured if the man had turned and attacked."

Marcus's eyes widened.

Rabi nodded with a solemn air. "A good soldier thinks before he acts."

"I'll be more careful. I promise." The heartfelt sincerity in Marcus's tone was quickly offset by a gleam of mischief in his eyes. The boy shot me a shameless smirk. "You'd be lost without me."

I gave him a warning look. "You remember that promise."

Mrs. C and her muffs scuffed across the plush carpeting of the aqua and lavender colored room. A shimmering concoction of crystal and wavy glass reflected the chandelier's light like the shimmers of the sun on ocean waves. She settled gracefully into one of the overstuffed chairs in the seating arrangement.

"Thank goodness, I had my knitting with me." She patted her ever-present, oversized purse. Then she reached in and pulled out the knitting conglomeration and settled in. "I shudder to think of the damage that crazed individual could have done to all my hard work."

"Yep," I said. "That was my big worry."

"What now?" Marcus leaned forward. "We need to make a plan. Go over clues."

"We're going to shelve clues and criminals for today," Kevin suggested. "I don't care if I go to jail. I'm done."

"Me, too." I melted into the soft cushions and waved a hand in the air. "I surrender."

Kevin aimed Marcus at the large TV. "Find a movie to watch. We'll order in."

Marcus stilled. He aimed his eyes on me, narrowing them to small slits. "Room service?"

I stared at him, then shrugged. "We're alive. Let's celebrate the victories."

Marcus's eyes widened to saucers. He glanced around. "You heard her?"

"Order quick," Kevin urged. "The real Tracy could wrest back control at any minute."

Hours later, with an over-priced meal and two movies under our belts, I was almost asleep on the sofa.

"We'll look for Ivan in the morning," Marcus said. "First thing."

I clicked my tongue and forced my eyes half-open.

My little PI patted my hand. "Sleep on it. Let your little gray cells fit the clues into the puzzle."

Mrs. C frowned. "Gray cells?"

"He's working his way through Agatha Christie mysteries," Kevin explained, pointing to his temple. "Hercule Poirot solves crimes using his mind rather than running after people. A method I wholeheartedly support."

"It's not as much fun," Marcus scoffed.

"Safer." Rabi, also looking like he was asleep, added to the conversation.

"You're a Brit." I roused myself to eye Mrs. C. "You've never heard of Poirot and his little gray cells?"

"I've heard the name, of course." She stroked her chin. "But I was never into literature."

Agatha Christie? Literature?

The ring of a rotary dial snapped my head toward Kevin's cell.

He glanced at the readout. "No name. Could be the DA."

I had no patience left. "Put it on speaker this time."

"I heard there was trouble. Was anyone hurt?" At Kevin's assurance that we were all unharmed, Elena Young breathed a sigh of relief before switching gears. "My sources tell me Pierce has found additional evidence against you."

"Any details?" Kevin's question shot out like a bullet.

"I'm working on it. You?"

"We have a lead we're following up on," Kevin said.

"Who?" Excitement underscored her single word.

Kevin stared at the phone with an enigmatic expression. "I don't like to say on this line. We've lost our last two contacts."

A long, pregnant silence greeted his response.

"Good idea." Young somehow made it sound like the cautious response had been her notion. "Keep me updated on what you learn. I'll work on Pierce."

I stared at the phone after she disconnected. "Nice to know someone else on our side has some skin in the game. Even if she's only interested in her political career."

Mrs. C exhaled a soft, slow breath, looking up from her ever-moving knitting needles. "Most people are looking out for number one, luv."

Her observation correlated with my own feelings. A wide streak of cynicism ran through each of our merry gang. Perhaps that was the tie that bound us, that and Marcus.

"We can't trust anyone." Marcus's warning could have come straight out of a horror movie. "Money and murder turn even the best people bad."

"Smugglers, or criminals in general, aren't the best people to begin with," I reminded him.

"That's not true," Marcus said. "I've known a lot of nice people who happen to be criminals. We've done illegal stuff on cases in the past, and we're the good guys."

I had no answer for him. I did consider how thin is the line that separates people who end up behind bars and those of us on the outside. Then I noticed a long cookie on the plate and lost my train of thought.

15

7 Across; 5 Letters;
Clue: A valuable person or quality
Answer: Asset

On Sunday morning I woke to the ambrosia-like smell of brewing coffee. I stumbled through the sunshine, past Rabi, who stared silently out the wall of windows, and aimed straight for the pot. A moment later, a long sip of the scalding liquid gave me sufficient energy to flash Rabi a smile.

Despite knowing my wallet had taken a hit last night, I didn't regret the room service or being locked away from the world. For a few hours, I'd been surrounded by movies, dinner, and dessert rather than bodies, murders, and mayhem. I sighed, raised my cup, and braced myself for reality.

Over the next hour, the others roused. We feasted on bagels, donuts, and fruit from a nearby grocery.

"The real T.R. woke up," Marcus groused. "No more room service."

Kevin smiled. "We knew it wouldn't last."

I called Crawford and brought him up to date. Then, since he had connections with the Vegas police, I asked him to find the cause of Winter's death. When he bellowed something about me handing out assignments, I hung up on him and did a little jig. "That's the way to start the day."

Marcus swallowed the last of his orange juice and thumped down the glass. "Time to search for Ivan."

Frustrated that I couldn't find a safe alternative for him, I grasped at straws. "Wouldn't you like to see Lake Mead? I would."

"Fine." He agreed with a shrug. "Go sightseeing while the rest of us hunt the seamy side of Vegas in a last, desperate gasp to save Kevin from certain doom."

Melodrama, no less. I should have known.

"O-kay," I drug out the word with an exaggerated sigh. "If we have to save Kevin, let's find our mystery man."

"Ivan Graham dropped out of sight two days ago." Rabi's unexpected announcement ended our banter. "One man been asking about him. Slim, brown hair, crooked nose."

A predator chasing its prey.

That was my first thought. My second thought was that this bit of news explained Rabi's absence yesterday afternoon. I had no idea the man had contacts in Vegas, but I knew enough not to doubt his information.

"Fedor." A heaviness underscored Kevin's tone. "My cousin. Late thirties. Master of disguises. I passed him in the hall once without recognizing him. He worked with Safina and me in our early training. Winning the game is everything to him. I'd bet he was our visitor yesterday."

"I guess we won't have to convince Ivan he's in danger." A

chill chased away the warmth I'd gained from my coffee. "If they're still searching, that means he's alive."

"Hopefully." Mrs. C's fatalistic mutter proved that knitting wasn't absorbing all her attention.

The glare I aimed her way was wasted. Her ears were open, but her eyes were on her needles.

"Either way, Ivan's a dead-end." I winced as I heard the words pop out of my mouth. "I mean a blind alley."

"Noooo." Marcus gave voice to a wail of regret. "We can find him."

"We have no breadcrumbs to follow." Kevin's voice held a note of finality. He thumped his mug to punctuate the decision. His fingers drummed a rhythm on the cup while his distracted gaze was clearly seeking another way to find our man.

Rabi's nod added another nail. "Man went to cover quick. No trace of him."

Marcus's chin sunk between his fisted hands. "Shoot."

Despite an answering mix of frustration and regret brewing like a volatile shake in my gut, I fought to keep my voice cavalier. "If Ivan's off the table, we dig into the background of the two victims. We also need information on the codex. So, we know what we're looking for."

We had to move forward. With the sniper attach and the break-in still fresh in my memory, I knew a menace was closing in on our heels.

"We can't afford to take our eyes off the players." Though Mrs. C's meditative words seemed to mirror my thoughts, there was no telling where she'd land. "Mr. Ivan Graham will be desperate. Few people have the experience required to hide out with any degree of success."

A sigh and a click of her tongue emphasized society's perceived failing at teaching people the skill of running for their lives.

The woman was toying with me, throwing out a hook baited with a juicy tidbit from her past.

With a full quota of puzzles, no way did I have time to pursue her intriguing comment. I set my jaw and shoved the questions about her background into my mental closet.

"Hiding successfully takes planning and preparedness," she continued, dangling the bait again. Her knitting needles settled slowly into her lap. Her pale green eyes rose to meet mine. "Simply bolting into the dark is setting oneself up for failure. You, of course, are the wild card. You have the clearest opening for a breakthrough."

"I have no path open to finding the man." I didn't understand what she was getting at. "Let's return to J.D. Darlington and Alice Winter."

A not-so-innocent ember smoldered in Marcus's dark eyes. "You want me to dig up dirt on the dead people?"

Ignoring his hoot of laughter, I shook my head at his sick humor. However, chuckles from Kevin and Rabi undercut my attempt to stifle the boy's weird wit.

It's a guy thing.

"Let's focus on the prize, people." Organizing this group was like chasing chickens. "Marcus, bring up what you have on Alice Winter."

The boy reached for the tablet at his elbow. A look of concentration overtook his features. His fingers were tapping on the keys when the hotel phone on the desk rang.

Everyone stopped and stared.

"No one uses a land-line anymore." Marcus's shocked tone implied the desk phone was already obsolete.

"Must be the front desk." I grabbed for it, but Rabi's long arm beat me.

He hit the speaker button in mid-ring then jerked his chin toward me.

I settled back. "Hello?"

Silence. No dial-tone. No static.

We had a connection. Then, we had heavy breathing.

I raised a brow and tried again, louder. "Hello?"

"Tr– Tracy B-B- Belden?" The scratchy voice spoke in a stage whisper.

My heart stilled. Not a voice I recognized. Every muscle in my body clenched. A new player? A new threat?

This case was making me crazy.

I gathered my scattered nerves.

"I'm Tracy." My voice carried more confidence than I felt. "Who is this?"

A slow intake of breath sounded over the line.

"Ivan Graham."

He spoke so fast I could barely decipher the name. For a moment I couldn't respond. Had our discussion pulled the man out of the ether?

"I need to speak with you." The voice continued at half the speed of light. "Today. This morning. Right now."

By the time the rapid-fire words stopped, caution and questions vied for attention in my brain. A glance around the room showed a range of skepticism, warning, interest.

Skepticism from Kevin and Rabi.

Avid interest from the two rogue agents.

"Hold it." I held a palm out to the phone as if that would stop the desperate demands. "If you're Ivan Graham, why call me? How do you know about me or where to find me?"

"I'll explain when we meet. I'm at a corner store." His voice rose then faded as if he'd pulled away from the phone. "I can't risk being on the street for long."

I couldn't stop myself from glancing at Mrs. C.

She was leaning forward, her red tipped, talon-like fingers clenched around her needles and yarn. A look of concentration blanketed her expression as she zeroed in on the phone.

If this guy proved to be Ivan, the older woman had definitely called it. He sounded like he'd reached the last knot in a short rope.

I reached a quick and easy decision. "I'm not meeting you blind. You could be anyone."

Including our resident shooter or Pierce setting me up for heaven knew what.

A gnashing of teeth seemed to carry over the phone line.

A mew of disappointment sounded from my son.

"I have information about the thumb drive." The man's voice clipped off each word with a knife-like edge. "Shawn told me details no one else knows. No one still alive."

Tempting. I reined in an impulse to dive in. "That's not enough."

Kevin touched my arm. When I met his gaze, he gestured around the table. "Friends. Family."

I nodded, catching his drift. "If you need help, why not contact someone you trust like family or a friend?"

"And ruin their lives like Shawn ruined mine?" The man's anger vibrated in the air. "He dragged me into this mess. Threw me to the wolves. Then died."

His violent reaction set me on my heels. Don't hold back. Tell me how you really feel.

"I may not survive the week. You think I'd do the same to someone I love?"

I had to admit the man made a convincing argument.

"You're a professional." The alleged Ivan continued venting. "You want the thumb drive and the golden... whatever it is they stole. You *chose* to be involved in this chaos."

Sure, throw that in my face. Though I realized he was the only person who didn't believe I, well, Kevin already had the thumb drive. That sounded promising.

I shared a measured look with my merry gang. Most of

their expressions matched my own grudging acceptance that our mystery caller probably was the real Ivan.

A long, shuddering breath indicated the guy had regained a measure of control, however slight.

"You have to help me." The commanding words couldn't hide the underlying plea. "I won't call again. If you ever see me, it'll be at the morgue."

His scenario was all too likely. My gut clenched. He was another anchor trying to latch itself to my leg. This one even more unwelcome than Shawn and the two murder victims.

I glanced at Kevin, shrugging in resignation. I could feel the slippery slope beneath my feet. Despite my reservations, I had a horrible feeling how this episode would end.

"I don't know who to trust." Ivan's hesitant tone reinforced his conflict. "I'm not sure I should be talking to you. You're a weak best over a bunch of bad options."

That's the kind of ringing endorsement I usually get. However, the man hadn't answered my questions. "How did you learn I was involved, my name, where to contact me?"

A long, shaky breath came over the line. "Shawn had an ace in the hole. He said if things went bad to contact Craw ford's rep. Friday morning, Alice Winter e-mailed me you were in town."

This was the first the first confirmation I'd had of Alice being actively involved. What was her role? How much had she known? Evidently, too much for her own good. "How do you know her?"

"Shawn, Alice, and I were in a class together. She heard you mention Crawford to Harrison in his office." Ivan's tone dripped with disdain. "Don't you know anything? Her connection with Shawn got her the job. Didn't you speak with her?"

When I looked around, Rabi's dark eyes bored into mine.

I hated the thought of scaring Ivan off, but I didn't feel right keeping the news of Alice's death from him.

In a few words, I told him how Kevin and I had found her. "Ivan? Are you still there?"

Electricity flowed off Kevin in waves. His hand grasped my arm.

My jaw tightened, but it was too late. The hook was set. I had to know.

"After Shawn dropped out of sight Thursday afternoon, I panicked and went into hiding." A weary defeat dragged at Ivan's tone as he continued. "I snuck out today and risked signing onto an online café. Once I read Alice's e-mail, I looked you up. You're not hard to find."

I rolled my eyes. So far everyone in town had located our little troop. "Tell me something I don't know."

"When you meet me," Ivan said, "I'll tell you something no one knows."

Another quick, silent consensus around the room. Even seeing the agreement on everyone's faces, I hesitated.

I was constrained by the same emotions tearing at Ivan - a reluctance to commit, combined with a large dose of caution. However, a more overpowering force pushed us forward: an almost total lack of options.

If I didn't do something to solve this case, violence would simply overtake my family and friends.

With a final wrench, I closed my eyes and forced out the words. "Where and when?"

16

14 Down; 8 Letters;
Clue: Secluding yourself
Answer: In hiding

E ver try to arrange a meeting when no one involved trusts the other side? It's not easy.

Trust me on that.

I won't waste time listing the cautions and conditions Ivan and I tossed around. I'd prefer to cut straight to the end, but Belden and company didn't exactly bolt out of the hotel. Quick escapes are beyond the scope of our small band.

I was deciding who to leave behind when Mrs. C bowed out. Shep had found a few intriguing facts related to our case. She'd made plans to meet him again for "another little coze".

The news lifted a weight off my shoulders. Wading into the unknown with a septuagenarian in pink muffs wasn't my idea of smart. However, unease crept up my spine at the thought of her being alone. Would she be safe? Who knew she was helping us investigate?

"Not to worry." Mrs. C waved away my concerns. "Shep lives at a retirement home for former city employees, mostly bobbies. One has to be buzzed in. All very safe and secure."

Kevin assisted her to her feet. "When are you meeting him?"

"He's expecting me this morning." She fluffed her hair. "Now would be lovely."

"I'll take her." Rabi stepped forward. "Then meet you."

"Good," Kevin concurred.

Then came the question of Marcus. Bringing my eleven-year-old to a possibly dangerous meeting was wrong. Irresponsible. Crazed. Yet, after chasing every option around my mind several times, I found no viable alternative.

Mrs. C had proved an unreliable guardian at best.

Rabi was needed more as a backup than a babysitter.

After yesterday, I couldn't leave my son alone in the hotel. Fedor or Pierce might snatch him. An urge to encase the boy in bubble-wrap and stick him on the mantel festered inside of me. Except I had neither bubble-wrap nor a mantel.

Marcus watched my tortured thought processes with his hands fisted on his hips. "I'm going with you."

I cast a silent appeal at Kevin.

"We're out of choices." Kevin never stewed over the inevitable. He turned to Marcus. "No more than six inches from my side at all times. Do exactly what you're told."

The boy snapped off a salute.

Despite his past transgressions, I had no doubt Marcus would obey. The boy was a survivor. He knew when the war-games were over, and the real battle had commenced.

I can't say how long it took us to get to the rendezvous or

even where we met. After all, it was a secret meeting. I can say the warehouse was hot, dusty, and dim. Completely lacking in amenities.

Mrs. C would have been appalled.

Rabi had arrived first and scoped out the warehouse. He texted that Ivan was alone inside, and no one was watching outside.

After receiving the all clear, Kevin, Marcus, and I took a side staircase to the second floor. A large open room greeted us, empty, but for a wooden table and three decrepit chairs.

Ivan Graham, former office minion with Westercamp Corporation, crept out of the shadows. He looked like a timid mouse fearing a trap; a dirty, pudgy mouse with brown, unkempt hair.

After patting us down for wires and weapons, Ivan started to unwind. Unravel might be a better word.

"I'm a computer geek, not a spy." He darted between the windows, evidently searching the quiet streets for movement. His hands never stopped, twisting over each other, gesturing to the universe. "Shawn told me he found proof that Harrison was using Westercamp's routes to smuggle stolen artifacts into the country. He had cops on the payroll. That meant Shawn couldn't go to the local authorities. His father said he knew a guy from the old days who was clean. Shawn was certain Harrison didn't suspect him, but a few days ago, Shawn's apartment was broken into. He said Harrison was onto him."

I mentally upgraded him from mousey to squirrelly. There was no telling if he'd started that way. Probably not. Mrs. C was right. Most people aren't prepared for the pressure and isolation of hiding.

I assumed he'd get to business then cut out. However, eight minutes in, the guy started to recycle his rant. He was determined to unload all the perceived injustices against him.

I bunched my muscles, prepared to pounce on him during his next circle around the cage and demand he get to the point.

He walked toward me.

I readied myself.

"Not vinegar," Kevin whispered, holding out a hand, low and by his side. "Honey."

I froze, foiled in mid-leap. Why did I have to dredge up niceness after everything I'd been through? Sugar and sweetness were so not my style.

When Ivan paused for air, Kevin slipped in a question. "Did Shawn mention when he found the files on the smuggling operation?"

The fugitive, surprisingly, stopped pacing and faced Kevin. "A week ago. When I asked him what he'd done with the information, he said, 'Nothing. Honestly, nothing.'"

The guy held up his hands, re-enacting the scene. Then, he dropped the play-acting.

"I could see in his eyes he wouldn't let it go." He slammed his fist into the door, shaking the wood in its frame. Agitated. Breathing heavily. Wild eyes filled with the fury of the storm. "I told him I didn't want to hear it. I assumed he'd dropped the matter."

Now we were getting somewhere. I folded my arms across my chest, determined to keep him on track. "Until when? This week?"

"A few days ago. Monday?" Ivan raked his fingers through his greasy hair. "Shawn insisted on going to this dive. I realize now he didn't want to be overheard at our usual watering hole. Once we got to the bar, he started doing shots."

Marcus nodded knowingly from his position by Kevin's side. "He was scared."

Kevin slid a glance at the boy. "Courage in a bottle."

A paralegal would need courage, even if it were fake, to take on a smuggler who feared being exposed. Still, getting drunk was crazy.

Ivan smacked his fist into his other palm with rhythmic precision. "As the night wore on, he started dropping hints. He said someone besides him had to know the truth."

Shawn must have been desperate, but to trust his drinking buddy was beyond risky. For all he knew, Ivan might betray him to Harrison or Westercamp.

I said as much.

Ivan pulled back. Outrage showed on his face, but guilt flashed in his eyes. "I told him to leave the matter alone. If he continued to dig, he'd only cause trouble for himself."

The computer geek had preferred to bury his head. The ostrich syndrome. A common choice. Is it crazy or courageous to do the right thing and risk destruction?

It's all a question of what a person can live with.

Ivan strode to the table. His voice rose with each step. "Shawn was bound to get caught. Once that happened, Harrison would suspect I knew as well."

"Guilt by association." Kevin cocked his brow in my direction. "Your career was derailed when you got messed up in murder."

I met Kevin's gaze. Our first blush with murder had been ten years ago when I'd cleared him of the charge. From that fork in my path, everything else had followed. Marcus, Rabi, Mrs. C, being a PI. Like I said, it all depends on what a person can live with. "I never regretted losing that job."

Unlike Ivan, who'd obviously been looking forward to an undisturbed future with no hiccups. Now a fugitive, he circled like a trapped tiger in a cage. The man was still consumed with his last encounter with the accountant.

"No one would believe I hadn't known what he was planning," Ivan repeated. "I'm dead. I just don't know when the bullet will strike."

I swallowed my impatience with difficulty. As much as I'd like to write his melodrama off to hysteria, Harrison or Pierce or another dirty cop had tapped the DA's phone and been sitting in those hills with a rifle.

Kevin glanced at the door. Muscles tense. Eyes narrowed. His bearing resembled that of a panther. Though Rabi hadn't alerted us, Kevin was ready for any signal to either fight or flee. "Did you mention Shawn's discovery to anyone?"

Sorrow flowed across the other man's young, aged face like an ocean wave over the sand, leaving behind despair as a mark on his soul. "I was tempted. Shawn's talk of smuggling routes might have been a test of my loyalty."

That made no sense. Why would Shawn test his friend's loyalty to Westercamp?

"Shawn and his father are both dead. So is Alice. They didn't deserve to die, and for what?" Regret weighed down the man's whisper. "He should have let it go."

"He didn't." Done with vague answers, I cut off the might-have-beens. A pitcher once broken can never again be pristine. I regretted the three deaths, but all any of us could hope for now was to gain a measure of justice for them. I stepped into the young man's path, forcing him to stop. "Shawn made his choice."

Ivan slammed a fist on the table. Ferocity gleamed in his eyes. "He made the choice for all of us. I'm a marked man."

"Yeah, you are," Marcus agreed blithely. "Do something about it."

"I did. I called you." The computer geek thrust his hand

toward me. "Shawn said Crawford's operative could be trusted."

I leaned forward. "Believe it. Once I find the copied files, I'll turn them over to the authorities."

He gave me the fisheye, hard to tell whether he doubted my honesty, my ability, or both. "The only reason you're here is because I have no other options."

I could have said the same but gritted my teeth against the comeback.

Kevin studied him with a cold expression. "Did you speak with Shawn after Monday night in the bar?"

"No. I left work early Thursday." Ivan's enigmatic expression may have been regret, but he shook it off. "At two o'clock he texted me that he had the downloaded files. After that, nothing. Friday morning, I heard he'd been identified as a victim of a hit and run driver."

A heavy silence fell.

"I knew he'd been killed." Ivan's haunted eyes dimmed as he forced a hard swallow. He sucked in air. "Shawn has no one to blame for his death but himself."

Marcus reared up to his full height. "How about the guy who ran him down?"

Ivan's expression turned mulish. "He brought it on himself."

"For trying to do the right thing?" Marcus retorted, scorn dripping from his words.

My heart swelled. I loved my little superhero. I gave him a nod of agreement and laid out my hand, palm up.

He slid his small, nut-brown palm across mine.

"At least Shawn tried," Marcus said. "You're just hiding."

"He's dead." Ivan pointed out. "I'm alive."

"In hiding," Kevin reminded him in a flat tone.

I'd spent enough time listening to justification. I snapped

my fingers, pulling Ivan's attention to me. "Tell us what you know."

He leaned close enough to share his rancid breath. His bleary eyes held a desperate edge. "You're the monkey wrench in everyone's plan."

The disjointed comment wasn't quite the news flash I'd expected.

"That's T.R. all right," my son agreed all too quickly.

In five minutes, I'd gone from a paid professional to a monkey wrench. So much for my growing reputation. "Get to the files Shawn downloaded. What do you know?"

The computer geek ran his fingers through his hair. The bags under his eyes appeared darker.

"I can't get out of town." Defeat underscored the words as Ivan's focus once again slipped away. He stared at the far wall. "I don't have the money to hide long term."

A glance at Kevin showed a neutral mask. Only long familiarity let me glimpse the disdain in the depths of his gaze.

Perhaps my well of sympathy was running low, or my patience had been stretched too far, but I had little use for this guy. However, I did need him. "Give me the facts. I can end this matter."

One way or another. Just don't ask me how.

The fugitive circled back. He bit at his already frayed thumbnail. "You finding the files and giving them to the authorities should eliminate Harrison or anyone else's need to kill me."

Sympathy, unexpected and unwanted, at his desperate straits sluiced through me. I tamped it down. Focus on the prize. Our man-on-the-run seemed to be moving forward rather than rattling around in the past. I had to keep him talking long enough to pull his conversation together.

"I'm more than ready to collect the thumb drive," I assured him. "Tell me what you know."

"First things first." He bit off the words. His tone was hardly louder than a whisper. His gaze darted to the stairs. He leaned close.

I moved in as well. Finally, the missing puzzle piece was at hand.

Ivan's lips parted. "Hide me."

17

21 Down; 11 Letters;
Clue: Connected pieces of information
Answer: Breadcrumbs

After the hostile conversation, a plea for help was the last thing I'd expected. "You barely trusted me to meet you. Now you want me to hide you?"

"I was driving to work two days ago. I didn't plan to run for my life." He threw his hands in the air. An expanding circle of sweat was encroaching on old, dried stains under his arms. Each band testified to his lack of wardrobe, and his desperation. "I have no money. No food. Harrison's cronies are watching my friends by now."

Kevin raised a brow. "They're definitely watching us."

A sheen of perspiration emphasized the gray pallor of Ivan's skin. "You said they didn't follow you here."

At the accusatory note Kevin jerked as if he'd sat on a cactus thorn. "Nobody tails me."

"We disabled the GPS tracking in our cells so they can't be traced." Marcus's confident tone interrupted the tense moment. "We're using walkie-talkies as an added precaution."

Supplied by guess who? I was now doomed to hear accolades of his Kit for Private Investigators forever, but at the moment, I had to clench my fists to get a grip on my impatience.

"You've made it this far." My conciliatory tone surprised even me. "Give me the information and return to where you're staying. It should only be another day, maybe less."

With the multiple players involved and bullets flying, I didn't believe any of us would last much longer than a couple of days. Besides, like a mug I saw in a truck stop said, "If you can't dazzle 'em with brilliance, baffle 'em with bull." When I've got nothing else, I sell hope. Sometimes, even I believe me.

If Ivan bought my version, I could get the facts, walk away, and get back to work.

"They're not going to kill you until you get the thumb drive or the stolen artwork." Ivan's gaze skimmed over Kevin and Marcus before landing on me. He ran a shaking hand through his war-torn hair as he delivered this less than comforting assurance. "Until then, you're safe. That's longer than I've got. Burying me is their only option."

Enough, already. I grabbed the man's arm. "Do you know anything to justify us helping you?"

Ivan's whole body jerked at my sudden move. A cunning gleam burned from the depths of his gaze, sparking new life. "I know the clues to both hiding places."

I exchanged a shocked look with Kevin.

"The golden codex?" Marcus's explosive outburst caused Ivan to pull out of my grasp. "Shawn told you where it was hidden?"

"No one else knows." Ivan's triumphant cackle rattled around the stale air, seeming too loud for the enclosed space. "They were too quick to kill Shawn. The knowledge died with him."

His wild certainty breathed life into his shattered shell. He held the high card.

I filtered the new fact into my crossword puzzle.

Ivan stabbed a finger at me. "You have to guarantee I get police protection in exchange for this information."

"I'm not the police. I can't guarantee anything." My instant rebuttal made him draw back. When his jaw stiffened, I hurried on. "Crawford has a trusted contact in the Las Vegas Police force. I promise I'll let them know you were instrumental in helping us."

Marcus crossed his arms over his thin chest. "Only if the information pans out."

Kevin drew a reassuring aura out of thin air. Exuding confidence and strength, he met Ivan's gaze with a solemn expression. "If the information in those files is as thorough as Shawn claimed, it should be enough to convict Harrison and his associates."

The fugitive stabbed a finger at Kevin. "Hide me until the authorities have the files and it's a deal."

Behind Ivan's back, Marcus nodded wildly. I exchanged a glance with Kevin over Ivan's head. His infinitesimal nod gave silent agreement. No other viable choice existed.

The guy caught the silent exchange. His head turned slowly toward me. Determination warred with fear in his eyes and his bearing.

An aching need to end this interview overcame me. I had to get outside where the sun could burn away the cloying stench of hopelessness. I met Ivan's gaze squarely. "You have a deal."

He studied me; his skepticism plainly visible. After a

minute, he straightened. He seemed to throw off the fear that had dug its claws into his soul.

For the first time, I caught a glimpse of the man who'd been Shawn's friend before Fate took hold of his life and tossed it into a meat grinder.

He met my gaze. "You'll need to pull off a miracle."

"I keep spare miracles in my pocket." No need to mention that Kevin's freedom was on the line. Saving the man I loved meant more than anything else in this case. "I don't quit cases."

Not until my crossword puzzle was completed.

"She's good." Marcus pointed at me. His voice held the absolute certainty only a child can pull off. "And she has a great team."

I had to smile at that last bit of arrogance. The boy was right. I couldn't have made it as a PI without my merry band. I shot my boy a wink.

Whether my promise or Marcus's assurance broke down Ivan's last wall, the man's bluster faded.

"When I tried to leave the bar, Shawn grabbed me. The last thing I needed was more attention. So, I stayed and listened." Ivan pressed his index fingers against a matching pair of scars in the table. "The thumb drive contains the files Shawn took, but the missing artifact lit the fuse."

Kevin's finger thrummed a beat on his leg. "Why did Shawn take the artifact? He had to know its absence would alert Harrison that someone was on to him."

"Maybe he planned to sell it." The prompt response from the former street rat drew surprised glances. Marcus shrugged. "Only four existed until this one was found. A new one would be worth millions."

No judgment colored his words. In his former circumstances, greed was, like breathing, a fact of life, a way to survive another day.

Kevin paced to the window, glanced out, then turned on his heel. His brow furrowed in thought. "Shawn could have been hiding in Rio weeks ago if he wanted the cash."

Ivan snorted. "He did it so Harrison couldn't move the codex before he exposed his crimes."

Shock froze the gears in my mind. My brain sorted through his words. I wasn't convinced that was Shawn's motive, but I couldn't muster a counter-argument either.

Marcus cocked his head to one side. "Stealing the codex to force Harrison's hand wasn't the smart move, but Shawn did trap all the players in town."

The stunning revelation worked its way into my mind like water seeping through tightly packed stones. Ivan's version actually explained several things.

"No wonder Harrison and your family are desperate," I muttered. "They're not going to leave a priceless artifact floating around waiting to be found."

"They'll never quit looking." Kevin managed to sound matter-of-fact.

His comment did nothing to thaw the glacier that had taken up residence in my gut. They'll never quit chasing us. I wasn't sure the words made it out of my mouth. I don't think so. No one responded.

I needed more information. My fingers hurt from my hard fist. "Did Shawn put the hiding place for the codex in the files he downloaded?"

Ivan's expression fell.

So did my hopes.

Kevin looked slightly less shell-shocked than I felt. He rocked on his heels. "Where are the drive and the codex?"

Ivan put out his hands. "All I have are a few hints."

"That's okay," Marcus waved his hand at the disclaimer. "T.R.'s good at puzzles. She's got this."

Again, no pressure.

I stopped a sigh. "Let's get the facts first. What did Shawn say? Exactly."

Ivan leaned in close enough so I could smell his breath, which was a huge endorsement for regular tooth-brushing combined with a good mouthwash.

"Two rivers lead to the same ocean," Ivan spoke in a voice an oracle might use. And the meaning was just as obscure. "The only other thing you need to know is how to beat the shell game."

While I stood there waiting for more, the man slumped as if the weight of Atlas had lifted off his shoulders.

"That's it?" A feeling of betrayal coursed through me. To say I'd expected more was an understatement. I raised a brow. I'd definitely gotten the worst end of this deal. "You expect me to hide you for that?"

That lit Ivan's fire. "Shawn died for this knowledge. You figure it out. You're the professional."

Sure, throw that in my face.

Kevin stepped closer, his tall frame and calm presence diffused some of the tension. "What else do you know about Shawn's scheme? Is there anyone else he'd have told? Who did he trust?"

"He and Alice got along well." Ivan responded to Kevin's smooth, measured tone. The man's decisive answer showed a hint of his quick mind before this chaotic week. "He tutored her in her classes after he got her the job. She'd only been with Harrison for a few months."

"Alice Winter." The woman's name flowed off my lips.

Our new ally tensed. Tight lines hardened his round face. "I assume the ocean reference points to her second job."

That grabbed my attention. I'm not shy about asking for help. "What's her second job?"

Ivan looked more relaxed by the minute. Sharing his

knowledge had eased his burden. Though dirt and sweat streaked his face, his color was now pink rather than gray.

He drew in another deep breath, as if learning to breathe without fear constricting his lungs. "She works... worked part-time keeping up fish tanks at the Bayside Casino's main lounge. She's good friends with the weekend evening bartender, Lisa. Shawn and I went there a few times last month."

Another lead. Another clue.

"Our next breadcrumb." Kevin summed up.

Marcus checked his watch. "Time's up on Phase One. Talking is over. Phase two. Decide and Go."

We had a plan. Shocking, I know. In an attempt to divert his abundant energy, I'd suggested Marcus develop a timetable. A reminder that both Rabi and Kevin had used airtight schedules in their former professions was all it took to sell the idea.

My son waved his hands in a hurry up gesture. Give him an assignment, and the boy turned into a little dictator.

Kevin and I exchanged a glance of understanding. I was ready to get away from Ivan and his despair.

The man in question stood with us, paler than a moment ago. "You're not leaving me."

"You're coming." Kevin held up a hand to silence the other man's belligerent tone. "Get your things."

Ivan scrambled to the far corner. He pulled an over-stuffed laptop bag and a jacket out of the shadows, clutching both to his chest. His expression was a mixture of relief and worry.

A burst of static from Marcus's walkie-talked skittered across my nerves. Glee lit his eyes. A grin split his face. "Street Rat to Black Ops. Come in, Black Ops. Over."

His smile widened at the chance to use the politically incorrect call names he'd invented.

When I shook my head, Rabi had just chuckled.

The man responded now with a professional air.

"The flock is on the wing," Marcus answered. "Four. Out the back."

Moments later, having driven to a new location, we laid down the law with Ivan.

Disposable cell phones. Call only my or Rabi's disposable phone. Go nowhere. Don't poke your nose out of the room where you're stashed.

Rabi didn't bat an eye as he took custody of both our new ally and Marcus. His unwavering support eased my burden.

As we parted company, Ivan gulped a breath. "I'm trusting you."

I tried to look reassuring, but I was too fed up to respond.

Kevin, however, stopped with one hand on the car door.

"I'm trusting you." Though Kevin's tone remained calm, the eyes he fixed on Ivan were as hard as cut, blue diamonds. "This information better be legit."

His matter-of-fact delivery made the underlying threat all the more chilling. And, from Ivan's hard swallow, believable.

When our car disappeared around the corner, I released my pent-up breath, leaned back, and hoped the air-conditioner would cool my overheated brain. I needed to think through the latest twists to this convoluted case.

Kevin pulled the Caddy into traffic. "The Bayside Casino is a big place to try to find a thumb drive."

"At least we have a breadcrumb." It wasn't much, but it was something. "I only hope we fare better than those two kids in the Hansel and Gretel fairy tale. They almost got roasted alive."

30 *Across; 5 Letters;*
Clue: Arousing feelings of doubt or suspicion
Answer: Fishy

With Ivan and Marcus safely in Rabi's hands, Kevin aimed the Caddy toward the Bayside Casino. We'd only gone a short distance when I faced the fact that this puzzle was not coming together. "Shawn died Friday morning. J.D. Darlington was murdered later that morning. Why is everyone so sure J.D. had the stolen files on him when he was killed?"

Kevin's fingers played along the steering wheel as if it were a piano. "Safina would know."

"Think she'll meet with us?"

"I don't intend to ask." A roguish gleam sparkled in his eyes. "You work best from ambush. All we have to do is find her. Between us, we can push her buttons."

"Safina said she had to be at the Westercamp booth for an

expo tomorrow." I perked up at the prospect of having a plan of attack. "I'm sure Marcus can find the schedule."

We drove through increasing traffic as we headed toward the Vegas strip. Lulled by the luxurious ride of the Caddy, I was surprised to hear the raucous tone of Kevin's burner cell.

I sat up straighter. Only the DA had that number. "Young's calling you?"

Leave it to me to state the obvious.

After a greeting, his fingers, tapping out a rhythm on the steering wheel, stilled. "You picked up a tail?"

I cursed under my breath. Was Pierce onto her? Another dirty cop? Harrison? If anything happened to the DA, we'd be whistling in the wind for a rescue. "Our safety net has a hole in it."

Kevin's eyes narrowed. "I don't like to give details about our contact. We have a lead on Alice Winter's job at the Bayside. We're headed there now. We'll keep in touch."

"If we all live long enough."

He was already signing off as I tossed out the comment.

The Bayside proved to be a sprawling affair with a sand-castle profile. Colors of cream with coral trim underscored the beach motif.

Kevin hit the entrance and took off with the precision of an arrow shot from a bow. "If Ivan is correct about Alice working every weekend, the bartender on duty should know her."

"Not with our luck," I muttered.

The entry to the lounge had several aquariums built into the wall. Stocked with tropical fish, they gave the upscale bar a cove-like atmosphere. On the wall behind the gleaming mahogany bar, a manicured beach, complete with shells and the sound of waves crashing against a fake pier, completed the faux seashore.

Definitely an upgrade from meeting with Ivan.

By the time we slid into two stools at the counter, the female bartender had been watching our... well, Kevin's approach for twenty feet.

I breathed a sigh of relief on reading her nametag.

Lisa leaned a little closer to my guy than necessary. "What can I get for you?"

Kevin spread out five twenties on the counter. "Two waters and a few minutes of your time."

Guarded curiosity, not to mention a glimmer of greed, seemed to ease her disappointment at his lack of interest. "What's this about?"

"Who," I corrected. "We're looking into the death of Alice Winter. She was murdered yesterday."

The woman stiffened. Standing at her full height, six-foot-plus with her heels, she stared down at us for a long heartbeat. "What's your interest in Alice's death?"

Noting her suspicious tone, I cued my usual spiel. My detecting vibes started singing when she demanded I pull out my PI license. I explained what led me to her, though I didn't spill Ivan's name.

Lisa nodded with the hesitant air of someone deciding whether to cooperate.

Kevin eyed her for a brief heartbeat. "We're not the first to ask about Alice."

The tall bartender scrutinized us. Her rigid shoulders and stiff spine were still in place when she turned away without another look at the string of Jacksons on the counter. "I'll be back with the water."

I eyed the money longer than she had. "I'll put that on my expense report."

"That's the least of my problems."

A minute later, Lisa returned. The absence had softened the woman's suspicious manner. She crossed her arms under her ample chest. "The police won't tell me squat about Alice's death."

I felt better as cool liquid slid down my throat. I set the glass down with a thud and filler her in on what I knew. "We need information to bring Alice's killer to justice."

Her chin quivered. A still chin and a few sniffles later, sorrow had melted some of Lisa's cold demeanor. Her shoulders slumped. "I can't believe anyone would hurt her."

"Who else came asking questions?" The sympathy in Kevin's expression invited confidences.

"Harrison came yesterday afternoon." Lisa's lips flatlined. "He claimed he didn't want us to hear it on the news."

I waited for the rest. When she didn't continue, I prompted her. "You didn't believe him."

She hesitated only a second. "He said the right things, but it was only hours after she died and he was determined to check her locker. He said he wanted to return her personal possessions to her family, but she was a widower with no children. She didn't have any close family."

My nerves locked up. Were we too late? "Harrison would have known that."

Kevin flipped a swizzle stick over his fingers. "Did he take any of Alice's possessions?"

"Nothing to take. She didn't keep personal items here." Talking about the other woman softened Lisa's hard tone. "The supplies she used are in the maintenance room; nets, food, and filters. He insisted on checking. That's when I knew something was up."

I let out a breath. I couldn't afford to have any of the other players find those files. In anyone else's hands, they'd disappear forever.

"Anyone else ask about Alice?" Kevin inserted the question smoothly into the conversation.

Lisa paused to think. "A woman called. She said she

worked with Shawn and needed some files he'd taken home. She asked me to contact her if anything turned up."

I gripped the glass, dripping with condensation. "What was her name?"

The bartender's forehead wrinkled. "Carol? No. Clair? That's not right."

An aura of energy exuded from the man at my side. "Was it Clarissa Hodges?"

Lisa snapped her fingers. "That's her. I have her number somewhere. Do you want it?"

Kevin pointed the swizzle stick at the bartender. "That would be good."

Dismissing Safina for the moment, I focused on Lisa. There was no telling where the thumb drive was hidden, but if Alice was involved, learning about her might provide the needed edge to ferret out the hiding place. From Lisa's emotional response, Alice Winter had revealed a different side of herself at this job.

"What did Alice do here?" I asked.

Lisa's expression softened. "She maintained the aquariums and the beach display. She loved reworking the seashore and introducing new fish. The place won't be the same without her."

Alice's desk had contained a set of scales with seashells stacked on it. My gaze roamed over the colorful display surrounding the bar. The cove had a natural feel to it, evidently a labor of love. "Sounds like you two were friends. She evidently spent a lot of time here."

"Water and waves were her creative outlet. We were her home away from home." Lisa blinked rapidly as she wiped the already pristine counter. "Shawn knew he could find her here. He came off and on."

Kevin pointed the swizzle stick he'd commandeered at the woman. "Did he visit more often lately?"

Lisa caught herself in mid-shrug. The towel in her hand stilled on the counter. "Shawn came by a couple of times last weekend, then again a few days ago. Wednesday, maybe? He seemed upset."

Excitement zinged through my veins. Shawn had had a busy week. Monday drinking with Ivan. Wednesday confiding in Alice. Friday dead. I sought to match Kevin's casual tone. "Did Alice say why he was nervous?"

Furrows marred the bartender's brow. "He didn't tell her. Or so she said. She left Wednesday, right after he did. She never returned."

The plaintive note in her voice hung in the air.

I had to stop myself from inching forward. "You're sure it was Wednesday?"

Her gaze met mine. "Definitely Wednesday."

Though Kevin's laid-back stance didn't falter, a buzz seemed to electrify him. "How do you know Alice didn't return? She could have come when you weren't working."

Lisa's long arm snaked out toward the display on the far wall. "One of the aquariums had fish that were in a bad way. I left a message for Alice to check them. When I came in yesterday, two angelfish were dead. She would never have let that happen. Besides, she mentioned she was busy this week helping to prepare for a legal conference at the convention center."

The display I'd studied at the Aquarius had also included a beach scene. Another piece of Alice's handiwork, no doubt.

"What did Shawn get her involved in?" Lisa's sharp tone seemed directed more at the accountant than at us.

I opted for the encapsulated version. In this case, too much information was definitely a dangerous thing. "Some files are missing from Harrison's office. I was hired to recover them."

The bartender's eyes, heavily made-up with mascara and

liner, narrowed as she digested the information. "You think Alice knew where they were? Is that why she was murdered?"

"It might be." I didn't want to involve Lisa any more than necessary. "The trail led Harrison and us here."

Kevin spun his glass in the ring of condensation on the counter. "Did Shawn's father, J.D. Darlington, stop by recently?"

Lisa shook her head. "I don't know him."

"Sounds like Alike was close to Shawn." I wanted to hear the woman's take on the relationship.

A pensive expression painted the bartender's face with the brush stroke of a Renaissance lady. "Alice never had any children. She lost her husband years ago to drug smugglers. For a while, she worked for a forensic accountant who did cases for the Border Patrol. She had contact with a lot of agents. She still teared up when she told me how some of them died on the job. I could tell she looked on the younger ones like her own kids. It was the same way with Shawn. She'd have done anything for him."

Her words hung in the air. Shawn's father had proven his devotion to his son. He'd died for him. Now, it seemed that Alice had died for the young man's ideals as well.

Kevin's jaw tightened. He pushed the money toward Lisa.

The woman stared at it for a long minute. Then she studied us through her dark lashes. "Are you going to find out who killed Alice?"

I rarely deal with absolutes. Shifting tides have dissolved the ground beneath my feet more often than I can say. But, as I'd told Ivan, in this case, there was no other option.

"Yes," I spoke without hesitation. "We're going to find her killer."

---

10 Across; 5 Letters;
Clue: Protection sought by people in danger
Answer: Cover

S weat trickled down my spine as Kevin and I matched strides through the parking lot. Even in November, the desert sun baked concrete to a toasty temperature.

Questions and clues danced in the shimmering heat waves. Ivan's comment about the shell game returned. Though puzzles were my specialty, I lacked Kevin's background in con games. "Shawn knew he was being watched. Yet, his only clues are a comment about two rivers and how to find a pea hidden under one of three shells."

"Any carnival huckster knows the trick." Kevin bestowed a dazzling smile on me. He walked with an even, relaxed stride. "Except I can't see how J.D. and Shawn carried it off."

I was about to ask about the trick when lightning struck. "Maybe that's what J.D. was trying to tell you when he was dying. You heard 'Con and Shill' because of your background. Maybe he was saying 'Shell', as in a shell game."

Kevin frowned, already shaking his head. "I know what I heard."

Typical male, refusing to admit he might be wrong. Still ruminating, I squinted against the reflected light of SUVs and minivans gleaming in the sun. "The Caddy's just ahead."

"The car's three rows over this way." Without warning, Kevin shifted abruptly to the left.

I pivoted on my heel and followed him into the shadow between two oversized SUVs.

A ding sounded. The windshield on a tall SUV sprouted a hole two inches behind my shoulder. A spiderweb of fractures spread across the surface then cracked into a thousand shards.

Shock poured through my veins.

Kevin pulled me to the ground.

My elbow hit with a thud, scraping the skin. Hard, hot cement burned through my thin shirt. My heart pounded.

A rapid series of metal dings filled the air. Car windows shattered. Pea-sized glass pellets rained around us like a hailstorm.

With his body covering mine, Kevin dug his phone out and dialed one-handed.

I was so close I heard the operator answer. "9-1-1. What is your emergency?"

While Kevin gave the location and our current crisis, I hoped in vain for Rabi to get off some answering shots. Except this time, he and Marcus were stashing Ivan.

Kevin pocketed his phone. "They're coming."

"Yay." I infused my tone with a dose of artificial joy to mask my fear. "Do you think the police will arrive before the gunman comes to finish the job?"

"The shooter's been careful not to be seen." Kevin

sounded far too composed when discussing our possible deaths. "He won't be prepared for a close hit. Too many witnesses. We keep our heads down. The cops will be here."

He smoothed my hair with his hand.

"If that's a hint to stay put, don't worry. I'm good where I am, but I've had it with snipers showing up on my cases." I couldn't stop my imaginings. "What if he has a confederate with a handgun?"

Kevin gave me an exasperated look. "Did you throw rocks at robins when you were young?"

"I like to think of disasters before they sneak up on me."

"I've noticed that."

The hailstorm ceased. Though pebbles of glass blanketed the cement, no more fell.

Raised voices sounded in the distance.

Kevin raised his head. "It's quiet."

A gruff tone identified itself as casino security and commanded everyone to remain inside. The thrum of traffic threaded through my brain again. Then, the heaven-sent sound of distant sirens joined the mix. That was sure to scare off bogeymen with rifles.

"Good thing only cars were killed." I let the tension seep out of my coiled insides. "If you hadn't pulled us to the side when you – "

"My car." Kevin's hands gripped my shoulders, horror filled his expression. "What if he hit the Caddy?"

He was up by the time the words penetrated my mind.

"It's. A. Car," I spoke slowly to make him understand.

He'd already crab-walked to the edge of the now demolished minivan.

I sat up. "What happened to keeping down?"

He inched his head around the bumper as he waved away my concern. "The sirens scared the shooter off."

"You don't know that." I got my feet under me, poised to grab his arm.

"I have to check the car." He bolted out of cover in a low, fast run.

He reminded me of those mechanical ducks at a shooting arcade. I was torn between hoping he got winged and prove me right, and scared spitless he'd get winged and prove me right.

Only when Kevin made it safely to the Great White Beast, did I begin to believe the gunman was halfway across town.

The sight of him inspecting the Caddy drove me from cover as well. If the shooter still had us in his sights, we might as well go splat together.

I fisted my hands on my hips. "Is your brain fried?"

"No worries." He patted the hood of the pearly white car. "Not a mark on it."

"That wasn't my concern." Boiling over with irritation, I did a slow three-sixty. Any number of buildings could have been the gunman's perch. He could still be there, biding his time. "We shouldn't just stand here. The guy could be waiting."

Kevin shook his head, his attention riveted on the Great White Beast. "He'd have shot us by now."

"That's reassuring." That blasted Caddy had addled his thinking. Now he was stroking the car. I felt like I'd lost him to the proverbial other woman. "How about we drive off and call it even?"

"We're suspected of murder. We can't leave the scene of a shooting. We have to talk to the police."

"Talking with the cops takes *forever*."

"We could at least get inside the vehicle." Being used as a bulls-eye was eating at my nerves. Two murders and two shootings in approximately twenty-four hours was a new record for me. "The guy would have a harder time hitting us."

Lines of worry finally creased Kevin's brow. He definitely looked concerned - about the Caddy.

I folded my arms across my chest. "You'd rather me be shot than the car?"

"No." His instant denial mollified me a bit, then his concerned gaze returned to my rival. "No."

The second denial sounded less convincing. Just then sirens burst into full volume. Two cop cars roared into the parking lot with lights blazing.

Kevin flashed a smile. "Saved by the sirens."

"You're lucky." I pointed a warning finger across the acre-wide hood. "At least this incident should help our cause with Pierce. Getting shot at makes us victims."

Kevin stretched to his full height. He looked toward the police cruisers at the main entrance. "Or, we're weak links that need to be eliminated, which would confirm our guilt."

I hadn't thought of that angle. "Now who's throwing rocks at robins?"

"Someone has to stay focused."

The ring of an old rotary dial sounded from Kevin's burner phone. After checking the readout, he raised a brow. "Why is Young calling again?"

"She could be monitoring police dispatches."

A hive of activity boiled around the demolished SUVs. More police arrived. I pulled Kevin behind a double-cab truck with monster wheels. It wouldn't do to have anyone overhear us talking with the DA.

"Hello?" Kevin answered, putting her on speaker.

"I heard a shots-fired call at the Bayside." Her bullet-like tone cut right to the point. "Tell me it isn't you and your partner."

"No such luck," Kevin responded in a breezy tone. "We still have a bulls-eye on our backs."

I gave him a silent glare at his word choice.

A hiss of breath came from Young. "Anyone hurt?"

"Three SUVs and a minivan," Kevin answered.

"I'm pushing my sources for information. Nothing concrete on who's after you or how they're tracking your movements." The DA sounded as frustrated as I felt. "Be careful. I need the information on those files. If you're killed, the smugglers will be blamed. My case could be derailed."

And people thought I had no tact. I glared at the phone. What is it with these people and their choice of words?

"Could Pierce be the shooter?" I asked Young as I shot a quick glance at the police now scouring on the scene. "If he's on the smugglers' payroll, he'd do anything to stop us. A dirty cop can't afford to be caught."

"He could be. He has a marksmen's rating with firearms." Young's terse response carried a hint of impatience. "Any cop on the take would prefer to see you dead. The other players want the thumb drive. They need you alive."

I exchanged a glance with Kevin. "At least until we find the goods."

"Exactly." The DA's voice cut across any reply Kevin had planned. "What have you learned so far?"

"We're not the only ones on the hunt." Kevin checked out the police response, evidently aware this conversation was taking too long. "No one else is having any success either."

A staccato tapping of drumming fingernails came over the phone. "Any leads on the location of the thumb drive?"

"Not so far." Even over the phone, Kevin kept his poker face in place. His glance met mine in a silent accord not to mention Ivan, the codex, or the shell game comment.

"I've gone out on a limb because I believe you're being framed." The sharp retort, like the slap of a hand on wood, echoed over the line. "If you hold back information, I'll charge you both with murder and see you rot in prison."

I pointed at the phone and mouthed. "She sounds miffed."

Kevin smiled even as his crystal blue eyes narrowed. He raised the phone closer to his mouth. "I've told you the truth. Neither Tracy nor I have the thumb drive or know its location."

"I almost wish you were lying." Frustration burned through Young's harsh tone. "My contacts confirm there's no buzz about a leak. The files are out there. Find them. Until then, lay low."

"What a novel concept." The click signaling the DA had disconnected underscored my comment. "Is it me, or is she hung up on stating the obvious?"

"She's frustrated." Kevin started walking toward the growing police presence by the shattered vehicles.

"I hate being questioned by the police. They ask too many questions and it's already past my lunchtime." When Kevin snorted, I threw up my hands. "I have to have priorities. Besides, I don't know anything helpful. Although, if Pierce is the murderer and the shooter, he wouldn't have bothered searching our suite."

Kevin's eyes narrowed in thought. "The searcher was Fedor. He wants the codex."

A uniformed police officer marking off the scene hurried toward us. "Ma'am? Sir? Did you see anything?"

"I called 9-1-1," Kevin said.

For the record, the police questioning did take forever. Well past my lunchtime.

The only good thing was Pierce didn't make an appearance. On the flip side, his absence made me uneasy. We'd been stumbling over the detective since the bodies started to fall.

Where was he now?

25 Across; 9 Letters;
Clue: A short pause
Answer: Interlude

When Kevin slipped the valet an eye-popping tip with a promise of more cash to keep the Caddy close, I didn't blink. I didn't want to cringe every time he turned the key. "Does it strike you as odd that neither Marcus nor Mrs. C has called me? I don't trust those two when they're out of my sight."

"Marcus is with Rabi stashing Ivan and Mrs. Colchester is surrounded by retired police."

As if either of those facts made a difference. "Is that supposed to make me feel better?"

"Count your blessings," he shot back. "The cops haven't called about either of them."

"I'll give you the point on that one." With those two, I take reassurance where I find it.

Kevin tightened his arm around my shoulder as he shook his head. "She has no appreciation for classic cars."

I took a big drink of coffee and leaned back, Kevin's muscled arm beneath my neck. "I'm tired of being behind the eight-ball. We need answers."

The crossword puzzle I was constructing for this case popped into my mind. My reverie was interrupted as the door swung inward.

"Hello, ducks." Mrs. C breezed in on the wings of a wide smile and a simmering contentment. "Shep has filled me in on the several intriguing cold files. I'm certain we could clean up more than one given the time."

I hoped her "we" referred to her and Shep, because I had enough on my plate.

The older woman nodded in greeting as she made her way to one of the overstuffed chairs. Her entrance reminded me of a queen waving to her subjects as the motorcade drove by. As she settled herself, she resumed her one-sided discourse. "Shep has asked me to visit again tomorrow so we can go over some of the finer points of the cases in question. Unless, of course, I'm needed here. I do so hate to abandon you in your hour of need."

She raised a brow in my direction.

"You go visit. We'll work on the leads while you're gone." No way would I admit I wasn't making any headway.

"Too bad this isn't a crime drama." Marcus slumped in the chair. "The autopsy and lab report would be in on Alice by now."

"Crawford was supposed to find out how Alice died." I reached for my purse and dug out my phone. "He still has some backdoor connections. I also want to know where the cops found her car keys."

The thought of crossing words with my boss pulled me out of my doldrums. Moments later, I'd updated Crawford on our progress, such as it was, including the second run-in with the sniper. That shut him up, momentarily. I skimmed over the account quickly. Though Marcus outwardly brushed off the violence, I didn't want to linger on the attack. "I have a lot of irons in the fire. I'm working all the angles."

"That's it?" His loud, growly voice made the speaker function unnecessary. I held the phone six inches away from my ear to protect my hearing. "You need to start making progress, Belden."

I frowned at the phone. "Tell me something I don't know."

"Are you writing all this down? I haven't seen any reports."

"I'm keeping detailed notes." I fought to infuse my words with sincerity, but it was hard. Basically, no one within hearing distance believed me. My best shot was to have Marcus fill out the reports. I chalked that up to assisting him with his essay skills. "I've only been on the case two days. What about your assignment? What do you have to report?"

The resulting bellow had me holding the phone out at arm's length. Marcus laughed so hard he fell off the couch

Once the hubbub settled, I repeated my question.

"Fortunately, one of us is a *real* detective. The cause of death is straight out of an Agatha Christie novel." A rustle of papers sounded over the phone. Crawford, being old school, had no doubt pulled a paper file out of the metal stand on his desktop. "Winter's killer got close enough to stab her at the base of her skull with a thin, pointed object. Severed the spinal cord."

While I was busy grimacing at the MO, Marcus slapped the coffee table several times. "I read that book. The killer used a letter opener. I think."

"Definite possibility," Crawford confirmed. Squeaking springs indicated he'd shifted in his well-worn office chair.

Sitting back and staring at the ceiling was one of his favorite positions for thinking.

Mrs. C leaned forward with unabashed interest. Her latest knitting project lay in her lap, momentarily forgotten.

"I had no idea you could kill someone like that." I grimaced as a replay of Alice Winter's murder ran through my mind. "Who would have that kind of knowledge?"

"Effective method." Rabi, poised by the widow, inserted the analytical comment in his usual brief style. "Little strength required. No blood. Quick strike."

"Death would have been instantaneous," my bossman confirmed. "As to the weapon, it could have been anything at hand. Strong. Slender. Four to six inches. A letter opener. A screwdriver. A long, metal pen with a sharp tip would have done the deed."

I did a slow double take at the phone. "I have none of those things on me in a parking lot."

"You don't have flour in your kitchen or eggs in the fridge most of the time." Crawford countered.

Kevin tapped a rhythm on my arm, his thinking mode.

Now that I'd had time to come to grips with the visual, I turned to the logistics. "Who would know how to kill someone using that method of murder?"

A gleam sparked in my son's black eyes, but his expression remained serious. "Agatha Christie readers."

I rolled my eyes. "That narrows the suspect list to a few billion souls."

Marcus's expression broke out in a wide grin. After a few seconds of indulgent laughter, he pointed at Rabi. "Military people. Cops. Someone who works in law enforcement and reads case reports. Another murderer must have used it sometime."

"No question there." Crawford's tone held a steely edge. Having put in his twenty-five years on the force, rising through the ranks from uniform to homicide detective, he took the possibility of cops turning to theft and murder as a personal insult.

"While every person involved in Las Vegas law enforcement is a slightly smaller pool of suspects than Agatha Christie readers, it's not small enough." I did not like the way Winter's death was shaping up. I shook off the gloom that threatened to envelop me. "What about her key ring? Was it on the floor? In her purse?"

"Not found." Crawford's voice had a meditative air. "Not in her purse or in the vehicle."

"I bet the killer took it." Marcus thrust an arm high in the air. His excited voice range through the spacious suite. "I have a thumb drive on the fob on my backpack. If she had a fob on her key ring, the murderer might have thought she had the missing files. They killed her and stole the keys."

A rock settled in my gut. It actually added up.

"Now that is the flawless deduction of a detective." Crawford's booming voice.

The boy bounced on the chair, wriggling in a dance-like motion. He pumped a fist and mouthed a silent. "Yes."

The full implications of his theory slapped me in the face. "Someone Alice knew and trusted is after those files."

15 Across; 6 Letters;
Clue: Unusual or foreign
Answer: Exotic

"Daylight ambush. The best kind." The Sunday morning sunshine glinted off Marcus's silky black hair as he bit off a piece of purple cotton candy. The spun sugar was at odds with his false, deep voice of dread. "The target sees you coming, but nothing can save them."

"No more film noir for you." Yesterday evening, I'd read all I could find on the players, but I still had the same empty crossword puzzle to show for my time. After another quiet evening in the suite, I felt ready to face Safina.

Thankfully, the International Import Expo was open to any business that imported goods from a foreign country, and Westercamp was here.

With my son two steps ahead of me, I matched strides with Kevin. Our clasped hands swung between us as I took in the publicity free-for-all. A large plaza by Vegas's old downtown area was alive with a carnival-like atmosphere of games, displays, and booths.

It seemed as if every company that brought in a berry from outside the United States was offering information, products, and freebies. The Westercamp Corporation was hawking samples and selling the organically grown, Latin American produce they flew into the states. Clarissa Hodges, AKA Safina Drummond, staffed the booth.

Rabi was in the crowd, hiding in plain sight. Mrs. C, thankfully, couldn't seem to get enough of Shep, his cold cases, and the former police officers at the retirement home.

Kevin watched Marcus's swaggering walk with an affectionate expression. "We should turn him loose on my sister then stand back and watch the fireworks."

A slight breeze carried the warm, seventy-degree air across my cheek like a caress. I looked over the crowd, hoping to get my bearings. "According to the map, our target should be down the next left turn, the third booth."

Sunglasses hid Kevin's eyes, but his expression didn't change. "The booth is straight ahead, roughly half-a-block."

As I rechecked the map, Marcus raised his glass of lemonade. "I'm going to need another hot dog."

"It's ten o'clock in the morning." Any good ambush should come with cotton candy and grilled franks. After all, an army marches on its stomach. At least this one does.

A moment later, following Kevin's directions, we arrived at the Westercamp booth. I pasted on a smile and stood in line while Safina oozed charm over a retired couple determined to buy every unpronounceable fruit on the table.

Marcus spun around on his heel and eyed me as he slurped up his lemonade. "Should I bother asking if you have a plan?"

I gave him a flat stare as I made a spinning motion with my hand. "Turn around."

"Do you want me to start you off?" His whispered question came with a mischievous gleam in his eyes.

"May I interest you in any of our products?" Safina's professionally cultured tone held just the right note of friendly interest. "We have a wide assortment of fruits and nuts, possibly as weight loss aids for the lady."

"Are any of them poisonous?" I raised my voice on the last word, drawing startled glances from three nearby college students, balancing on six-inch stilettos.

Safina's laugh put them at ease, as did her promise of twenty percent off their purchase. Once she shifted them to her associate, she turned her attention to us.

"Are these all free samples?" Marcus pointed his now empty paper cotton candy tube at a row of shallow bowls containing various pieces of dried fruit.

"Absolutely, take your pick." While her voice remained fluid, a wariness shone in the depths of her gaze.

His innocent question seemed to throw her off stride more than any calculated attack of mine.

I hid a smile. The boy was a natural.

I picked up an ugly looking coconut thingy and raised it to eye level. "I need a timetable for Friday, along with background information."

Safina's mask didn't falter. "That is an excellent choice. It has a host of nutrients that smooths out wrinkles."

I tossed the hard-shelled fruit in my hand like a baseball I was about to aim at center field, or at the blonde's pretty little head.

"Let me weigh that for you." Evidently worried about my restraint, or lack thereof, she grabbed the hairy fruit out of my hand. "Please step over to the scales."

When she shifted on her platform sandals and walked to a

side table, I followed. Kevin and Marcus lingered behind. The shifting tide of people quickly separated us. Under the guise of checking out the products, both kept their eyes on me and Safina.

The other woman raised her chin, giving a good imitation of looking down her nose at me. "Kevin's going to be on death row before you have a clue what's going on."

Truth hits the hardest and inflicts the deepest wounds. Fear that she might be right fueled my temper. "At least I put his safety above scamming a few lousy bucks."

The only sign my arrow struck home was a slight flare of her nostrils. As my jaw tightened, her delicate eyebrow rose. An enigmatic expression shown in her eyes. "You need to cut him loose."

Taken aback, I frowned in puzzlement. "What are you talking about?"

A light glowed in her expression, brighter and sharper than I'd seen yet. Her hard, jewel-like eyes had softened to chocolate. "Fedor and I can get him a new identity. Get him out of the country."

It would be like old times.

The hope lay hidden but vibrant behind her words. Somewhere inside that hard-shelled, hostile, irritating piece of fluff was an eighteen-year-old girl waiting for her brother to return.

Kevin had walked out on her and, as far as she knew, never looked back. For the first time in her life, Safina had been forced to face the world without her stalwart defender.

An additional decade of dealing with love and loss, helped me distance myself from my boiling emotions.

Kevin was a rock. Easy going. Intelligent. Loyal to a fault.

I'd known him for ten years. The very thought of facing life without him felt like an abyss had opened beneath my feet.

My animosity slipped away like smoke on the wind.

I hate it when that happens. Now all I had left was sympathy.

Safina's sharp gaze bored into mine. Her offer hovered in the air.

I would rather have him safe without me than loyal and loving in jail. However, the decision wasn't mine. "Your brother will never return to scamming."

"Dump him." She studied me through narrowed eyes. "Break his heart. Tell him you don't want him."

Her suddenly cavalier attitude made me wonder if the glimpse of her eighteen-year-old self had been my imagination or a carefully crafted trap. Sympathy didn't make me an idiot. "I don't lie to Kevin, and I am going to clear him."

As Safina drew on her professional demeanor with no more effort than a blink, Kevin and Marcus stepped to my side.

"I should have known you wouldn't be up to speed on even the most basic facts." Blond tresses flowed over her shoulders. She delivered the barb in honeyed tones. "What do you want to know?"

"Is anyone in Westercamp helping Harrison smuggle artifacts?"

"Not that I know." She weighed and packaged the fruit as we spoke. "All indications are that they're clean."

My son deposited a handful of golf ball sized objects. "I want some of these purple and orange ones."

His voice carried into the people milling around the table. Perfect cover for our extended tête-à-tête.

"When did Harrison become aware someone had accessed the hidden files?"

Safina's gaze narrowed. "A few days ago. When he went looking for the artifact to give to me. He uses several drop locations. The only place they're listed is in those files."

"Did he have proof it was Shawn?"

"Who else was there? The old woman?" Her tone and expression had an annoying "well, duh" attitude, but unlike Marcus, on her, it was not cute. "Harrison set an electronic trap for anyone who accessed the files again."

Something about Safina's timeline didn't track, but I couldn't put my finger on the flaw. I still didn't know how Alice got involved. Shawn wouldn't have pulled her into a dangerous situation.

The thought lit up my brain. I flipped the image. Shawn wouldn't endanger Alice, but if Alice found a problem, who would she turn to? Who else but her friend Shawn?

Alice as the instigator of this whistleblowing scheme made so much more sense. The possibility almost took my breath away. Keeping my expression neutral, I returned to the business at hand. "So, what happened?"

As Safin expertly weighed and sacked our purchases, she cast me an eye-rolling glance. She glanced at Kevin for good measure, in case he hadn't realized what a weak reed he'd chosen.

I didn't care. I wasn't about to expose my hand. I still didn't see why Shawn took the artifact. He had to know that would alert Harrison. And why had he accessed the files again? He had them already. Or did he? If Alice was the original whistleblower, how much of this chaos could be laid at her door?

"For a smart man, Shawn made several mistakes. He was an amateur." Safina's tone was matter-of-fact.

Her judgment contradicted everything I'd heard about Shawn. Smart. Shrewd. Computer genius. That was how Ivan and Lisa described him. Shawn wouldn't have made the mistakes that exposed him to Harrison's retaliation.

Alice, however, was a different story. Lisa said she'd looked on the border agents as her surrogate children. She'd cried for them when they fell in the line of duty. She would have rushed in without thinking to prevent a smuggler from profiting. She most likely gave no thought to the danger she'd unleashed.

"J.D. signed onto a computer in the business office of the convention center Friday morning." Safina's pleasant expression looked so natural I would have believed it, if I didn't know her. Her low-pitched voice couldn't have carried beyond our tight little group. "He used Shawn's sign-on, entered a thumb drive, and copied the accounts. Once he signed off, he made a bee-line to meet you."

Marcus fanned himself with one of the colorful flyers he'd picked up. "He had a tail on him."

Kevin slipped off his sunglasses. "He was watched the whole time?"

"Every second." Safina made a show of adding literature and flyers to our bag. "He stopped nowhere and spoke to no one until he turned into that corridor."

Safina held the bag out to me, careful not to glance at Kevin. "And we all know what happened then."

"Actually, no one knows for sure, or we wouldn't be here." I took the purchases from her. "Thank you. You've been so helpful."

Several minutes later, I breathed a sigh of relief as we left the last of the crowd behind us. Rabi rejoined us, seemingly out of nowhere. We headed to the Great White Beast lost in the jungle of an endless parking lot.

I took a deep breath and related my theory of Shawn and J.D.'s true motive. "Shawn and J.D. were trying to protect *Alice*. They died to conceal her involvement."

I cast a quick glance at Kevin. A vengeful fire burned in his eyes.

Rabi's expression could have been carved from stone. "No one left behind."

I nodded slowly. The former Special Ops commander had a special respect for people who protected their associates. "So much for J.D. being nothing but a shyster."

Marcus, walking backward, raised a brow. "What were you and Safina talking about before we came over?"

Like I'd told the other woman, I never lied to Kevin. Unlike her, I didn't equate manipulating loved ones with breathing. By the time I finished, Kevin's gaze was locked on mine.

I knew the answer before I looked in his cobalt eyes.

Safina's plan never had a chance.

Marcus shook his head, equally unconcerned. "Even if you dumped him, Kevin wouldn't leave. He'd stay in town to share custody of me."

The illogic of the boy's argument swept away the shadows left from interacting with Safina. I hated to remind my son that as a foster child, he wasn't covered under any custody arrangement. "Kevin wouldn't get even partial custody."

I have no idea why I argued. Kevin wasn't leaving, so our breaking up was a moot point.

"That's pretty harsh." Kevin injected a hurt tone into his comeback. "I'd expect at least one week a month along with a couple of weekends. Fair is fair, Belden."

I shot him a flat stare. The man only played along to egg Marcus on and, as usual, it worked.

"Yeah, T.R." My son spun around to walk beside Kevin. He nudged Kevin's arm. "Maybe a full month in summer. I could sleep on the sofa. We could watch horror movies and eat pizza."

The two males notched knuckles. They loved joining forces against me.

"Wait." Marcus held up a hand. "What about Rabi?"

Kevin dismissed the worry with a wave of his hand. "We'd

share custody of him, too."

The man in question breathed a heavy sigh of relief. "Good."

"Drop it." I threw up my hands. "No one is going anywhere, except to Langsdale after we clear Kevin."

"All right." Marcus nodded decisively. His straight black hair bobbed around his golden colored skin. "You can't break up a good bunch like us."

"On to more important matters." The clock showed it was early, still several minutes before eleven, but my stomach demanded attention. "I'm hungry."

"Oh, no." Mock horror sounded in Marcus's voice. "We don't want that."

"Absolutely not," Kevin agreed between chuckles. He spun the key ring out of his pocket as we approached the Caddy.

A moment later, I was settled in the front seat, watching the expo fade into the distance.

"Crime-solving is hard work." I grabbed my phone and checked for calls or texts. "Mrs. C hasn't called. I wonder if she's planning on eating with Shep."

Despite my deliberately casual air, worry gnawed at my gut. My thumb hovered over the quick dial for her when the beginning notes of "God Save the Queen" rang out. Relief melted the tension in my bones. "There she is, right on time."

I was so anxious to hear her British accent, I didn't care if it was real or fake. I was even looking forward to her next crazy theory.

"It's about time," I said in a teasing tone. "You eating there, or are you ready to be picked up?"

Silence.

The smile froze on my lips. A single second had never seemed so long. Or so chilling.

"Damn." The gloomy voice in my ear was neither British nor female. It was Shep. "She's not with you?"

4 Down; 9 Letters;
Clue: Form a theory without direct evidence
Answer: Speculate

My heart seized. Mrs. Colchester couldn't be missing.
I swallowed hard and sought for words that usually came so easily. "She isn't with you?"

Kevin's hand covered mine. Marcus and Rabi went rigid in the backseat. Collective shock seemed to leech the air supply from the car.

My shaking thumb put the phone on speaker.

"I was hoping she'd left with you and just forgot her phone." An unhealthy dread colored Shep's wobbly voice.

Focus on the facts, I told myself. "You're still at the retirement home?"

"Yes." The single word dripped with despair. "We've searched the whole place. She's not here."

My fear meter climbed to the red zone.

Worry carved itself into Marcus's face.

Kevin subtly increased his speed as he met the boy's gaze in the rearview mirror. "We'll find her. I promise."

I swallowed my own sense of hopelessness. "When did anyone last see her?"

"We were discussing crooked cops an hour ago." Shep's voice hitched as he took a breath. "She muttered something about a crucial detail and scurried off. She said she'd be right back. People come and go. You know how it is."

Shep's tone took on a desperate, pleading note.

Darn that woman and her crazy intuition.

"She's not in the building," the older man repeated, taking a quick breath. "We found her phone on the front table. We hoped one of you had picked her up."

"No." Chilled at the alternative, my tone came out harsher than intended. Then my throat closed.

"Maybe she called a cab and she's on her way to the hotel." Hope colored Shep's suggestion.

Marcus leaned forward as far as the seatbelt allowed. "She doesn't like cabs."

His strident tone betrayed his fear.

Rabi squeezed his shoulder.

I took a deep breath. We'd been playing catch-up on this case since we hit town. The blows landed thick and fast, with little time to breathe and no time to think.

I met Marcus's worried gaze and forced a calm I didn't feel. Mrs. C was my responsibility. She was also my friend. "Shep, get a taxi. Bring Mrs. C's phone to the Aquarius."

Rabi raised a finger.

I acknowledged him with a nod. "We'll be there soon. Rabi will meet you in the lobby. Don't call anyone or do anything unless I tell you. Got it?"

"On my way." The line went dead.

I hung up, returning my gaze to my son.

Rabi moved closer, his steady presence, like an unshakeable oak, calmed the boy. "We'll bring her home."

"Absolutely." I weighed in with my own measure of confidence. "We're a team. We don't leave anyone behind."

Kevin's hand covered mine, stilling the trembling. "We'll find her."

I reveled in the feel of his skin on mine. "How did this happen? A place full of former police officers should have been able to keep an eye on one woman."

Rabi's gaze narrowed. "Who goes unnoticed among cops?"

Well, smack me over the head with an onion ring. I raked my hands through my hair, destroying any claim to a coif. "One of their own. Another cop."

Kevin's teeth ground together. He fisted a hand as if that would contain his fury. "Mrs. Colchester's first inquiry could have leaked to Pierce."

From the dark fury on Rabi's face, he looked ready to blow as well, but with iron control, he locked down his emotions.

Panic burned hot in my son's eyes while he fought to hold onto a defiant expression. "How will we find her?"

"We don't have to," I assured him. Time to put on a good front for the boys, not to mention myself. "Whoever took her will call us. We have what everyone wants."

Marcus cocked his head to one side. "The only thing anyone wants is the files on that thumb drive or the golden codex."

"Exactly," I assured him.

Kevin's eyes cut to mine. He wasn't fooled by my brave words. "We can't bluff. We need the real deal."

My son watched us both, logic momentarily crowded out concern. "No one has been able to find either one of them."

His thin voice rose higher with each word as the Aquarius Convention Center and hotel loomed in front of us.

"No one is looking." I let the words sink in. "They think Kevin took the thumb drive as J.D. lay dying and they're all hoping he's recovered the codex."

Kevin's shoulders lost some of their tension. "You are a genius."

I spread out my hands, forcing a quick, seemingly light-hearted comeback. "You didn't know that already?"

"That doesn't help." Marcus shot down my balloon with a direct hit. Despair had deflated his usual cocky confidence. "We don't know where the drive or the codex are any more than anyone else."

"Yes, we do." His down-in-the-mouth attitude spurred my false confidence higher. "What do you think we've been doing running around town for the last two days? We have all the clues we need to solve this case."

Our arrival at the hotel interrupted our conversation. Minutes later, safely ensconced in our suite, we picked up the discussion.

Marcus eyed me, wanting to believe I held the solution, terrified of the alternative. His eyebrows rose, and his slim body followed. He popped up like his inner spring had been rewound. "You really know where the thumb drive and the codex are stashed?"

My sharp nod conveyed absolute confidence. I had to plan for success. Any other outcome was unthinkable. "Kevin has a solid lead."

My guy raised a brow. "I do?"

"As good as." I pinned him with a narrowed gaze. "Ivan's talk about the *shell* game. Don't think I forgot. You said the thumb drive had done a vanishing act."

While realization dawned in Kevin's eyes, I marshaled my dominos. I hoped my guesses proved to be correct. Attitude alone wouldn't save Mrs. C. I pointed a finger at Kevin. "Spill."

A generic ringtone from my phone interrupted any chance of a revelation.

"Who is it?" Marcus tensed.

"Unavailable." My gut twisted. The kidnapper? I motioned for silence and hit the speaker button. "Hello?"

"I have the old woman." The computerized voice held a mocking undertone.

I tensed as a knife-like pain sliced into my chest.

"You have the drive." The computerized voice tore through my thoughts. "Did you find the codex?"

I couldn't deny it. Where would that leave Mrs. C? "How did you know about Darlington's meeting with me?"

A harsh mechanical laugh sent shivers up my spine. "I know everything."

"Hardly." I sneered at him. "If you knew the details, you'd have both prizes instead of me."

"Don't get smart," the voice growled. "J.D. thought he had it figured out, too. Right up until he died."

A dark laugh sent slivers of ice slicing through my veins.

Yet J.D. *had* pulled a switch. He secreted the files before the murder, and I was banking he'd left a trail.

"You mouth off again," the low voice continued, "the old lady's going to pay."

A red haze blinded my good sense.

"You put one bruise on that woman and after I e-mail these documents worldwide," I stabbed a finger at the phone wishing it were the man's eyes, "I'll come for you."

Dark electronic laughter echoed over the line. "You don't know who I am."

"You're named in the files." I kept my tone even, taking a measure of satisfaction as a cold silence answered my thrust.

"You can't know that. You can't read them."

Interesting. The guy knew the documents were encrypted. Not useful since I didn't have them, but interesting. I shared a quick glance with the guys.

"I don't need to read them." I didn't bother to hide my derogatory tone. "If you weren't fingered, you wouldn't care."

"You'll do as I say." The lack of humanity in the stilted voice made the command all the more chilling.

"Let me talk to her." I channeled the fury raging through my blood into the task of blocking out my fear. I fought to keep my voice steady. "Right. Now. Or I will make sure the files on the thumb drive do as much damage to as many people as possible."

Scatter pellets in a wide enough area, and you're bound to draw blood. That was my Uncle Buck's motto. Though he hunted a different kind of animal, Buck's words have served me more than once.

"Calm down." The computerized voice commanded. "She's here."

A moment of silence managed to stop my lungs from working.

"Hello, ducks." The breezy British accent rang out loud and clear. "Quite the muddle, eh?"

I wasn't sure how long we'd have to talk. "Are you all right?"

"Absolutely," she assured me. "Nothing is what it seems though, is it?"

Great observation when dealing with con artists and criminals.

I met Kevin's gaze, grabbed the hand he held out, and straightened. He clasped Marcus's shoulder with his other hand.

Fear lurked in my son's eyes. The game had become real.

Rabi stood poised and ready. His steady gaze never wavered.

"Enough." The stilted voice returned. "Now we deal."

I swallowed my panic and set my mouthy meter to high. "We both have something the other wants. We make the exchange and walk away."

"You're finally getting smart."

I so did not like this guy's attitude. It reminded me of Safina and Pierce's derogatory comments. Cold fury overcame me. Let them underestimate me. Others had before them.

I hadn't failed to solve any puzzle in the past.

I would not fail this one.

"You keep your gunman clear." The voice warned. "I'd hate for anyone to get shot by mistake."

My gaze shot to Rabi. "Fine. He'll stay out of it."

Above Rabi's cold smirk, his eyes glittered like black diamonds.

I doubted the kidnapper believed me either. Given the chance, he'd kill us all. We both intended to achieve our ends.

"I want to talk to her one more time." I couldn't think what I hoped to prove. I was breaking protocol. I didn't know why. I only knew I had to hear her voice before I finalized the trade.

After an initial refusal, the guy agreed.

"Not to worry." The British accent rang out again. "I'll be back soon, playing those words games Kevin loves."

"Playtime is over." The stilted computer voice sounded abruptly.

"Time and place?" I needed as late a time as I could get. I still had to recover the two items Kevin supposedly had in his possession.

The guy insisted on the Tropical Rainforest right here at

the Aquarius. Seemed like a weird place to meet. While I wondered at his reasons, I refused to meet any sooner than ten o'clock tonight. We'd barely concluded the details when the readout went blank.

Tension sucked the air out of the room. The phone shook in my hand.

I fought to recover my false bravado. Inside, my gut was hardening like quick-set concrete. Mrs. C was under my care. Sure, I'd told her not to come. Sure, she annoyed me at times, leading Marcus into mishaps again and again. Sure, she'd charged headlong into trouble.

She was also my responsibility. She was my friend. She was family. You don't leave family behind. Yet, I had nothing to follow but guesses and ghosts.

"You bought us some time." Kevin's calm, steady voice was like a lifeline in a hurricane, drawing me out of the storm.

Marcus straightened. "Now, all we have to do is find the prizes."

I tossed my head with careful nonchalance. "That's why I gave us several hours."

Marcus's shrug indicated he'd bought into my false confidence. "A few hours are all we need, T.R. You're the puzzle guru. You put the pieces together. We'll do the snatching."

Oh, the confidence of youth. What I wouldn't give to recapture that sublime certainty. I wasn't sure who was fooling who. Right now, I couldn't string two thoughts together.

Kevin's attention never left me. After one more squeeze, he released my hand. "Concentrate on what we know."

"Shawn's clues." Rabi, constantly on alert, didn't move. Yet I could feel his attention shift to the problem. "No one else has that intell."

A new attitude infused the air, or maybe the change was

in me. The dark despair that clouded my mind retreated. The timer in my brain, set for the exchange at ten o'clock tonight, started ticking.

Word games and breadcrumbs. That's all I had to solve two murders, rescue Mrs. C, and unmask the killer. Sure. No problem. "Mrs. C mentioned Kevin. Let's start there."

Marcus's ragged sneakers instantly went toe-to-toe with my sandals. The plush carpet of the five-star suite gave way beneath his slim frame as he raised himself up on tiptoe. "She said Kevin played words games, but he doesn't. It's a clue."

"Thanks, I never would have figured that out on my own." Sarcasm laced through my comeback.

Marcus rocked on his heels. "Then tell us what it means."

I work best under pressure. Looming deadlines clarify my thoughts. However, I had no thumb drive, no plan, and no idea what Mrs. C's enigmatic words meant.

I sidestepped Marcus's laser-like gaze. My own personal interrogator. I needed to move. As I paced the spacious suite, my mind clicked through the past thirty-six hours like a roulette wheel. A spark flared deep in my mind. I stilled, willing it to life. "Con and shill."

"J.D.'s last words." Exasperation colored Kevin's tone. "They started it all."

"Your *interpretation* of his last words." My tone came out harsher than I intended. My certainty had crystalized, and I couldn't afford to lose the connection. "J.D. knew Shawn's secret. He used Harrison's name to point us to the smuggler. He only had seconds to convey their whole plan. What if he was saying conch shell?"

Energy invigorated the room.

My brain went into typhoon mode, swirling ever quicker. "Alice put prints of the seashore on her wall. Ceramic shells are all over her desk. Let's assume she found the files. Maybe

Harrison thought he'd shut down his computer or a report, but it didn't close. Alice saw it and realized what it was from her days of working for that forensic accountant. She sounds rash enough to have moved the codex. That's what brought the hammer down on them. Shawn wouldn't have given away his hand with such an obvious mistake."

"What about con and shell?" Kevin drummed a rhythm on the glass-topped table. "Shawn told Ivan the shell game was one of the keys to solving the crime."

Marcus popped up to sit on the back of an overstuffed chair. He balanced one foot on each arm of the chair, then planted his fists on his thighs. The boy looked like an armed missile ready for flight. "Darlington was a hustler. He'd be tricky."

A revelation danced on the fringes of my mind, skirting out of view when I turned to look at it. I remembered a conversation with Kevin years ago. "You told me more than once that a good hustler lets everyone believe they're smarter than he is."

Kevin nodded. "Much easier to get the drop on someone who's blinded by their own brilliance."

The partial epiphany hit like a bulb at low wattage. "That's what Darlington and Shawn did. Everyone believes they failed."

"They're dead," Marcus spoke in a quiet voice. "That's not a win."

The desert sun beat down on the city outside the windows with an unyielding glare.

"Helping Alice was their objective." How to explain that sometimes a higher goal takes precedence? "They got the goods. They made everyone look at them. Harrison never suspected Alice. We have to get the prize to the authorities."

Marcus chewed his lip while trying to wrap his head

around the concept that a victory could be salvaged for the three victims. He cocked his head to one side. "You think if we get the files, J.D. and the others would be satisfied?"

"He and Shawn knew the risks when they signed on." Kevin stepped forward. Drawn in by Marcus's need for clarification, he met the boy's gaze. "When the killer confronted them face-to-face, they hid the location of the stolen files and the codex. So did Alice. They protected the secret to their last breath."

"They were sticking up for each other," Marcus spoke softly.

Just as I and the others had stuck up for one, small orphaned boy over the past three years.

Rabi stepped forward, moving for the first time in several minutes. "Family comes first."

Marcus's chin stiffened. "We could win for them."

"That's right." A renewed determination swept through me. The two anchors that J.D. and Alice had tied to my ankle solidified. After discovering the motivation of the two victims, I'd stopped fighting the obligation. "We have to figure how they tricked everyone."

My son's black orbs sparkled with flashes of color. A shift came over his features as he did a one-hundred-eighty degree turn from PI to street hustler. "J.D. wouldn't have had the goods on him."

I noted he was now on a first name basis with the first victim. "There are witnesses."

"That's it." Marcus raised his hands above his head. "He was seen."

Kevin's eyes glowed like embers. This was his kind of crime. "Of course."

The two exchanged high fives. Even Rabi nodded, a knowing gleam in his dark eyes.

I frowned, frustrated at being left out of this boy's club. "How does repeating what I said solve anything?"

The three turned to me with matching Cheshire Cat grins.

I pointed a warning finger at Kevin. "Don't say, 'he was seen' or I'll bake chocolate chip cookies in your oven."

"No. Please." Kevin threw up his hands as if to fend off my threat. "Anything but that."

Marcus snorted in laughter. It took a moment for the boy-child to regain control. "The firemen will ruin your apartment putting out the flames."

Kevin palmed a pair of dice, then opened his hand to show only air. "Shawn told Ivan the secret. It was a shell game from the beginning."

A small tilt of Rabi's lips creased his long, thin face. Admiration glittered in his eyes. "Shawn and his father kept all eyes on them. As long as everyone knew where the files were, no one looked elsewhere, or earlier."

"Speak English. No one ever wins the shell game." My frustration tilted near the boiling point. Then my gaze darted to each of the guys. For a moment, I'd forgotten who I was dealing with. "Unless they know the solution."

Marcus slapped a hand to his forehead. "Everyone knows the trick behind that game. It's obvious."

"If the trick were obvious, no one would fall for it." I pointed out. Still clueless, I glanced at Kevin and Rabi, only to meet two knowing expressions. "Stop it. I can't be the only one who doesn't know."

Kevin patted my shoulder in a consoling gesture. "We love that honest streak in you."

Marcus spread his hands. "The pea is never under any of the cups."

"But… " I paused, then looked at my handsome guy, the master con artist.

He confirmed Marcus's revelation with a nod. "The scammer palms the pea or the card before the game begins."

Lightbulb. A few of the answers filled in on my crossword puzzle. "Shawn downloaded the files and took the thumb drive out of play days before the chase began."

"Exactly." Kevin rolled a pair of dice around his fingers while his brow creased in thought.

"The vanishing thumb drive J.D. downloaded that morning." I reviewed the steps to get the facts straight in my mind. "The meeting. The handoff."

Marcus waved a hand. "Staged."

A new playing board presented itself. My gaze darted around the room, stopping on Rabi. The lean man stood by the window, eclipsed by the blazing sun behind him. One more shadow in a game of shadows. "Shawn visited Alice regularly at the Bayside this past week."

Marcus jumped out of the chair. "He probably executed the plan before he gave Ivan the clues."

My gaze ricocheted around our small band. My mental gears spun at typhoon speed. The aura grew heavy, waiting.

A knowing smile spread across Kevin's face. "While all eyes were on J.D. and Shawn, Alice hid the thumb drive and the codex."

Marcus threw himself into one of the overstuffed chairs. The air exploded out of the cushions with a loud whoosh. "We did it."

I gave an unladylike snort. "Hardly. We need to find the as yet unseen thumb drive and this golden codex."

Rabi's phone buzzed. After a quick glance, his lean frame arrowed toward the door and disappeared into the hall. "Be back."

The door to the suite was closed by the time my brain deciphered his words. Only then did I remember Shep.

Rabi returned as silently as he'd left. Shep, however,

hurried in, huffing and puffing, keys rattling on his belt. His walking stick thudded on the floor through the thick aqua carpet. He sank into the couch cushions with a weary sigh. His white hair pointed in all different directions. New wrinkles lined his round, gnome-like face.

I clenched my jaw. In the six years I'd known Mrs. C, I hadn't been able to dodge her hawk-like interest and her probing questions for even a day. How could he have lost her in a few hours?

That's what I would have liked to ask, but I could hardly blame him. I couldn't contain her either. Besides, the guilt in his gaze and his slumped shoulders said more than words.

Marcus made him a cup of tea with the one cup brewer, and I brought our resident gnome up to date on the kidnapper's call, the timetable, and our suppositions.

"Did Mrs. C give any clue as to what she was thinking?" The woman is as subtle as a tornado. "What was she harping on?"

"Reputations." Shep tapped a finger to his lips. He'd recovered his color and, judging by the gleam in his eyes, he was ready to jump into the mix. "She said insiders can't be fooled."

Marcus, leaning across the coffee table, nodded sagely. "Cops know which of their own are dirty."

Kevin stood guard behind the couch, directly opposite Rabi's position by the windows. The two looked like a pair of sentinels.

A frown marred Kevin's brow. "Crawford's twelve years gone from the LVPD, but his sources didn't mention Pierce being on the take."

Which meant the police detective was either sneakier than anyone gave him credit for, or Safina's eyewitness account was a lie. She could have murdered J.D. A barrage of implications assaulted me. I dismissed them with a shake of my head.

"We have no time for speculation. Since Mrs. C didn't leave any solid facts, we have to keep our eyes on the prize." My stern tone drew all gazes to me. "I think I know where Alice hid both the thumb drive and the codex."

23 Across; 7 Letters;
Clue: A goal or objective achieved
Answer: Touchdown

B reaking and entering always made me nervous. Sneaking into Harrison's office in broad daylight, even on a Sunday afternoon, was the height of stupidity, but what else could I do?

What had J.D. said? Con and shill? Conch shell?

The whispered words of a dying man. I took my best guess. I hoped I was right. We were short on time and out of options.

The sun hung directly above the Caddy, zeroing in on us like a spotlight from a police helicopter.

Marcus, Kevin, and I were driving around Harrison's office building in a perimeter several blocks wide, drawing closer, then farther away. Rabi was inside, borrowed janitor cart in hand, cleaning rooms on Harrison's floor. In the front seat, the laptop balanced on Marcus's legs showed the image from the tiny camera clipped to Rabi's shirt.

I sat in back, gobbling the last bag of fries. I wasn't even hungry. If I were a cat burglar, I'd pack on thirty pounds. I craned my neck to see the speedometer. "You should slow down. We don't want to be stopped for speeding."

Marcus exchanged glances with Kevin. His incredulous expression was clear. "If he drives any slower, we'll stop traffic."

I sat back, too nervous to watch the view on the laptop. My fingers ripped a hole through the bottom of the bag searching for more salty goodness. "Any more fries?"

"They've all given up their golden, potato lives for you." Barely contained laughter underscored Marcus's solemn tone.

The two guys exchanged a laugh.

A red brick corner of Harrison's building became visible through the trees. Worry ate at me. "Seriously, is there more food?"

Kevin jerked his thumb toward the front seat. "A fried cherry pie is hiding in the sack."

I was already filled with guilt at sending Rabi into the front lines of battle. "I got that for Marcus."

Kevin glanced at my son. "He ate a combo meal with fries and a large shake. Where do you Beldens put this food?"

"It's medicinal." Marcus held out the tempting morsel. "You need it for your nerves."

I held out for a nanosecond, then snatched the grease-laden goody. "Shep better report soon, or I'll need new pants."

Shep had e-mailed that Harrison agreed to come to the police station, but I wanted to ensure the lawyer arrived.

I couldn't remember what ruse the older man had used, especially on a Sunday. I didn't know where the lawyer had been before the call. Didn't matter. We couldn't take the chance Harrison would waltz into his office. I only prayed my guess was right. I bit into the pie. "This could be a fool's errand."

Marcus chuckled. "Then we're definitely the group for the job."

"None better." My recently minted boyfriend gave him a thumb's up before casting me a reassuring glance in the mirror. "Your bullet points are sound. Alice hearing Crawford's name told her that J.D. had changed the game. He planned to meet you without her and the exchange ended badly. If not, J.D. would have called her."

Hearing the logic calmed my nerves, but it didn't assuage my guilt. Even though Rabi had volunteered, I hated sending him into danger based on a chain of logic consisting solely of my guesses.

It was broad daylight. If this went south, he might be seen and remembered. Admittedly, it was Sunday so the place should be deserted, but you never know. Also, Kevin had confirmed he'd spotted no security cameras in the lobby, elevators, or halls. Still, anything could go wrong.

A sharp intake of breath sounded from the front seat.

"Shep confirmed Harrison is at the station." Marcus tapped his Bluetooth earpiece. "Fox is in the henhouse. You're a go."

I focused on my arguments for this venture. "Alice's hiding places for the thumb drive and the codex would be locations she could access without anyone questioning her presence."

"Absolutely," Kevin agreed, playing the game along with me.

One more reason to love him.

A glance outside the window showed the residential houses had given way to a smattering of small businesses. In the gaming mecca of Las Vegas, every grocery and laun-dromat flashed signs offering high paying slot machines.

"The dead lady could have hidden the drives anywhere." Marcus chimed in without taking his gaze off the screen. "It took genius detectives like us to figure out where."

Grateful to be included in the genius category, I nibbled on gooey cherry filling and pastry and continued reviewing the scheme, mostly to keep my mind off our criminal enter-prise. "Alice had no personal possessions at the Bayside. She was gone from home most of the day. That leaves her desk as the most obvious place. No need to be covert. No one knew she had the prize."

Silence. Kevin drove into residential streets where small-ish, older homes showed their age.

Marcus's attention remained glued to the laptop.

I filled the quiet with a faithful standby: guilt. "We shouldn't have brought Marcus to the scene of a crime."

"You can't leave me behind. You need me." Sunlight reflected off his hair as he shook his head. "Besides, nowhere is safe."

His voice descended to the realm of a horror movie narrator. Then a new energy infused him. He shifted in the front seat. "Rabi's outside Harrison's office."

A volatile mix of hope and dread swirled in my belly. "I should have gone in."

A bark of laughter exploded out of Marcus. "You're the worst burglar ever. You get nervous, and you talk too much."

That pricked my ego. "I do not."

"I could get in easy. I'm small. I'm sneaky."

My snort of derision interrupted him. "That would leave me to explain your arrest to your caseworker."

The woman had never believed I was parent material. If Marcus had been eleven months instead of eleven years, he'd be in one of the finer neighborhoods with an up-and-coming young couple.

"You can't even pick a lock." Marcus retorted.

"You act like that's a bad thing." I countered. "Picking a lock is not a necessary skill."

"It is today." Marcus snapped his fingers and pointed at the laptop. "Rabi's in Harrison's office."

Kevin drove slowly, letting a green truck from a side street pull ahead of him. Our speed remained constant. The quiet streets flowed by.

I sat forward, resting my chin on the seat. Now that the moment was at hand, I was impatient to get the goods, retrieve Mrs. C, and nab the murderer.

If there was crime scene tape on the outside door, I'd missed it. The view on the laptop showed the interior office, looking much the same as it had two days earlier.

Rabi turned and locked the door behind him. Latex gloves. Nice touch. He strode toward Alice's desk, stepped behind it. The same place Kevin had stood when he checked her files.

This was the biggest leap in my logic.

Alice knew we were there for the thumb drive. But when she tried to interrupt, I barreled my way into Harrison's office without a backward glance.

Then, the unknowable happened. Someone called her. Or had she called them? Had she learned of Shawn's death? J.D.'s murder? Either way, she left without waiting for us. Without knowing when she'd return, she'd have left a message.

I hoped.

That's when I pulled out my ace in the hole. Kevin's training as a scam artist. "You memorized her desk when we arrived. It's automatic with you, like tracking the passing time, memorizing license plates, counting cards. You saw the desk after she bolted. What was different?"

In the face of the Caddy's AC with sweat beading on my lip, I held my breath.

Now, with Rabi in position, Kevin once again described what he'd seen. "Shells and little beach toys line the front of her monitor. To your left, is her pen caddy. A ceramic treasure chest was moved behind the caddy while we were with Harrison."

Rabi's hand pulled the chest out of the shadows. After trying to flip open the magnetic catch with his thumb, he drew it close for inspection. "Glued shut."

Air escaped my lips. A smile tugged at the corners of my mouth. I'd guessed right.

A police siren sent my nervous system into a seizure.

Heart. Lungs. Brain. Nothing worked.

"Black Ops." Marcus's code name for Rabi came out in a calm voice; however, the note of warning was clear.

"I hear." Came the almost lazy response. On the screen, a knife blade pried at the chest lid.

Kevin glanced in the rearview mirror. Flashing lights of blue and red reflected from the mirror. The car slowed. He pulled to the right. "Everybody breathe."

I forced my gaze to remain locked forward. Putting on my poker face, I cleared my mind for alibis, excuses, ad libs to come forth.

Marcus stilled. A street rat knew better than to draw attention to himself, even from the perceived safety of a car in broad daylight.

The wailing tone drew closer.

On the screen, the tip of the knife cut at the seam of glue.

The scalding alarm reached a crescendo.

I glanced back and to the left. Anyone would.

The cruiser closed in, lights ablaze. Full alert, then, they sped past us.

Kevin pulled into the street.

My fists clenched tighter. "He should take it with him."

"Can't." The knife blade carefully slit the glue lining the lid of the treasure chest. "It's in the police photographs."

The siren faded. The rapid-fire thumping of my heart didn't.

The cruiser continued toward the office building. How could anyone know? Were they listening? Was our suite bugged?

The lid to the chest popped open.

I caught my breath. Leaned over the seat. Closed my eyes then opened them. The image remained.

A single USB thumb drive lay clearly visible against the white ceramic interior. The treasure.

"Get out." Kevin's speed hadn't changed, but his tight tone carried a solid dose of urgency.

The small device rolled out of its confines and into Rabi's palm. The drive and the knife disappeared. The chest returned to the shadows.

In seconds, Rabi was out the door and in the hall. I'd have been running full tilt, but his deceptively calm pace ate up the distance to the elevator.

Marcus's tight fists betrayed his anxiety. "We can meet you by the rear door."

"Stick to the plan." Rabi cautioned in his low drawl. He pushed the janitor's cart onto the elevator. "I'll be there."

The police cruiser had vanished. The sirens were silent. Out of range? Quieted on purpose? Or headed to Harrison's office?

I gripped Kevin's upper arm. "We could do a drive-by to see if the cops are out front."

"No matter what happens, stay in character until the game is done." He quoted the lesson from his childhood without blinking. The set to his jaw and his no-nonsense tone brooked no argument. Behind his laid-back attitude and casual exterior lay a brick wall of stubbornness. "He was hired for the day from an outside cleaning service. Anyone who finds him has to prove differently."

Which they easily could. Goosebumps crawled over my flesh.

The tension in Kevin's muscles and his iron-grip on the steering wheel were clear indications he was more tempted to break protocol than he let on.

Resolve stiffened my spine. I shoved the hysterical part of me into a closet. Deep breath. Straighten the shoulders. Time to encourage the troops.

I rubbed Kevin's arm as I shot Marcus a reassuring look. "Rabi will be fine. We can't be the only B and E going on today."

My attempt to break the tension drew two feeble smiles. With everyone's nerves balanced on the knife's edge, Kevin drove toward our rendezvous point, a block away from the office building.

Our Special Ops, fake janitor slid into the car four and a half agonizing minutes later. He settled into the seat next to me, then met my gaze. "Want it?"

"Absolutely not." Was he crazy? "My heart can't take much more. You keep it."

Anyone who could get the thumb drive from Rabi and escape to tell the tale deserved the prize.

Now it was time to get the second piece of the puzzle. First, I needed ice cream.

24

12 Down; 6 Letters;
Clue: Mentally braced for a demanding situation
Answer: Nerves

The golden codex was in plain sight. Sort of. At least the conch shell was there for all to see. I hoped we'd find our second piece of treasure inside.

The bartender told us Alice Winter created the display in the main hall at the convention center. She'd been there every morning and evening. Easy to keep an eye on the golden treasure. Easy to recover the item when needed. Had she not been murdered; she'd have been the one to dismantle the display at the conference's end.

On my first day in Las Vegas, I'd spent over an hour walking in front of those exhibits while cursing J.D. for being late. The display with the nets and shells was particularly eye-catching. Especially the conch shell and the small sailing book tangled together in a fisherman's net high up beyond the casual reach.

According to Marcus's research, the wafer-thin pages of gold could be folded together, forming a book roughly four-by-five inches and two inches thick. A hollowed book with the cover glued shut would hide the priceless treasure.

My mental focus pulled back from the close-up, widening like a movie camera. Back from the ceramic conch shell and the paper book to my view outside the convention center. We'd been in the Aquarius for the past few days. We all knew the layout. I much preferred the patio outside the Pearls of Pleasure, a dessert shop where we'd landed for the moment.

Marcus took a bite of his ice cream. The sun reflected off his straight, black hair. "At least we don't need to reconnoiter."

"We need a diversion," I observed. How else could we retrieve an item from plain sight?

Rainbows danced in the droplets of the water spray from the nearby fountain. Prisms hovered in the air while the sound of splashing water and popular music almost drowned out my words.

Marcus licked his ice-cream cone. "If it's a diversion you want, I'm your guy. I have an idea, too. It'll be great."

I grimaced. I didn't want to know. I didn't trust the boy and his ideas.

Kevin and Rabi, however, both looked encouraging.

"What's your plan?" Kevin prompted.

"Lizards." Marcus strung out the word. "One of the janitors told me the hotel brought in a bunch of them for the rainforest. They have them in a back room. The lizards are from six inches to two feet long. There's a party tonight. If we let them loose, it'll be chaos."

"You can't be serious." I picked up my feet. My eyes darted around the screened in patio. "Are you serious?"

Kevin gave me a searching look. "You're scared of lizards? Why am I just learning this now?"

"I'm not scared." Okay, maybe a little. "I just don't like them. They're skulking, creepy, little alligators."

Kevin and Marcus exchanged a look.

Rabi, who had spent time in South American jungles and practically lived with lizards and snakes and all manner of crawling critters, tried to look sympathetic.

"They're snakes with legs. They have claws." I crooked my fingers so they could get the full picture. Something brushed my arm. I slapped at the source and jerked away.

Kevin held his hands up, palms out. "Come down off the ledge, Belden. We don't have the reptiles yet."

"See?" My son pointed my way. "People will panic. A perfect time to snatch the codex."

Kevin settled his arm across my chair. "Sounds like a plan."

Marcus elbowed my arm. "I know how to get them inside, too. Mrs. Colchester and I walked through the delivery entrance when we arrived. There's a hallway that leads to the main room."

That managed to distract me from the image of man-eating reptiles running amuck. "Why didn't you enter through the main door?"

"I think she got lost." My son whispered as if Mrs. C were there to take offense. "Like my teacher says, knowledge is never wasted."

Trying to banish a wave of worry at the mention of the older woman, I heaved a sigh. "I don't think this is what she had in mind. Besides, you can't be involved."

Marcus rolled his eyes. "You say that every time."

"Taking a child to a crime is always a bad idea." I sought for an alternative but, as usual, found none.

"Rabi will be with me." Marcus's dark eyes flicked to the watchful man. "You and Kevin are too obvious."

"He's right." Kevin is much quicker to come to terms with the inevitable. "We can't show up until the last minute. If anyone suspects the codex is part of the display, our bargaining chip will be lost. We might be detained."

"Or jumped or stabbed." The recent murders didn't stop Marcus from offering up random methods of attack with ghoulish abandon. "If anybody grabs me, I can scream and cry like a little kid."

Which he was, bravado and his own opinion notwithstanding.

"During the chaos, Kevin can grab the book. Even if the cameras spot him around the display, he's too quick for them to see what he's doing. He'll get the book." Marcus continued in a carefree tone. "That's when you reclaim me. What can they do? I was helping recover wild, dangerous lizards someone let loose."

People in authority could do lots of things. Unfortunately, we were on a time crunch, and I had no better plan. A rush of impatience pushed me to agree before I had time to think through this crazy idea. "Where do we find the creatures?"

I couldn't wait to fill out this expense report. Crawford would have a fit.

Turns out they didn't want my assistance. I've never been so relieved in my life. Marcus waved away my apologies to Rabi for sticking him with lizard wrangling.

"He's having fun," Marcus assured me. "What would he be doing at home? Watching TV?"

We parted company, keeping in touch by phone and text. I didn't ask details of how they planned to get the lizards past the omnipresent security cameras. Unless I got a frantic call that they'd been caught, I didn't want to know.

Thankfully the last message I received was the one saying the pieces were in place.

Moments later, I sauntered into the convention center, eerily close to where I'd waited for J.D. that first day. A few feet behind the displays, tables brimmed with food. The convention attendees were seated at closely packed tables.

Within minutes, I got a text.

Lizards on the move.

I hurried forward, clinging to the shadows. Insidious doubts warred with my confidence. The codex was in that small book by the conch shell. It had to be; because if it wasn't, I was out of ideas and this was all for nothing.

A hulking figure stepped in front of me.

Pierce. Holding Marcus by the arm.

Ten seconds in and the bottom had fallen out of our plan.

Years of experience in telling tales helped me mask my shock. I drew myself up and squared my shoulders.

The police detective glared at me. "You should keep better track of your son if you want to keep custody of him. I'd hate to tell his caseworker how often he's been roaming around a casino unsupervised. He could end up in juvenile detention."

Maternal instinct overcame caution. No one threatened my son.

"If you paid more attention to catching who killed J.D. Darlington and Alice Winter rather than pursuing an old vendetta, you'd have realized Marcus wasn't in the casino. He was in the convention center with a family friend. She must be worried sick that you've snatched my son without warning and without permission."

I inched closer to Pierce.

Marcus scanned the room behind me. He backed up, giving me room to confront the police detective head on. His arm rose. He pointed behind me. "T.R."

I held out my hand, warming to my rant. Something

flicked across my ankle. I looked down as pointed claws dug in and scampered across my foot. I caught sight of lizards moving over the food tables.

My lungs gasped for air. I danced back. A blood-curdling scream started in my toes and tore through my throat.

"Lizard!" I screamed at the top of my lungs. One hand clutched Pierce while the other pounded him. "Lizard!"

The police detective raised both hands in a futile attempt to fend me off.

I spun in a circle, looking for the rest of the killer horde. Holding onto the detective, I dragged him with me, using him as a human shield. Feet moving like an Irish dancer, I held onto the police detective, ready to throw him to a man-eating reptile without compunction.

I have to confess when my survival instincts kicked in, I gave no thought to my son. My one concern was keeping Pierce between me and the wild monsters.

Don't judge me. Marcus is quick. He can outrun twelve-inch killer lizards.

I had a vague impression of my cry catching on and echoing through the two-story atrium. I give full marks to the architect. The place had wonderful acoustics. Screams, both bass and soprano, reverberated and carried through the air with astounding clarity.

The chorus seemed to reach a crescendo as it rose. Crashes of tables, chairs, and shattered dinnerware served as counter notes to the crisis. The noise doubled and tripled. Displays tottered then crashed.

If there'd been a chair handy, I'd have been on it. If I could have climbed on Pierce's shoulders, I'd have done that as well. If I had any connections with the military, I'd have called in a platoon with missile launchers.

Looking back, I confess, it wasn't my finest moment.

Good thing that retrieving the codex was Kevin's assignment.

At some point, Marcus pulled me away. Giving no thought to the mission, I grabbed his hand and fled. We met the others at a hotel room Rabi had rented earlier under a different name. It didn't compare to our suite, but no one knew we were here.

Rabi stood by the window. Marcus sat crossed legged on one bed, while Kevin sat beside me on the edge of the bed with his arm around my shoulders.

"T.R., you were great." Marcus hadn't stopped talking since we'd locked the door. His eyes crinkled in amusement. "I've never heard anyone scream so loud or so long. Pierce didn't know what hit him."

His laughter burst forth, and he fell on the bed.

Feeling like a limp dishrag, I gave a casual shrug. "All part of the plan."

Kevin's eyebrows rose into his hairline. "Really?"

"By the way," I spoke in a nonchalant tone, refusing to concede I'd lost control. "I've decided I don't like lizards."

We hadn't been able to recapture them. I use the term "we" loosely since I didn't try. I don't know what happened to the man-eating monsters. I only know I hope I never see them again.

At some point amidst the resulting chaos and overturned displays, Kevin snatched the conch shell and the small book next to it. He gave me a comforting squeeze. "If we wanted a commotion, we got it. I've never seen such hysteria in my life, and I've survived earthquakes."

"It was like a rolling wave." Marcus, still trying not to laugh, spread his arms wide. "The screams swept through the crowd like a tsunami. It was so cool. I wish we could do it again."

My heart tripped over itself. "Not in my lifetime."

Rabi put out his hand to forestall any such event. "My heart couldn't take it."

"Amen." I met the amused gleam lurking in Rabi's eyes with a heartfelt sigh. I tossed the ceramic conch shell in the air and caught it. "We got what we needed."

I clasped the shell in both hands while Kevin drew forth the small child's book from his inner jacket pocket. He'd already cut through the glue that sealed the cover shut. A quick flip opened the book. Remnants of glue clung to the two halves.

The interior was empty.

My lungs deflated.

Kevin's hands flew too fast for me to follow. The paperback book flipped and twisted. Suddenly, the golden codex appeared, seemingly out of nowhere. The prize, five-by-three inches with several leaves folded together, lay in his calloused palm. The burnished gold shone like a dark, deadly treasure.

Marcus made a grab for it. "Now, we can save Mrs. Colchester."

Kevin's arm jerked. The codex popped into the air.

I moved to secure the prize, but it was gone. I froze, too shocked to move. I jolted forward, desperate to find the prize that had caused three deaths. "We can't lose that."

Kevin's touch on my leg stilled me. He flipped his hand with a flourish. The codex lay in his palm.

I heaved a sigh of relief. "Stop that."

Marcus grinned.

Kevin flicked his wrist, then flattened out his empty palm. With another gesture, he pulled the coveted object out of thin air. Then the faster-than-the-eye tricks ceased, his expression turned serious. "Now, we contact Crawford. He can take these files off our hands and have his computer genius rig us up a convincing copy for our exchange."

Concern over our ability to rescue Mrs. C had me tied up in knots. I'm sure the added stress contributed to my lizard reaction.

Kevin's fancy moves helped ease the pedal back on my worries.

Who better to con a killer?

Marcus's grin widened as Kevin returned the codex to its hiding place in the hollowed-out book, then slipped both into his inner jacket pocket. "I'll contact Shep and make sure his people are in place in plenty of time for the exchange tonight."

I gave a nod of satisfaction. What better allies then retired police officers with a guilty conscience? They'd been eager to help. After all, Mrs. C had disappeared on their watch. My confidence rested on a bubble, but now we had a solid foundation. "We're going to get Mrs. C back."

Rabi's profile hardened to stone. "No one left behind."

Marcus shook his fist in the air. "We'll teach him to mess with our people."

We had the bait. We had the plan.

I just hoped no one else died.

25

6 Down; 5 Letters;
Clue: Uncontrollable fear, causing wild behavior
Answer: Panic

Four minutes to go. The knots in my gut were weighted with ball bearings.

Though the time had been my choice, the location had been at the kidnapper's insistence, the not-yet-open Tropical Rainforest at the Aquarius. Plants, waterfalls, and paths were in place. Security cameras not yet installed. Barriers and construction signs should limit the players to those directly involved.

Thankfully, the structure was on the opposite side of the center from where lizard mania had taken place. I wasn't worried about the critters. I had enough on my mind.

With a seventy-plus woman to rescue and an eleven-year-old boy to protect, the smart money said to leave the front-line action to Kevin and Rabi.

"This is like a live version of a Clue game." A fern plant muffled Marcus's whisper but couldn't hide his scoffing tone.

I said staying behind was smart. I didn't say I was going to do it.

Kevin hadn't believed me anyway. "You and Marcus wouldn't last ten seconds waiting for a call."

Rabi and Kevin had both insisted they'd feel better if they knew where Marcus and I were from the beginning. So, my son and I crouched amidst the outer ring of plants. An emergency exit was ten feet behind us to the right. A dozen feet to the left, the greenery broke through to a gravel path. Several yards straight ahead, a well-lit clearing marked the center of the garden.

"Anything?" I whispered. My job was to watch Marcus and be prepared if the plan went south.

Marcus's assignment was to relay to Rabi any sign of extraneous personnel. He sat against a stone wall, elbows balanced on his knees, his eyes glued to the binoculars.

Mrs. C's binoculars. Ironic, right?

"No movement," Marcus whispered.

"Bizarre place for an exchange," I muttered. A dozen yards away, tourists and gamblers sought fun in Sin City.

Marcus his thin shoulders. "Easy to slip away once you have the goods. Blend in with the crowd, and you're gone."

The voice of experience. I put my hand on his back, feeling his spine underneath his shirt.

He shifted the binoculars. "Woman at nine o'clock. Skulking in the shadows."

"Safina?" My nerves prickled. Would she confront her brother with Mrs. C's life on the line?

Marcus shook his head. "It's the DA, Young."

"How did she know?" My brain vaulted to suspicion. "I wonder if she's having us followed. Do you see Mrs. C?"

"Young's alone." Marcus's mouth, visible below the binoculars, twisted into a grimace. "JAFO: just another flipping observer."

Anxiety tightened the screws on my nerves. This exchange left no room for glitches. My hand clenched, bunching Marcus's shirt in my grasp. I couldn't leave him, but neither could I allow Young to throw a monkey wrench into the works.

"You better get her." Marcus's voice barely reached my ears. "She's going to cause trouble."

My grip convulsed, further wadding his t-shirt.

"I won't move." His tone had that eye-rolling quality. "Go."

Delay was pointless. Crouching low, I slipped through the outer band of shrubs and trees, where the lights weren't installed.

The other woman was using a bush with monster leaves as cover. She whirled at my touch. "I thought I had the wrong place."

My irritation boiled over. "What are you doing here? This isn't a party."

"My contact got wind of this meeting. I had to warn you. Pierce has been out of touch all afternoon. He's up to something."

Who wasn't? Including me. Young's news ricocheted through my mind. If Pierce was in league with Harrison and the smuggling operation, he could be waiting to exchange Mrs. C, then turn around and arrest Kevin. "Do you have cops here?"

"I didn't have time." Her voice sharpened. "Why didn't you call me like we agreed?"

Because I only feel bound to uphold agreements that are in my favor. Besides, Kevin was the one who actually agreed to keep Young in the loop. "I couldn't risk Mrs. Colchester getting hurt."

And because I like to be in control.

The niggling voice in my mind sounded suspiciously like Kevin.

"Follow me," I ordered.

As I turned, Young thrust her face close to mine. "Do you have the thumb drive?"

"No." The denial was automatic. I'd learned long before coming to Las Vegas to hold back your high cards. Besides, technically, I didn't have the goods. Kevin and Rabi had one each.

Her incredulous expression was almost laughable. "What's your plan?"

"To get my friend back." Irritation ignited into anger. She didn't get to be critical. No one invited her.

Young's eyes narrowed. "You need those files, or your boyfriend is going down for a double murder."

Her worried tone had me rethinking my growing grudge against her.

Young touched my arm. "Where's your shooter? At least tell me he's in position."

Rabi, I breathed his name in silent prayer, our ace in the hole. Good thing I'd told no one about him.

At my silence, she started to rise. "I've delivered my warning. I'm leaving."

I pulled her back. "You're staying until my people are safe."

She stared at my fingers clutching her Armani jacket. "Do you realize who you're dealing with?"

If she thought I cared, she didn't know me. I was ready to shove a sock in her mouth. "Move."

Pulling her with me, I aimed for Marcus.

The boy greeted Young with a businesslike nod.

I got in position just in time.

Kevin's solid frame broke through a pair of ferns on

steroids. He raised his arm, from his hand dangled the infamous thumb drive. His arm, bare all the way to the t-shirt ringing his bicep, reminded me of a magician. "See? Nothing up my sleeve."

A shift in the air caused the air handlers to kick in. The game was afoot. I tightened my grip on Young. "You interfere, and your successor can file a murder charge after they deliver your eulogy."

I was too tense to care about a death threat to a DA. Labored breath. Shaking nerves. Sweaty palms. You name it. I was a mess.

The foliage along the path leading to the far door waved like wheat in the wind. A figure sauntered out of the shadows. Knee-high boots. Skintight jeans.

My blood roared with the heat of an inferno.

Safina. Her blond hair was knotted at the base of her neck. Her expression was as casual as her brother's on his best day. She walked up to Kevin, brandished a slim tablet, then held out her hand.

Kevin gave her the thumb drive.

My breath hitched in my throat. We'd staked our entire pot on Crawford's computer expert's decryption of the thumb drive.

Young leaned forward, drawn into the unfolding drama.

So was I. I didn't know what would happen next. Any general will tell you - once the battle begins, nothing unfolds like you expect.

Safina inserted the thumb drive.

My son reached across the DA, his long fingers twined with mine. His dark eyes met mine. He looked more confident than I felt.

In the circle of thorns, Safina's attention was locked on the tablet's screen. Her gaze froze. She looked up.

Expressionless?

Suspicious?

I couldn't tell. Kevin simply looked impatient.

My pulse pounded in my ears. My heart threatened to quit altogether. More than anything, I wanted my landlady to scuff into view on her precious, pink muffs.

Safina pulled the thumb drive out of the tablet. The small device disappeared. Her head jerked.

Was that a nod? A denial? A furious rejection?

She spun on her heel.

My throat closed.

Kevin's hand shot out, flipped her hand over and open.

The thumb drive popped into view.

As quick as a pair of striking cobras, each twin grasped an end.

Kevin's gaze hardened. "This is an exchange. Not a gift."

My admiration for him soared at the disdain in his tone. The man knew how to play a scene. My body was wired like an electric charge. Yet my lungs were too locked to draw in air. I still wasn't sure.

Had they bought it?

Safina managed to look offended behind her icy mask. A delicate eyebrow rose. "Of course."

Marcus's smile shown bright as the long-gone sun. His fingers tightened on my wrist.

Young's gasp sounded loud to my ears. "You had the thumb drive all along."

Her accusation came fast and low.

I shushed her, too absorbed to answer.

Keeping her gaze locked on her twin, Safina turned her head to one side and nodded.

That's what happens when you have the files. Crawford's computer whiz had unencrypted the files, kept the folder names, and replaced the content. They looked good, but who could tell? How much did Safina know?

Evidently, not enough to see through our ruse.

During my reflection on our trickery, the tableau remained unchanged.

"You have what you requested." A mocking smile tipped the edge of Safina's lips. She raised the small tablet. Her thumb skimmed the surface. Her smirk grew as she turned the screen so Kevin could see it. "You made a handsome deal, but the location of the other item had better be on these files as you promised."

While my emotions took a dive, my heart rose to choke my throat. What was she trying to pull?

Marcus's grip dug into my skin.

Kevin glanced at the readout with a baffled expression, which morphed into anger. "I made no such promise. I can't access those files. I want Mrs. Colchester returned alive and unharmed. Now."

A furrow marred Safina's brow. Her eyes shifted to the right. "What is he talking about?"

That's when I realized she had a Bluetooth device in her ear. Who didn't these days? Better than having a wire taped to your skin.

Her razor-sharp gaze studied Kevin.

He towered over her with an aura of contained fury.

His sister's face settled into a marble mask. The hard edge of her jaw betokened the white-hot anger of betrayal.

"He's not lying." Barely contained fury colored her words with fire. "Kidnapping was not part of our deal. Where is the old woman?"

Add one measure of treachery. Mix lightly with a double-cross, and out comes complete confusion. At least, on my part. Why would they give Kevin money? Why betray Safina? Was there no honor among thieves?

"You didn't have time to download the files." Safina's gaze never left Kevin's, but her stiff tone indicated she was speaking to her Bluetooth connection. A smirk of satisfaction crossed her face. "You're worried about my cousin being angry? Trust me, you don't want to meet my gram when she's in a temper."

Safina's eyes met Kevin's.

His tight expression eased as a knowing smile teased his lips. He met his sister's look and gave her a nod.

Safina smiled in return. The twins for once in perfect accord. Their reaction made me both curious about their gram and relieved the old woman wasn't present.

Safina's gaze shifted to her brother. "No hard feelings."

I couldn't decide if she was talking to Kevin or her partner.

She paused for a heartbeat, then continued.

"Of course, we're still on the same side." The distracted look in her eyes dissipated. She focused on Kevin, facing the tablet toward him. "The money's been withdrawn."

His cold expression, threatening posture, and clenched jaw remained immovable. "I want Mrs. Colchester."

"She's coming." Safina waved the tablet over her shoulder. "It was a misunderstanding. We can still be friends."

She took a measuring look at her brother. "Do you know where the other item is? We've torn Shawn and J.D.'s lives apart trying to figure out where they could have hidden it. What about Wonder Woman? She's the puzzle guru. Surely, she has an idea."

Yesterday, she sneered. Now, I was a puzzle guru.

Safina's expression softened. "You could come with me. You could help us find it. We have the private buyers all lined up, waiting for their one-of-a-kind artifact. It could be like old times."

"Old times." Kevin's tone held nostalgia, but no anticipation. He looked into his sister's eyes and shook his head. "Different worlds. Different dreams, from the day we were born. I have enough adventure in my life. Alice Winter hid the item, not Shawn or J.D."

A cocoon of warm honey enveloped me. Marcus and I were Kevin's world, his dream. A bubble of happiness rose up in me, but I had no time to dwell on the feeling or appreciate Safina's shocked expression. The scuffling sound of slippers sent an eruption of joy swelling through my body.

Mrs. C appeared behind Safina. Pink slippers. Oversized purse. Slightly dazed smile. All there. She'd never looked so beautiful. She stopped in the dead center of the clearing. "Hello, ducks."

"I had no idea you'd been taken." Safina glanced at the older woman. "I hope you weren't hurt."

"He took all the precautions, ski-mask, blindfold." She waved a dismissive hand. "I do appreciate the professional touch."

Any ex-MI6 agent would, I noted silently. So, the guy was experienced. Perhaps a certain police detective?

Kevin reached out to the older woman without taking his gaze off his sister. He pointed behind him, positioning his body between her and Safina. "Go, Mrs. Colchester."

I gathered my legs beneath me, grabbing Young with one hand. Marcus clasped her other hand. The seconds crawled by while Mrs. C shuffled toward the shrubbery with glacial speed. She had six feet to cross. Each second rang in my skull like a gong. I bit my lip, fearing dawn would arrive before she made it to cover. Finally, she slipped through the branches.

Leaves rustled. Twigs broke. Then, silence. That woman could call up stealth a cat burglar would envy.

An aura of subdued excitement tightened Safina's cherubim expression. "You have what you want, and I intend to find what I want. Thanks for the tip. As always deal's a deal."

Kevin tossed her the thumb drive. "Except when it's not."

Suspicion skimmed over his sister's eyes.

Then blackness fell. Literally. The lights went out.

I'd expected the darkness. After all, I was at the planning meeting. Still, shock rippled through my body.

Young stiffened, started to rise. "What the he--"

"Don't move," Marcus whispered. "Not yet."

Adrenaline coursed through my veins. I bunched my muscles, counting the seconds. The power should pop on –

A blinding flash. The lights blazed to life.

I jumped to my feet. Marcus was already up. Between us, we dragged Young into a semi-upright crouch.

"Go," I ordered and swung left.

Young dug in her heels. "You don't know where you're going."

"Of course, we do." Marcus countered. He put his hand on the small of her back and pushed. "This is part of our plan."

---

9 Down; 8 Letters;
Clue: A plan of action to achieve a goal
Answer: Strategy

D id I forget to mention we had a plan?
Heart-stopping trepidation will do that to a person.

Though Young sputtered a few choice words, the woman seemed unable to string together a coherent thought.

That's what happens when you miss meetings. Then again, she hadn't been invited.

Marcus pushed from the rear. "Phase Two, people. We're falling behind."

His low-pitched voice was aimed at the Bluetooth earpiece which connected him to Kevin and Rabi.

The boy had a new byword - timetables. He especially loved Phase Two. Time for action.

I started forward, feeling both relieved and worried.

Recovering Mrs. C was only the most important of our many hurdles. While Kevin was even now rushing... well, taking her to safety. Rabi was close by to ensure everyone else got out unhurt. I was still planning... okay, hoping to trap the killer.

I twisted and turned through the plants. While Rabi's assurance that no sniper chose this closed-in location eased my fears, the puzzle gnawed at me. The kidnapper brought us here for a reason.

I picked at the problem while dragging Young behind me. Marcus crowded on her heels. Fortunately, the path of the rainforest matched the layout Marcus had unearthed from the Internet.

I glanced over my shoulder. "Stay close."

The DA's nod didn't hide the antagonism in her eyes, but she remained silent.

"The sniper is unaccounted for," I reminded her, my son, and myself.

Harrison and Safina believed they had what they wanted. A bit of fakery and sleight of hand had pulled off that maneuver.

The sniper wanted us dead.

Fulfilling that wish was not part of my plan.

The gravel path snaked right. Directly ahead stood a large bush with red-veined leaves. I offered up a silent prayer. With a hand far steadier than my shaking nerves, I parted the branches.

An old man crouched among the forest greenery. The first of Shep's friends who'd volunteered to help. Below the man's pot belly, his weathered hands held a gun with the ease of long experience from his years on the Vegas police force. He jerked his head to urge me forward.

I slithered through the branches. Not daring to relax, I kept a tight hold on Young's hand. I wasn't losing her at this point. She might get shot. Our carefully managed script didn't account for drop-in allies wandering through the escape route.

A few short steps left the retired police officer behind. He remained in position to cover our escape.

For anyone else who missed the meeting, I'll tell you now that retirees from the LVPD littered the place. They wanted to vindicate themselves. After all, Mrs. C had been snatched from under their noses. And, honestly, they were bored.

In moments, our threesome had shimmied through more shrubbery, spotted a few more gray hairs with guns, and was walking down a covered walkway. The sounds of tourists and locals losing money wafted through the air. I breathed a bit easier, but my heart still pumped double-time.

Marcus flipped the binoculars under his arm. Hardly the oddest sight to be seen in a Vegas hotel.

"All clear." He tapped the Bluetooth receiver in his ear then gave a thumbs-up. "The others will meet us at the rendezvous point."

Young tried to pull her arm out of my grip. "You can release me."

Probably a good idea, but I couldn't make my hand relax.

"You could let us both go." Marcus wiggled his arm as well. "You look like security escorting us off the grounds."

Which is what they would do with a child his age.

A young couple in a tux and wedding gown gave our trio a wide berth. Noise and laughter filtered through my tension-filled haze.

I took a lungful of warm, evening air. Perhaps I was more wound up than I'd thought. I forced my hands to relax and released my grip on both of their arms.

Marcus tapped his device again. "The rabbit is in the hat."

I rolled my eyes. Him and his crazy codes.

Young clenched her teeth. "What does that mean?"

The boy gave a cheeky grin. "I can't reveal our codes for just anyone."

His derogatory tone sent a ruby flush rising up her neck.

She ground her teeth, then eyed me with a laser-like death-stare.

I bit my lip and fought not to laugh. I'd like to state for the record that my amusement was not aimed at her. It was the release of tension. Once I had control of myself, I held up a hand. "I'll explain everything in a few moments."

A strong compulsion to remain on guard refused to release its grip. Perhaps it was the abundance of windows in the walkway leading to the main building that kept my nerves balanced on a needle's point.

Young pulled on her cloak of authority. "You've ruined everything."

"That's standard procedure for me." I almost laughed in her face. "Besides, I consider the night a success. I rescued my friend."

"I realize the importance of that fact." Her sincere tone quickly dissipated. Ms. Pushy DA soon to be Congress-woman Young had her own agenda. "However, giving up the thumb drive negates any chance to clear your boyfriend."

"I don't agree." Flush with the glow of success, I was almost tempted to confess we had the real drive and the codex, but now was not the time.

We left the connecting walkway for the safety of the hotel. I breathed easier, releasing some of my tension into the thick walls.

A cacophony of bells and voices announced the presence of slots and gaming to our right. We turned left. The mostly deserted hall boasted a string of slot machines fed by three geriatric gamblers. Our last checkpoint, though I wasn't sure if they were all former law enforcement officers.

The grin on my face felt forced and hollow. We were

almost home, yet my inner alarm was clanging. As we came to the end of the corridor, I put a hand around Marcus and pulled him close to my side. "We made it this far."

"Nothing to it." His thin shoulders shrugged. The bright lights glinted off his glossy, black hair. "We're professionals."

"Now what?" Young swiveled to face us, blocking the narrow hall. "You plan to walk away? If you'd informed me of your plan, I could have brought in the police. We could have caught the person who kidnapped your friend. He's most likely the murderer. It's too late now."

I brushed past her, eager to see the others. "Those crimes are a matter for the police. They can find the murderer, so long as he doesn't find us first."

Young caught up, once more wearing her professional mask. "Why did the kidnapper think the files on the thumb drive were the correct ones? The files Shawn hacked were encrypted."

"We knew that." I stepped up my pace. I was only half-listening. My gaze darted around the quiet hall. "The files couldn't be unlocked without the code thingy."

"T.R. means the key code." My son, with his chronic mistrust of authority, also kept quiet on our recovery of the codex. "All Safina saw was a directory. We figured the contact wouldn't have time to do more than glance at the files before letting Mrs. C go."

Young's eyes narrowed. "J.D. Darlington had that thumb drive when he was killed."

"I told you from the first that Kevin didn't take anything off J.D.'s body." I brushed off her unspoken accusation, petty enough to feel a flush of satisfaction at Young's mistake. Like everyone else, she didn't realize J.D. never had the stolen files with him.

I refused to enlighten her. I wasn't being paid to do the

police's work for them. I'd been paid by Crawford to get the files. And despite what everyone believed, I had them.

Well, okay, Rabi had them. Same thing.

And, bonus, I had the golden Mayan codex.

All right, Kevin had it. Again, same thing.

A few yards from another intersection of halls, Young grabbed my arm. Not hard, but enough to stop me. "Pretending to find the Mayan codex was ludicrous."

Her voice hardened.

I shot a narrowed glance at her hand on my arm.

She glanced behind us.

One of the oldsters had disappeared. Another one appeared to be gambling in his sleep. The lone woman had eyes only for the coins counting up below the three crowns on her readout.

"The information on the Mayan artifact was on the files, and they were encrypted. Only Harrison has the code." The skin over her high cheekbones tightened as she clenched her jaw. The words came out in a whisper. Her fingers dug into my forearm. "I want an answer."

I debated whether to brush her off, but Young's impatience had clearly reached the boiling point. For once, I couldn't wait to hear Mrs. C's British accent, real or fake.

"Fine." I was ready to be done with this conniving. "I discovered information that Alice found the files on Harrison's computer. She downloaded them, not Shawn. She took the codex from its hiding place and hid it elsewhere. Shawn and J.D. were trying to cover for her."

Surprise. Disbelief. Eagerness. The different emotions flowed over her face like a roadmap. "I need those files for my case. Do you have the real ones with you?"

"Ummm, yes." Sort of. Her sudden urgency took me aback. Right now, my attention was divided between reuniting with the others and a voice in my brain yammering for attention. One part of the puzzle refused to come into focus.

The DA faced the T-junction at the end of the hall. She marched forward. "Let's go. Hurry."

I cast her a puzzled frown. She was one driven woman. My son's face held a fight-or-flight expression I hadn't seen since his days of living on the streets.

The worry glinting in his black eyes knifed through my haze. In the past two days, he'd faced murders, break-ins, and random shootings without blinking an eye. Why worry now?

It took a nanosecond for a fist to slam into my gut like a rock. Rabi as the second gunman. Encryption.

I'd been a fool. Like anyone caught in the force of an undertow, now that it was too late, I saw my mistake. I ached to tell him, but I couldn't risk alerting Young.

My feet faltered, then recovered. Despite myself, my muscles tensed beneath her fingers. Thinking fast, I nudged our ensemble toward the right branch of the hall.

On the other side of the DA, Marcus frowned.

Our gazes had barely locked when Young reached around Marcus and snatched the Bluetooth from his ear. She pulled him in front of her and pushed him down the left corridor. In the same motion, she veered against me, pushing me along her chosen path.

"I have a gun in my purse," she whispered.

Sure enough, her right hand was lost in the depths of her shoulder bag. "If you want your son to remain unhurt, don't do anything to attract attention."

Like I said, perfect plans don't exist. Of course, it helps if you have a roster separating the heroes from the villains.

27

17 Across; 6 Letters;
Clue: To pay attention, understand what is heard
Answer: Listen

Young's pasted-on smile was one for the papers, not to mention the cameras imbedded in the ceiling. "If you try to alert security or start to run, I'll shoot your mother."

Red spots blazed on Marcus's cheeks. Fury darkened his eyes. "I don't run from a fight, and I'd never leave T.R. behind."

I had to buy time. While Marcus's Bluetooth had gone silent, the mic I wore should be transmitting. Unfortunately, if our guardians in the hall had lost sight of us, neither Kevin nor Rabi nor Crawford's ace-in-the-hole police contacts would know where to find us.

I tamped down my emotions. My mind launched into calculation mode, searching for a way out. "Don't worry, Marcus. We'll get out of this mess."

"Yes, you will," Young responded with a smooth tone and a sincere smile. "Cooperate, and no one will be hurt."

Did she seriously expect either of us to believe that?

Glancing around, I gauged our location. An exit lay at the end of this corridor. I couldn't risk her taking us outside. From there it was one short car ride off the grounds. After that, we'd never be seen again. At least, not alive.

"You realize the comment on the artifact was a mistake." I pointed out. "As well as knowledge of the encryption."

"Only Alice, J.D., and Shawn knew that detail," Marcus interjected.

"J.D. and Shawn died right away." I picked up the story-line. "But Alice spoke to someone before she died. Someone she trusted."

"An honest DA would've mentioned that," Marcus spoke in a censoring tone. "Which means you're one of Harrison's minions."

The DA aimed a look of veiled rage at my son. "I am no one's *minion*. Who do you think gave him the idea? Who do you think put him in touch with the right people? Who protected the smuggling all these years? This was my operation."

She spat out the word through clenched teeth.

Marcus looked into the face of her fury. A shrug accompanied his patent indifference. Both threw fuel on a blazing fire.

With fear for my son roiling in my gut, I jumped in with both feet. "Which means your payoffs are in those files. That's more than enough to destroy you."

Fire. Fury. Vehemence seethed from her very pores. Her purse vibrated with the force of her shaking hand.

"Big brother's watching." I put my arm around my son's shoulders and pulled him to my side, scared he'd pushed too far. The image of her finger tightening one iota too much on the trigger almost made my heart seize. "You don't want anyone to notice us."

I shot Marcus a cautionary look.

With a visible effort, Young pulled her gaze off him and stared straight ahead. Her muscles slowly relaxed.

"You still need the thumb drive." I deliberately reminded her she also needed us. "I'll give it to you, but we have to stay in the building."

Her narrowed gaze darted to the door of a nearby meeting room. "Step in here."

"The Rose Room?" Marcus wrinkled his nose. "You think they have real roses in there?"

I opened the door to a conference room, twenty-feet-by-twenty. "No roses."

Once we filed in and the door shut on the possibly life-saving cameras, I searched for a way to stall. "You know what your second mistake was, after mentioning the encryption? You asked about our gunman. I was too nervous to realize that neither Kevin nor I mentioned he was with us."

"I didn't make a mistake." Young's jaw tightened. "He provided covering fire for you at the park."

Oooh, she was touchy at being called out.

"The two gunmen could have been connected. He could have been with the police. How did you know he was with me?" I raised a brow. "You also made a comment at the park about the *second* gunman. You weren't surprised by the first shooter, but you didn't expect a second one."

Marcus patted me on the middle of my back. "Good catch."

"Yesterday, it would have been great. Now, is a tad late." I forced a rueful smile. My pulse was booming in my ears, but I fought to appear calm. "You really did want Kevin and me to find the files and get them to you. Did you mean to kill us from the first or was that someone else's doing?"

Young scoffed. "This isn't a book or a movie. I'm not going to confess."

Marcus bumped against my hip. "She wouldn't do her own dirty work. I bet the shooter was *her* minion. She had him try to get the files off J.D. at the Aquarius the day of the murder."

Ding! Another piece fell into place. Again, too late. That was who Safina had seen stabbing J.D. Not Pierce, another long-time police officer with the same build and the same loping gait of someone on the beat for decades.

"J.D.'s killer was a police officer who helped you scuttle cases against Harrison. What happened? Did you lose control? Did he want to kill us before we got too close?"

If so, he'd vastly over-estimated the progress Belden and company had been making on this case.

The weapon shook in Young's white-knuckled grip.

Evidently our guesses were striking too close to the truth.

"All I ever wanted were those files." The woman's teeth were clenched so tight she was in danger of cracking her dental work. Young took a deep breath. The weapon in her hand never wavered from my chest. "You should have trusted me. I could have arranged backup and ensured the thumb drive was handed over to the police."

"No, way." Marcus peeked around me. "They'd have disappeared and you'd blame us."

I kept my body positioned in front of him.

"This isn't on me." The DA raised the gun. "There was no need for any of this to happen."

Stunned at her self-serving rationalization, I decided now was not the time to provoke the person pointing a gun at me and my son. However, instead of calming her down, my silence seemed to agitate her. Her hand tightened, then shifted on the weapon.

She shook the gun at me. "You made a mess of this situation."

Why does everyone blame me when these cases go bad? All I wanted was a nice, quiet weekend in Las Vegas with my guy. Not another showdown with a cornered criminal. "Alice didn't tell anyone where she hid the codex, but I'll give you the drive. Then, you can lock us in a closet and leave."

Young's steely gaze met mine. "Hand it over. No tricks."

I held up my hand palm out. "Anything you want."

A knock sounded on the door.

My whole body jerked.

The other woman gestured downward with the gun.

I obediently dropped my arms while she slipped the weapon into her purse.

My whole body was clammy. I wiped at the sweat on my lip. With a firm hold on Marcus, I stepped back, pushing him with me. I had no idea where I was going. The rows of chairs filling the meeting room provided scant protection at best.

The door eased open.

An old man in a blue and gray uniform jerked to a stop on the threshold. His hand froze on the cleaning cart.

"How do," he said, starting forward. "I didn't know this room was in use. Won't be a minute. Just need to empty the waste can."

For a moment, none of us moved.

Though two of the gamblers in the hall had been retired police officers, I wasn't sure they'd seen us take the wrong turn. I wasn't sure the mic I wore would carry far enough. As for this guy, I had no idea who he was. Former cop? Actual janitor?

Without a roster, it was anyone's guess. My nerves were stretched as thin as Young's. I felt as if one of the lizards was crawling over the gooseflesh on my arms.

Young shook herself as if waking. "Could you give us a

moment? We have a matter of some importance to work out. If you could start on the other rooms, we should be done soon."

The old man had already raised a small trash-can. "Won't take me but a minute."

"Danny," Rabi's familiar voice drawled from the hall. "You almost done?"

My heart seized. My hands clutched Marcus, safely tucked behind me and poking me in the back. I hardly dared breathe.

The DA clamped her jaw tighter at the second interruption.

With Marcus tapping unneeded Morse Code on my spine, I kept my gaze glued to the doorway.

Rabi swung into view.

I almost flat-lined from relief. It took all I had to keep my knees from buckling.

The skeleton-thin man, guardian angel incarnate, didn't spare a glance at anyone but Danny. "C'mon, man. It's break time."

For one telling flicker, Young's gaze followed Rabi's.

Mine didn't, probably because I was too keyed up. I clamped onto Marcus's wiggling frame and kept my gaze on our own personal cavalry. Even then, I didn't see him move.

One second, he was in the door, arms at his sides, looking bored. The next, his right arm was ramrod straight, pointing a large, steel-gray gun at Young's head.

His move didn't so much as rustle the air.

Danny paled. The waste can fell with a clatter. The old man's muscles shook as he ducked behind his cart.

A blink of an eye would have covered the entire drama.

The DA's body seemed poised with a fatal indecision.

Rabi's black eyes met hers. "You'll never make it."

A chattering of teeth and moans rose from behind the cleaning cart.

"This is Detective Rodriguez of the LVPD." A commanding voice boomed from the hall. "I have several officers with me. You have nowhere to go, Ms. Young."

He paused, evidently to let his words sink in.

I inched toward the corner. Not that I doubted Rabi's marksmanship. I just wanted some maneuvering room in case Young went crazy. Which seemed increasingly likely.

"Ms. Belden's wearing a microphone." Detective Rodriguez continued. "We're also in possession of the thumb drive and the stolen artifact."

Rabi could have been carved from stone. An ashen-skinned, immovable statue. Except for his coal-black eyes, which burned like twin infernos.

That was what Elana Young was staring at when her shoulders slumped, and she drew her empty hand out of her purse.

To be honest, the rest passed in a blur.

I remember almost collapsing, then getting a bear hug from Kevin.

I remember Rabi, swallowing hard as he put a hand on Marcus's head. When he raised his gaze to meet mine, tears of relief were running down my cheeks.

I remember hearing Mrs. C's British accent in the background. "I knew she was the bad apple. I was confirming her confederate, retired police detective Gaffney, when I was snatched. If I'd only been able to speak with someone, I could have cleared up the entire affair."

28

27 Across; 4 Letters;
Clue: To fasten several strands together
Answer: Knot

E xplanations always leave me torn between "Nobody told me that" and "I should have seen it".

Young said all the right things. She looked and sounded sincere, but, like Pierce and Safina, she was always around, always in touch. Things happened so quickly that I didn't have time to confirm or eliminate anyone as a suspect. I truly thought Pierce might be the sniper and/or the kidnapper, trying to bury his association with the smuggling operation. In the end, I wasn't convinced of her guilt until she made her move.

I'll skip over the unending police questions and cut straight to the good part. It was Monday morning. The authorities had Young and Gaffney for murder. The files provided evidence to put Harrison away for smuggling and theft of international artifacts, plus a whole slew of international crimes for ransacking archeological sites.

The Westercamp company was guilty of nothing but being clueless. Harrison and Young used their transport system for his own benefit. Pierce had the satisfaction of arresting Harrison at the airport trying to make his getaway.

The powers that be were tracking down the smugglers' operation and everyone listed in the secret files that had cost three innocent people their lives. A federal task force was at work recovering the artifacts and antiquities listed in Harrison's records. Ivan was home, and, most importantly, Belden and company were headed to Langsdale. Bags were packed, and the luggage cart was loaded.

"Come on, people." I clapped my hands. "I want to be on the road before Pierce knows we're gone."

Strong arms swept me up in a bear hug from behind and spun me around. Kevin planted a kiss on my lips.

I put my arms around his neck and returned the favor.

"I thought you wanted to get on the road." Marcus's accusing tone interrupted the moment. "I'm riding with Rabi if you two are going to kiss the whole time."

Kevin grinned, keeping his arms around me. "What if I promise not to kiss her while I'm driving?"

Marcus eyed my guy for a moment, then shook his head. "I call shotgun with Rabi."

"Did you forget Rabi flew here with a friend?" I asked. "You're stuck with us for the duration."

Marcus slapped his forehead. "Oh, no."

I laid my head on Kevin's shoulder. "Remind me never to plan a trip to Las Vegas again."

Mrs. C shuffled out of the bedroom. Her oversized purse bulged at the seams. She patted it gently. "I've socked away the little soaps and goodies from the loo. They replenish them daily. I've quite the collection."

I rolled my eyes as she walked past.

After a quick hug, Kevin released me. "I don't think you need to worry about vowing off Las Vegas. After this weekend, we'll be banned from the city, certainly from the Aquarius."

Moments later, we had the luggage cart loaded and in the hall. Marcus made a show of pulling from the front, directing everyone toward the elevator as if it weren't straight ahead of us. He looked at me over his shoulder. "You should split the money you get for this case with all of us."

That was so not going to happen. "I would never cheapen this delightful weekend by offering money to any of you. Look at the fun you've had, you got a free trip to Vegas. You got to solve a mystery. Now, we get to go home."

Marcus hit the button then spun to face me. Fists on hips. "Mrs. Colchester got kidnapped, and Kevin nearly got shot. They deserve something."

"I did my part," I protested. "I put the rescue in motion. I got the players on hand. Young fell right into my trap."

That drew raised brows from everyone, even Rabi.

"Okay," I backpedaled. "Our trap. The kidnapping was obviously a gambit to get the thumb drive, rather than another attempt to kill Kevin. The guilty party was bound to show."

"Absolutely right, luv." Mrs. C patted my arm. "Fortunately, Detective Gaffney, your sniper, had given up trying to kill you. I had a lead on him when visiting with Shep. There had been rumors he was on the take, but he grabbed me while I was confirming the fact. He'd gone a bit crackers after murdering poor Mr. Darlington. He was certain you'd unmask him. He hoped Kevin's death would effectively end the investigation into Mr. Darlington's murder."

Rabi gave a quick shake of his head. "Young lost control."

Marcus climbed on the edge of the cart and pointed at me over the suitcases. "Good thing you called Crawford to get help from Vegas PD. They arranged the wiretap. When Young made her move, Shep's buddies saw us go down the wrong way."

I slipped an arm around Kevin's waist. "Ivan was right. Once the contents of the files became known, Harrison and Young's secret was out."

Kevin rubbed my shoulder. "He also realized there are some battles you can't fight alone."

When Shawn's rattled friend had asked us to hide him, I thought he was crazy. On reflection, I realized the wisdom of his request.

He hadn't driven to work prepared to run for his life.

I hadn't come to Vegas prepared to run a dangerous game.

We both needed help.

He'd turned to us. I'd called Crawford and Shep. Their contacts in the Vegas police force, both active and retired, provided backup and helped get the decoded files to the right people. Some cops might be crooked, but ninety-eight percent of law enforcement consists of honest men and women trying to do their best.

The elevator dinged. We all shifted and maneuvered to get on.

"Crawford did his part," I admitted. "But don't tell him I said that."

"The police got the kidnapper who took Mrs. Colchester. The guy turned on Young before he got to the cruiser, but he'll go to jail." The boy smiled at Kevin. "Safina and Fedor got away clean, but they didn't get the codex. No one saw her after the lights went out. Why was she at the exchange?"

Kevin shrugged in answer to Marcus's question. "Could

have been a test of her loyalty, or, more likely, she wanted a shot at the computer files to find the codex."

I had to smile. "Poor Harrison didn't see what hit him."

While we were still being questioned by the police, Kevin received an e-mail from Rodef with the tag @gamers.com. It took me a few seconds to see that it was Fedor spelled backward. There was no subject.

The message consisted of a forwarded e-mail dated late that day, presumably from Harrison. In it, he admitted he had taken photos of the codex. Though not as clear as the real thing, he believed a facsimile could be recreated in enough detail to fool anyone who had never seen the codex. In exchange, if the real item were never recovered, he would be given a percentage of the sales.

Below this was a short message. "Too bad for him, it's been recovered. Good work, cuz. Sorry for the mess in your suite. Say hi to your lady. Perhaps we'll cross paths again in the future."

There was a small image that looked like a leprechaun tipping his hat.

Kevin chuckled. "Fedor and Safina have never returned empty-handed, except once."

The ill-fated scam that ended with Kevin walking away from the clan.

I had to laugh as I read the message. After all, the private collectors knew they were buying stolen goods. They should know there was no honor among thieves. "At least Gram will be happy."

Detective Pierce could have told Harrison that trying to outwit a Feilen was doomed to failure.

I settled against the wall of the elevator with a sigh. "I so wanted Pierce to be guilty of something besides being a jerk. Safina really did think Pierce murdered J.D."

Kevin nodded. "I knew she believed what she was saying, but it didn't jibe with what I knew of Pierce."

"I thought she was lying. Then, I realized that Safina never saw the face of the killer." I'd gone over what she told me more than once before I saw the problem. "She saw Pierce tailing her. She saw someone of similar build - with a distinctive gait of a cop - from a distance. I think that, like me, she wanted Pierce to be guilty."

Mrs. C clicked her tongue. "It's Ms. Winter I feel bad for. She was completely taken in by Ms. Young."

When the police found Alice Winter's missing key ring shoved in the bottom of Young's purse, the DA pointed the finger at Gaffney. She swore he'd called Alice the morning of the double murder due to her connection with Shawn and Harrison.

I interrupt at this point to clarify that her story fell apart when the police accessed Young's phone records. The DA was the one who called Winter when Kevin and I were in Harrison's office. I continue with her story but the correct person.

Young, who knew the incriminating files and the codex had been stolen, spun Alice a story that Shawn had contacted the DA's office about the smuggling. When Alice admitted the files were on a key ring thumb drive, Young assumed Alice had them with her.

When she met the woman, Alice refused to come clean. She gave Young the same hints she'd given Ivan, that the conch shell held the answers. She held up her keys with a small shell thumb drive attached, evidently as an example. Young wanted to recover the files far more than she wanted the Mayan codex. Without waiting for the whole story, the DA grabbed the keys and killed Alice with a letter opener she'd stuffed in her purse.

Alice never had a chance to explain that the real drive was hidden elsewhere.

Young realized too late she'd stolen nothing more than vacation photos and a few PowerPoints.

My reverie was interrupted when the elevator doors whooshed open onto a sunlit, bustling lobby of the Aquarius Hotel.

Marcus fell in step with me. "I'm ready to do some sightseeing."

"Oh, no." I slid him a sideways glare. "You had your chance."

He held out his hands in a pleading gesture. "You and Kevin could be alone. Have a romantic brunch."

"Nope." I continued toward the main entrance. The pearl-white Caddy was waiting just outside. "I'll get my alone time with Kevin at home where people aren't trying to kill me."

Marcus didn't say a word. He just aimed his shining black eyes directly at my face and straight into my heart.

I was strong. Eyes forward. Head high. I walked straight to the main entrance of the Aquarius and the beckoning sun.

I could feel Kevin's amused gaze.

I was almost home free.

Until I made the mistake of meeting my son's gaze. I wouldn't have gotten past the city limits anyway. "I suppose we have to eat, and there must be a rooftop roller coaster somewhere in town."

Rabi gave me a knowing wink and a little nod.

Mrs. C waved her hand. "With an eating establishment on the roof as well? I do love a panoramic view when dining."

I threw up my hands and surrendered with a smile. "I'm sure we can find a restaurant with a view of the city."

Kevin slid his arm around my shoulders. "You're such an easy mark. That's the sign of a good mom."

As the doors of the Aquarius opened, Marcus launched

himself toward the unsuspecting city. "Las Vegas, here we come."

With my arm around Kevin's waist, I watched the boy run into the sun-drenched day followed closely by Rabi and Mrs. C.

I hoped Sin City was ready. Marcus was on the loose.

ADVENTURES IN VEGAS
CROSSWORD

The crossword puzzle related to his book (w/ the solution) can be solved online at: http://crossword.info/ Paws42/mystery_puzzle_3

A QUESTION OF MURDER

CROSSWORD PUZZLE COZY MYSTERY
BOOK FOUR

CHAPTER ONE

23 Down; 7 Letters;
Clue: Frequented by a ghost
Answer: Haunted

So far, my first foray with Ghosthunters 101 was not only lacking in ethereal spirits, I'd lost a son. While the rest of my group was in the second-floor music room of Rycliffe Castle listening for spirits, I was playing a worried mom and trying to find Marcus, my eleven-year-old Korean foster son.

I'm Tracy Belden, full-time cynic, part-owner of a handyman business, part-time PI, and a lifelong lover and creator of crossword puzzles. At the moment, I lurked in the semi-darkness at the top of the polished staircase.

Evidently, electricity interferes with manifestations, so the hall was lit only by the white light of January's full moon. The soft light shining through the intricate stained-glass windows painted dancing colors on the wall, lending an appropriately eerie feel to the evening. The ornate chandelier seemed to glow with an unearthly light.

The molding along the ceiling and the delicate wood carving spoke to the mining money that had built the four-story house at the height of the silver rush in Langsdale, Nevada.

I was contemplating my next move when a white form glided out of the rear sitting room. The shadowy figure came straight at me. Arms outstretched. White hair shining through the dimness.

My breath caught in my throat. My pulse spiked. Then the figure solidified into Mrs. Colchester, my widowed friend and apartment manager. My relieved smile froze a second later.

The woman looked as white as the ghosts we were hunting. She sped along as if her pink slippers had jet-pack power. Her eyes were glassy and unseeing. Her face was etched with horror.

My heart stuttered as my long legs closed the distance between us. When I reached her, her red, taloned fingernails dug into my arm.

"Is it Marcus?" Fear spread through me at the panic filling her pale green eyes. "Did something happen?"

"Not Marcus, Daniel." Her voice broke on the name. "I killed him decades ago. Why can't the dead stay buried?"

Any thought that she might be putting me on vanished. She was as frightened as I've ever seen her in our seven-year acquaintance. I sputtered for possibly the first time in my life.

Had I heard right? She'd killed a man?

"I killed him once," she repeated in a low, fast whisper. "Now he's come back. He's found me."

Her English accent, which had appeared out of nowhere several months ago, deepened as her agitation grew.

An almost over-powering urge to ask about her mysterious past rose up. Regretfully, I swallowed the impulse. "Are
you sure you saw a real person? The organizers might be
playing a trick."

Before Mrs. C answered, Marcus sprang out of the
shadows.

I swallowed a gasp and scowled at the boy. "Where have
you been?"

My former street urchin son ignored my question. He
had always had a taste for trouble. He'd come hoping to see
or hear a real ghost, but given his rabid interest in murder, a
corpse would be an acceptable substitute.

"You saw the ghost of a dead guy?" Marcus crowded close.
"Who? Where?"

I cringed at the way his excited voice reverberated
through the hushed corridors.

While I'm an actual PI, albeit part-time, I have no desire
to solve crimes. I especially didn't want to mess with a
murder. My interest is the money it adds to my bottom line.
Marcus and Mrs. C, however, take a morbid and enthusiastic
interest in my cases.

Mrs. C put a hand on her thin chest and drew a deep
breath.

"Daniel Weatherington. In there." She pointed over her
shoulder. She started to turn. "I must face him, clear the air."

"No way." Marcus shifted to block her. "Never go toward
trouble."

"Especially dead bodies," I seconded the need for circum-
spection. With my arm around her thin shoulders, I helped
Mrs. C to a padded bench against the wall. In the dim light,
her ashen face made her look every day of her seventy-plus
years.

The brick walls and brushed fabric wallpaper of the old

mansion seemed to have been designed as a backdrop for drama.

"He found me. He wants vengeance." Mrs. C clutched my arm. She shook so much the wrinkled skin on her cheeks and neck quivered. She took a deep breath and appeared to regain control. "I evaded justice once. I won't run again."

She started to rise, as if planning to drift offstage like an aged screen star intent on one, final, dramatic scene.

I stood transfixed. Who was this woman? I'd seen her face down a gunman in a cemetery. Now she was giving up without a fight?

She placed one red-tipped hand over her heart. The parchment-like skin looked transparent in the light shining through the windows.

"No need for you to get involved." The hushed air seemed to gather around Mrs. C. "I'll speak with the bobbies. I'll tell them everything."

"Seriously?" On my best day, I couldn't get a straight answer from her. Now she was ready to confess to someone else? No way. I had more time invested in her mysterious past than the bobbies, er the police. If anyone deserved answers, it was me.

Marcus, my little force of constant motion, planted himself in front of the older woman. "Smart money says keep your mouth shut. Don't volunteer nothing."

Though I cringed at the syntax, I seconded his attitude.

She touched his straight, black hair. His golden skin appeared dusky next to her almost translucent hand. "You've always been such a good boy."

Talk about a final scene.

Marcus's black eyes pleaded with me. "We have to save her."

"Mostly from herself," I muttered.

Mrs. C's gaze remained riveted on the door of the sitting room.

I put my hand on her cheek and gently turned her face toward me. Though I hadn't forgotten the "I killed him decades ago" confession, I had to deal with the matter at hand.

"Take a deep breath," I urged in a soft, calm tone. "You've had a shock, but it's dark. They may have rigged an effect to make the image of a body appear."

Langsdale, a resort town of twenty-five thousand residents, lies three hours north of Las Vegas. The town pulls in upper-crust tourists with attractions that include golf-courses, art galleries, and pricey boutiques to gourmet restaurants and numerous concerts. Rycliffe Castle often hosts appealing activities, such as Ghosthunters, 101.

The mansion had been built by the Rycliffe patriarch who'd made his fortune mining silver in the late eighteen-hundreds. Located on the edge of town, the turreted, castle-like structure had been home to several generations of Rycliffes. The family history of intrigue, arguments, and violence was the basis of the hauntings credited to the building.

"There's money to be made from the dead." I cringed at my words. "I mean from the ghost trade. They'd pull out all the stops to get a good story going."

"It's him." From her blank expression and distant gaze, she didn't appear connected to the here and now. "I thought I was safe. I let down me guard, didn't I?"

"You're sure he's dead?" Marcus didn't hide the ghoulish interest in his voice.

"Blood on his temple." A shudder shook the older woman's thin frame. "A blow to the head. Just like the last time I killed him."

"Shhh!" I checked the empty hall for witnesses lurking in dark corners.

"Don't say that," Marcus whispered at the same time. "Never confess."

My son balanced on his toes, obviously eager to see for himself. He eyed me with a hopeful yet guarded expression. "I could go check."

I hesitated, but I had to know what we were facing. Though I was unsure what the older woman had seen, she was too overwrought to be left alone.

"Don't touch anything," I warned the boy in a hard, low tone. "Look and come right back."

I watched his undersized form dart down the corridor. Soon, his black hair blended with the darkness. He disappeared into the sitting room.

Before I could breathe or blink, he was dashing toward me.

My alarm meter shot to high. This couldn't be good.

Tension radiated from the tight set of his shoulders. He put a hand on my arm. "There *is* a dead guy. He's got blood on his head. It's dripping down his neck."

I filed away the image of gore. Containment. That was my priority. I couldn't let the older woman talk to anyone. Whatever she had done now or in the past, she was too frightened to make sense. Her confusion might land her in prison.

Luckily, only we three rebels had strayed from the main group, but it was a matter of time before we were missed.

I grasped Mrs. C by the shoulders and bent from my five-foot-nine-inch height to meet her gaze. "Did this man hurt you?"

She nodded. Her shaking hands touched the loose skin on her throat. "He threw me against the table. The Tiffany lamp shattered on the floor. His hands were crushing my throat. I couldn't breathe."

Though the hall was cool, Marcus pulled his shirt away where it clung to his skin. "That's self-defense."

"Wait a minute." A full-blown attack and I hadn't heard a sound? That made no sense. "He just now attacked you? Who is this guy?"

"He's followed me across the ocean, across time." Mrs. C looked frantically around. "I have to confess."

Marcus put a restraining hand on her arm. "No."

The street ethics Marcus had grown up with before hooking up with me gave no thought to guilt or innocence. Protect your own was the first rule.

"We need the whole story before you do anything." I put a hand around her shoulders. "First, let's get out of here."

Marcus and I helped Mrs. C to her feet.

"T.R." A note of urgency rang in my son's tone. "Is that tape recorder still running?"

My breath caught in my throat. One person in each group carried a handheld tape recorder to catch any happenings. Lucky me, I had the one for my group. I'd hung it on my purse and forgotten it. My first impulse was to destroy the offending instrument, but I didn't dare. Instead, I thrust it at Marcus. "Erase it. We'll wait here."

He took the recorder, pushing some electromagnetic thingamabob detector he'd been given at me. "Keep quiet."

He walked several feet away. His expression intent. After a moment, he wiped the recorder with his shirt, then set it on a nearby table.

I pointed him toward a room on the far side of the stairs. If there was a dead body, I wanted the three of us to be elsewhere when it was found.

I put my arm around Mrs. C's shoulders. "Not another word about the past, bodies, or vengeance. Marcus can't be involved. He might be taken away from me. We might never see him again."

Gut-wrenching fear shot through me at hearing my own personal nightmare aloud. Though the current caseworker was a good sort, I lived in terror of losing the boy I loved. Besides, I had to cut through the older woman's confusion.

Mrs. C's shoulders stiffened. The blank look in her eyes dissipated. "Quite right, dear. I can't drag you or the boy into my troubles. Not a word."

I put my hand on her shoulder while Marcus waved us forward. Once in the child's room, deserted but for us, I aimed our trio toward a door that connected to the music room. With luck, no one in the main group would notice we'd gone missing.

"Not a word," I repeated. "We stay together from now on."

Marcus nodded.

Mrs. C stared straight ahead.

I squeezed her shoulders. "Remember, think of Marcus."

She took a deep breath. "Right."

Slipping into the main group was amazingly easy. Between the darkness and the attempts to communicate with spirits, no one so much as glanced our way or seemed to realize we'd been missing.

I breathed a sigh of relief until I realized the real murderer would have been able to leave and return just as easily. I glanced at the shadowy ring of figures and wondered which of them was the killer.

A new worry sprang up, full blown. What if the murderer had seen Mrs. C head for the library? Even worse, what if they overheard her confession?

Coming Summer 2021

Dear Readers,

Welcome to the adventures of Tracy Belden and her son, Marcus, along w/ their adopted family: Kevin Tanner, Mrs. Colchester, and Jack Rabi as they are drawn into Tracy's cases as a PI. While Tracy would prefer to drink her flavored coffee and create crossword puzzles, like most of us, she has to pay the bills and keep food on the table. So, she puts her puzzle solving talents to good use as she dives into her cases.

While most of her cases are simple, the ones involving murder are often so complicated she despairs of solving them. However, Marcus, with the confidence of youth and his pride in the detecting heritage of the Belden family, never wavers in his belief that the Belden Agency can solve any case as long as they work together.

Among the many books I read while growing up weas the YA mystery series involving Trixie Belden and her group of young friends. While no part of this book is based on those stories, Tracy did tell Marcus that she was a distant cousin of Trixie's. Her good intentions were based solely on her efforts to get him off the streets, but her alleged relationship with Trixie is a claim Tracy is never allowed to forget.

I hope you enjoy your time in Langsdale, Nevada, and the adventures of Tracy and her adopted family. If you enjoyed the book and have the time, please leave a review at your favorite bookseller or at Goodreads.

Thank you for giving me your time to read this book and your support by buying it. I don't take either for granted.

Louise Foster

MEET THE AUTHOR

I didn't pursue a writing career until I was well out of college. However, a lifelong love of reading and solving puzzles proved to be good training when the writing bug bit. While I enjoy reading many different types of books, from thrillers to fantasy to science fiction, mysteries have always intrigued me.

Working on jigsaw puzzles as well as crossword puzzles with my family has also been a constant part of my life. A habit that carries through to today.

In the Crossword Puzzle Mystery Series, my love of writing and solving puzzles came together. I hope you love the quirky characters and their high-spirited adventures as much I enjoy writing them.

To learn more about the Crossword Puzzle Cozy Mystery series, visit my website www.louisefoster.com and sign up for my newsletter. You can also solve a crossword puzzle related to each of the books as they're released, either on-line or by downloading it.

Find me on Facebook: Louise Foster, Author

https://www.facebook.com/Louise-Foster-Author-107517717508196/?modal=admin_todo_tour

I love to hear from readers:

Louise.louisefoster@gmail.com

ACKNOWLEDGMENTS

I'd like to acknowledge a few of the many people who helped make this book a reality:

My editor, Mary-Theresa Hussey, for her awesome input.

Lee Hyat, who created my beautiful book covers.

Debbie Manber Kupfer, who used her skill and talent to create the crossword puzzles in this book and on my website.

Keith Jones for setting up my wonderful web-site.

ALSO BY LOUISE FOSTER

Made in United States
Troutdale, OR
06/11/2023

10556407R00169